THE COTTAGE AT WHISPER LAKE

PHILLIPA NEFRI CLARK

Storm

To request permissions, contact the publisher at rights@stormpublishing.co

Ebook ISBN: 978-1-80508-086-2
Paperback ISBN: 978-1-80508-087-9

Cover design: Eileen Carey
Cover images: Shutterstock

Published by Storm Publishing.
For further information, visit:
www.stormpublishing.co

ALSO BY PHILLIPA NEFRI CLARK

Rivers End Romantic Women's Fiction

The Stationmaster's Cottage

Jasmine Sea

The Secrets of Palmerston House

The Christmas Key

Taming the Wind

Martha

Bindarra Creek Rural Fiction

A Perfect Danger

Tangled by Tinsel

Maple Gardens Matchmakers

The Heart Match

The Christmas Match

The Menu Match

Detective Liz Moorland Series

Lest We Forgive

Lest Bridges Burn

Last Known Contact

Charlotte Dean Mysteries

Christmas Crime in Kingfisher Falls

Sadie headed for her Lexus, shoving sunglasses on as she passed a middle-aged couple on their way in.

'Did you see her?'

The woman's whisper was loud enough to get Sadie's attention and she slowed her steps.

'That was her. You know, Sadie Forest.'

'Out here?'

'I'm sure it is. Oh my gosh, I just love her.'

Be still my heart.

Was her face so familiar, even here? No reason why not. Only a week ago she'd finished filming the final episode of a documentary about homeless teens in Sydney. Heart-wrenching, and one of the reasons she was here today, although she'd never admit to being burned out by the emotional drain of the past few months. But there were no more excuses to use and after the most recent plaintive phone call from her mother and an unusual break in her schedule, Sadie had packed enough for a month or so away from her apartment in Sydney. The drive down took three days because she'd stopped frequently, needing every extra minute to prepare herself.

Back in the car, she fixed her make-up and pulled her hair out of the ponytail. Her eyes were puffy from tiredness and dabbing more concealer on made little difference. She tossed it and the lipstick into her bag. It wasn't as though she was going on set or had anyone to impress.

At the exit she idled, her eyes drifting in the direction she'd come from earlier. She could be in Melbourne by nightfall if she left now. Find herself a hotel somewhere before going back to Sydney and the life she'd made. But she turned the car toward Rivers End and barely drew a breath all the way down the hill.

As she crossed the bridge over the wide, lazy river, her mood lightened. She'd paddleboarded down Temple River as a teenager, ducking low beneath the bridge and singing through the arch of rock to hear her voice echo, before bursting into glaring sunlight. The board would eventually bottom out in the lagoon. Sometimes she'd take a picnic and go with friends. Those days were the best. That and hiking through the hills outside the town limits.

Rather than turning into the main street, she continued to the second road, passing the inn on the corner, then nosing the car into the carpark from the driveway in the next street. She found the furthest spot from the office. Her heart hammered as she climbed out.

No other vehicles were parked. Was Mum even here?

Although it was early in the week, Sadie had expected some guests at this time of day. The inn was the only one in Rivers End and catered for travelling business people and, in the school holidays, tourists who needed a cheap place to stay. Those with more disposable income or wanting something nicer than a plain room would book into Palmerston House, the local B&B, or find an Airbnb.

She pulled the handbag strap over her shoulder and locked the car and before she had a chance to turn tail and run, Sadie marched past the six inn rooms to the office at the end.

The screen door squealed in protest at being opened. Behind it, the wooden and glass door was closed and she thought locked, but the handle turned and she stepped into freezing air blasting from the old unit on the wall. Sadie reached up and pushed the on/off button and with a groan, the machine stopped.

Apart from the temperature, the office was no different from many small-town inns. A counter with a chair, phone, computer, and guest book. To one side a stand of brochures displayed local attractions and services. And a door at the back led into a living room with a basic kitchen and bathroom.

Nobody lived on the premises. Even at its busiest it wasn't necessary when the owners were only a few minutes away.

'What's wrong with the darned thing now, because if I have one more thing go...' Pam Carson might have been intent on checking why the air conditioner had stopped working but whatever choice words she'd meant to say trailed off. She stopped dead in the doorway, eyes wide, and a hand covering her heart.

Sadie's throat constricted.

How did you get so old, Mum?

It wasn't *that* long... was it?

'You're here.'

'Hi, Mum. I said I'd visit once I finished filming.'

Her mother's mouth opened then snapped shut but Sadie recognised the flicker of self-control in her eyes. Pam had something to say. When she was ready.

Stepping around the counter, Sadie embraced her mother, squeezing until Pam relented and hugged back. Another thing which hadn't changed. Lavender perfume. The cheap stuff. Well, there were gifts in her suitcase for later and one was a scent much nicer and longer-lasting.

'Are you sniffing my hair?'

Sadie released her mother with a shake of her head. 'Never.'

'Go inside and sit and I'll make some coffee. But I'll fix this thing first.' Pam headed for the air conditioner.

'I turned it off. It is like an iceberg in here.'

'It is? Oh.' As her hand hovered over the on/off button, Pam's brow furrowed. 'Why did I have it set so cold, I wonder?' She glanced at the front door then back at Sadie. 'Was anyone outside? Any guests I didn't hear?'

'Nobody. I was surprised how quiet it is. Are there any bookings?'

'None.'

'What time are you going home?' Sadie asked as she went

into the back room. The curtains were drawn and the sofa had a pillow and blanket folded at one end. On the coffee table was a partly eaten sandwich and empty coffee cup beside a paperback novel which was open and facing down. The air was musty.

'Mum?'

'I'm right here, Sadie, and before you ask again, I wasn't going to leave tonight.' Pam picked up the book, closed it, and put it down. 'There's bound to be someone looking for last-minute accommodation and quite frankly, I can't afford to miss them. Not these days, with the cost of living.'

'But you always had a system for that. The phone at the front door so they can call you at home and nobody ever minded waiting a few minutes for you to drive back across.'

'It takes me a good twenty minutes to walk over. I couldn't let some poor person wait around so long.'

The van hadn't been in the carpark. Dad's van.

'Is the van being serviced?'

'I don't care to drive such a short distance.'

'But Mum, wouldn't it—'

'Enough, Sadie. You've been here five minutes and want to tell me how to manage my life. But let's go now. Let's go back to the house and once you've settled in then I'll walk back.'

Pam grabbed a handbag and was at the front door before Sadie had a chance to process what was going on. Her mother didn't seem angry, despite telling her off, but she had a purpose about her. A focus of where she wanted to be and what would happen and that was nothing like the mother she remembered.

'Very fancy,' Pam said for the second time since they'd got into the Lexus. She sat bolt upright in the passenger seat, her feet flat on the floormats and hands on her lap. 'Plenty of fancy cars in Rivers End nowadays with new homes being built and people having holiday houses. Some even leave their yachts in Willow Bay year-round. But this one is *very* fancy.'

'Thanks, I think. Since when did we get a marina?'

'Oh, no marina. You remember how secluded Willow Bay is though. I've heard there's twenty or so yachts there all the time and most only get used for a few weeks each year. Rich folk. Boats. Big houses up in Rivers End Heights on little blocks of land. And *fancy* cars.'

Sadie shot a look at her mother who gazed straight ahead. But the corners of her lips twitched.

Who is in my mother's body?

They travelled away from the town for half a kilometre then turned right. Growing up, theirs was the only house on Ryan Road but now at least half a dozen others, all modern and on sprawling parcels of land, dotted the landscape on either side of the narrow, kilometre-long road.

'Who lives along here?'

Pam shrugged. 'Families. Most of them have swimming pools and ponies and the like. Green Bay's growing, with lots of jobs, and being only a short drive away I think people are happy to work there but live where it's a bit quieter in Rivers End.'

Slowing the car to round the final curve, Sadie's stomach was back to churning. Eight years since she'd set foot in the family home. She'd only been home that one time after leaving almost fifteen years ago. And if Dad was alive, she wouldn't be here.

The entry to the property was straight ahead where the road ended. The wooden gate she'd once swung on was gone, leaving the driveway open. Overgrown bushes on either side hid the house from the casual observer. Very overgrown.

'Careful on the left as there's a bit of a hole.'

Bit? A person could get lost down the pothole she had to swerve around. These were all things Dad took care of. Trimming bushes. Maintaining the driveway. Mowing. Pam couldn't handle the grounds here and run the inn. Well, she wouldn't have to for long. Sadie would help her sell the business so she could retire and finally stop being on her feet all the time.

The driveway curved in a U-shape but instead of following it around, Sadie parked in front of the double weatherboard garage at the side of the house. A few panels at the top swung down, held by their corners. A bird flew in.

'You might need to show me how to get out.'

'I'll come round.' Sadie dived out and opened the passenger door, offering a hand to her mother. 'It's quite a bit lower than your van.'

Pam let her help her out and stood for a moment to straighten. 'The van needs some new tyres, I think. I might need to have it looked at. Would you get my handbag?'

Carrying both handbags, Sadie slid her arm through her mother's as they climbed the three steps to the front door. Cobwebs and dust gathered in the corners and a pot plant had long since gone to God beneath the grimy, narrow window beside the door. Why was everything so run-down?

'Here we are, then.' Pam unlocked and pushed the front door open and kept going, her shoes echoing along the long hallway.

Sadness bubbled up as Sadie closed the door. She leaned against the wall and peered through the window. Nothing was the same, after all.

TWO

'I don't think there's much here for dinner, love.' Pam stared into the fridge, then, leaving the door open, wandered to the pantry and did the same.

Sadie closed the fridge after a quick glance confirmed the meagre contents. 'Any Uber Eats out here yet? Or would you like to go out for dinner?'

Pam shut the pantry door with a thud. 'Out for dinner?'

'Don't sound outraged, Mum. I imagine one of the pubs does counter meals. Are there other restaurants? Something you'd prefer?'

'How can you even suggest such a thing? Your father is only two months in the grave and you expect me to dress up and sit at a bar? What on earth will people think of me?'

That you are having dinner with your daughter?

It wasn't worth the argument. Sadie opened the fridge again. 'How old are the eggs?'

'Joan up the road gave them to me only a couple of days ago. She has chooks running around her place.'

There was an unopened block of local butter and a handful of mushrooms which weren't too bad. 'Still have a veggie garden?' For the first time, she took a proper look at her mother, who was far too thin. Not slender and fit as she'd always been but gaunt. Something told her it was from more than grief of losing her husband. If anything, his death should have freed her from decades of being micro-managed.

'What's wrong?' Pam frowned. 'You suddenly look very angry. Have I upset you?'

'No, not at all,' Sadie said, forcing a smile. 'Just working out a recipe to use what you have. So, anything in the vegetable garden we can pick?'

'Do you know, I've not been there in a while. Not since... well, you know. I think I'd like to go there now. Shall we take a look?' Without waiting for an answer, she stopped long enough to pick up a large metal bowl and headed for the back door. 'Coming?'

The back garden was almost as bad as the front. Dad only died recently yet everywhere Sadie looked showed months of neglect. Overgrown plants, weeds in the formerly perfect flower beds, and a pile of unchopped wood near the small shed. The pieces were grey with age and the block splitter was buried in one large stump.

'Watch your step, Sadie. The footpath fell apart a while ago.'

Pam led the way past the shed and between a few trees and then they were out in the open again. This part of the property was her domain. Dad rarely came out here unless to bark an order. He'd built ten raised garden beds when Sadie was a child and that was pretty much his contribution to the area. But Pam loved it. Or she had. So did Sadie, who learned what to plant and when, what grew well together, and the joy of digging up potatoes. These days she lived in an apartment but still kept a herb garden on the balcony.

'Oh dear, it does look rather unkempt.' Pam fussed around at the first bed. 'I'm sure I planted some cauliflowers in here.'

'Isn't that a winter veggie?'

More weeds, some huge and prickly, overshadowed what might once have thrived.

'Winter? I guess.' Pam roamed from one garden bed to another, lifting leaves and pushing back weeds, all the while talking softly to herself. Sadie uncovered a hand fork and spade and used them to take a proper look without getting prickled. It wouldn't take much to sort these out, just a few hours' weeding and then her mother would have no reason not to enjoy being out here again.

'I think these are onions, Mum, may I pull a couple out?'

There wasn't a reply so Sadie went ahead. Two perfect white onions came out without too much effort and Sadie shook off the dirt and some fat worms. In another bed was a tomato plant which was huge and heavy with dark red fruit. She twisted a dozen off. Finally, in the furthest bed, oregano and basil vied for sunlight but were doing well enough to spare some leaves.

'Quiche for dinner?'

'Don't think I have any frozen pastry. Or flour.' Pam's eyes widened at the sight of the produce in Sadie's hands and she held out the bowl. 'I found rocket. It grows in all the places I don't plant it.'

'Rocket, tomato, and onion salad on the side and a crustless quiche. I'll cook and you can put your feet up for a bit and talk to me.'

'Talk? What about?' Pam gazed around the vegetable garden, her shoulders drooping. 'How have I let this happen? I can't find the lettuce. Or beetroot. And why wouldn't the pumpkins grow?'

Whatever had happened meant less to Sadie than getting her mother to sit down and relax for a while. For that matter, the driving and stress was catching up with her and she'd not eaten since breakfast. Taking the bowl from her mother, Sadie slid her spare arm around thin shoulders. 'This can wait for another day, but I think both of us could use a meal and a chance to catch up.'

At least there'd been no more talk about Pam returning to the inn tonight. Arguing with her didn't appear even at number one-thousand on Sadie's to-do list. But it was hard to know what subjects were safe. Asking about going out to dinner should have been a simple yes or no but sent her mother into a spin and it was only now, after they'd both eaten and moved into the living room, that she seemed less tense.

'Nothing on television these days,' Pam said. She'd settled into the armchair she'd always preferred, closest to the window and beside a coffee table where she placed her phone next to a pile of paperbacks.

'You have a nice collection there,' Sadie said.

'The books? I always loved to read but you know what your father was like. Considered fiction a waste of good time. There's a new bookshop in the town and every so often I pop in while doing grocery shopping.'

'I've read the second and fourth ones from the top and you will love them.'

Pam leaned forward to check which books then smiled at Sadie. A real smile. 'Then I shall read them next. Why don't you make books into television shows?'

Sadie couldn't remember the last time they'd talked about her career. Leaving Rivers End drove a wedge between mother and daughter and for a long time it hurt Sadie. Only years later did she realise Pam had to choose between supporting her daughter's dreams or managing life with her husband. Instead of resentment, Sadie only felt pity that her mother chose the latter.

'I'd love to do that. We have so many talented authors here

and so many incredible stories would be perfect for the small screen, but I'm more journalist than producer so my skills are best utilised in the documentaries I help make.'

'What kind of documentaries, love? Do you mean like those reality shows about people marrying before they meet?'

Even as a chuckle formed, Sadie registered Pam's first words.

How do you not know what I've done?

'Um... no, not like those shows. The one I just finished filming is about homeless teenagers. We followed three brave youngsters for a week to produce something we hope will change how the average person views homelessness.'

'Can we watch it yet?' Pam reached for a remote control on the coffee table.

'Not for a few months. But there are others.'

'On television?'

'On a streaming service... do you have any?'

'Your father wouldn't waste money on them. There was a show I really wanted to see four or five years back. I told him I'd pay for it out of my own earnings from selling some of the preserves I'd made but he reminded me he owned the property, therefore any money I made from the produce I grow belongs to him. I never asked again.'

There was nothing to say.

Too many times Sadie had tried to get her mother to stand up to her husband and she'd had to give up. Had to stop encouraging and cajoling and then guilting her into even trying.

'Would you like a glass of sherry, love? I would.' With that astonishing offer, Pam stood and although her face was strained, she smiled. 'There's a bottle in the kitchen cupboard.'

Surprise after surprise.

'Don't believe I've ever tried sherry, but why the heck not.'

'That's my girl.'

When her mother returned a few minutes later, she seemed

quite ready for a solid evening of sherry drinking. A whole bottle, two small glasses, and a bowl with ice cubes were on a tray which she fitted beside the books.

'I quite like it over ice.' Pam tipped some of the ice into one glass and glanced up.

'Sure, let's do ice.'

After opening the bottle, Pam poured two small amounts and then handed one to Sadie. 'Shall we toast something? How about to Sadie and her successful career?'

Unsure if there was a dig at her in that, Sadie tapped her glass to Pam's. 'And to being together again.'

'Yes, that's a nice one. I do like toasts.' Pam lifted the glass to her lips and swallowed the sherry in one long gulp. Without wasting a second she refilled the glass – but this time to halfway and then she leaned back in the armchair and crossed her legs.

Sadie took a cautious sip. It wasn't horrible, but she'd have preferred a decent robust red wine, preferably from the Barossa Valley. 'Isn't sherry used in cooking?'

'Why else would I have a bottle?'

That expression was back on her face. Pure innocence with a touch of humour, like the one in the car when she'd ever so gently teased.

'Mother, since when do you drink alcohol?'

Lifting her chin, Pam gazed directly at Sadie. 'Since the day after your father's funeral. He wasn't here anymore to tell me how sinful it was. For some reason he never minded me cooking with it, sherry in cakes or even brandy in some things, but drink it?' She shook her head. 'The nectar of the devil himself.' The glass met her lips again and she drank another large mouthful.

Well, good for you.

It wasn't about alcohol. This was about unshackling a woman from the invisible chains Ronald Carson had used to enslave and control anyone who let him, or loved him. Sadie finished her glass and helped herself to another. A nice, full one.

And then she topped up her mother's and tapped her glass against it again.

'To cooking. Long may it provide such delightful extras.'

Pam giggled. She actually giggled. Stupid tears prickled at the back of Sadie's eyes. She wasn't one to cry. To show emotions. But how long since she'd heard her mother laugh, let alone like a teenager?

Perhaps it was the sherry. Or just being in the same room together again. But for the first time in... forever, Sadie saw her mother in a new light. This evening, Pam Carson was a woman. Not a mother. Not a wife. And not a browbeaten human who had accepted the dominance of a man rather than forge her own path. Sadie had learned from her mother and done the opposite. Lived her life and lived it well, keeping men at arm's length and her bank balance on the high side.

'What's next, Mum? You said earlier that Dad told you he owned the house but it's yours now. As is the inn.'

Pam's eyes widened. 'The inn. I should go back.'

'Nope. Nada, no. Has anyone called to say they want to stay? Anybody at the door of the office?'

'Well, no. I'd hear the phone if there was. But still...'

'Still nothing, Mummy. The inn is fine. You need a night off and I'll stop drinking now and listen for your phone. Anyone calls, I'll run down and sort out a room. Okay?'

The uncertainty on her mother's face tugged at Sadie. How long had she tried to manage the inn and her grief and all the changes in her life? Or had this gone on for much longer?

'Mum? When did Dad stop managing the inn?'

And there it was. A mix of relief and shame filled the face of the woman who'd supported her husband for forty years.

'Sadie? I'd prefer you drink with me tonight. Forget the inn. Turn off the phone. Just for one darned night I need to be free of it all.' As if to prove her point, she picked up the phone, turned it off, and put it face down on the table. 'Top-up, love?'

THREE

Sadie woke from a dream, startled. She was sitting, partly out of the bed – the same one she'd slept in until she'd left home. Sunshine streamed through the window and she squinted at the light, trying to estimate the time. Once her heart stopped bouncing around in her chest from whatever woke her, she pushed back the covers and stood.

Little was different in her room, apart from the things she'd taken with her. Same bed, same desk, same cupboards. Even some of her old photographs were still on the desk in frames. She might take them home with her this time, unless Pam wanted to keep them. Or she could have copies made. She'd slept well. Days of driving followed by an evening of drinking sherry was probably responsible, yet she had no headache despite having had quite a few of the little glasses.

So had her mother. But the conversation hadn't evolved. No more mention of her father or the future of the inn. Pam wanted to reminisce about past moments which were special. Sadie's tenth birthday. The day she got her driver's licence. Stuff which didn't matter to Sadie but somehow was entrenched in her mother's thoughts. Before going to bed, they'd hugged.

After a quick shower, Sadie dressed and went in search of her mother but the house was empty. It was barely past seven. There was a note attached to the fridge with a magnet.

Rest up, love. If you feel up to it later, pop down to the inn and we can have lunch together. But I have accounts to do this morning. See you later, Mum.

After making coffee, Sadie wandered around the garden again, sipping as she walked. In the morning light the condition of the place was worse than she'd realised. The house itself was in dire need of a repaint and repairs to the guttering, a few weatherboards, and the paths. It was nothing a decent tradie wouldn't fix though and it raised more questions about how long her father had been neglecting the jobs he'd always insisted on doing. He wasn't one to spend money on getting help unless he couldn't manage something. Well, she had a few weeks' free time and would help Pam get the property back to a manageable state.

From the vegetable garden the view was lovely. Their few acres backed onto vast tracts of open land and a small forest. Further away were rolling hills within an easy walk and Temple River in between. Sadie had spent many a day hiking on her own and had often longed to own a pony to ride further. But a pony was out of the question so she'd used her legs and, in hindsight, it taught her to rely on herself and stay fit. She wasn't much of a jogger or runner but regularly walked along the beach near her apartment.

The coffee was finished and she took the cup inside. Pam was busy for a few hours. The shops weren't open yet so she couldn't replenish the pantry and fridge until later. And she wasn't one to sit around. With a grin, Sadie grabbed a hat, her phone, a bottle of water, and the house keys.

.   .   .

'Still believe you're fit?' Sadie muttered under her breath as she forced aching legs up a hill. Surely it was steeper now? Perhaps there'd been some kind of reverse erosion. More likely her teenage self was in better shape.

At the top she flopped onto the ground, panting. This was hardly a mountain but it was part of the higher area of Rivers End where once a railway line had carried timber from the local mills. The easier way up there was to head up the hill to the cemetery and turn inland. But doing things the easy way wasn't as much fun.

Rivers End had grown. She picked out familiar shops and some of the houses she'd visited as a child or teen. Her primary school was bigger with a new building added on and what looked like a new estate was being developed on the road to the Otway Ranges. It was worth the climb to see the town laid out. Along the couple of streets of shops most of the buildings were old but well maintained. There was a charm about the small town. Apart from the inn. Even from this distance, it was out of place.

Her father had the inn built to his specifications before she was born and the design was plain. Plain ugly. Half a dozen guest rooms plus the office and a lockable laundry and storage area was about the size of it, along with enough parking for the guests. Despite its looks the inn had brought in a good wage for her parents and paid the bills.

With a deep sigh, Sadie pushed herself to her feet and got her phone out. She took lots of photographs and then moved to the highest spot to take panoramas. Some were nice enough to make into prints or put onto stretched canvas. Checking them, she stopped on one image behind the hill... between it and the next rise, which would reach the far end of the road the railway line was on.

She pinched the screen, zooming in on a clump of trees near a small lake. How had she never come across it in all her wandering? Dangling her feet in a lake for a while was appealing. Very appealing.

Sadie stopped a couple of times on the way to check the photo. There was a narrow valley she needed to reach which was easy to miss beneath a canopy of redgums but she found a way down and stepped into the cool. Filtered light danced with butterflies. Underfoot, the ground was cushioned by decades of fallen leaves. The freshness of the air almost hurt as Sadie inhaled and she lingered in a glade alive with tree ferns, slowly turning in a circle, her face to the roof of the forest and her fingers outstretched as if to capture the magic.

At the edge of the redgums a deep green pasture invited her to take off her shoes. How could it be so soft and the hues so intense in the middle of a dry summer? The grass tickled the bottom of her feet and with every step a sense of calm and freedom from stress seeped into her soul.

The valley widened into an area of ten or so acres of completely flat land broken by the lake Sadie had photographed. A few metres from the edge of the water, a little white weatherboard cottage was the last thing she expected to see.

She had to leave if this was private land and that meant retracing her steps with a long climb ahead. Alternately, if there was a cottage there'd be a road somewhere close by and with a bit of luck it would make for an easier walk home.

Sadie put her shoes back on and skirted around the edge of the land, keeping an eye out in case anyone saw her. She'd explain herself, of course, but didn't wish to startle someone who would hardly expect a stranger to appear from nowhere.

All was quiet. Eerily so with no breeze to disturb the lake nor any sign of life.

Almost no sign of life.

Sitting directly in her path was a green-eyed, jet-black cat.

. . .

'I'm quite sure you're not lost. Look at your lovely coat.' Sadie stroked velvety fur as the cat wound itself around her ankles. 'Somebody loves you a lot.'

With a yowl and its tail held aloft, the cat trotted away.

So much for that.

There was a track ahead, leading from near the cottage to a break between the higher ground. Sadie changed direction to intersect it. A sad meow stopped her. The cat was trotting parallel and meowed again.

'You can't come home with me. You live here. Don't you?'

The cottage was close enough to see a rocking chair on the verandah.

Another yowl, which was even more insistent, and then the cat ran to the cottage and pawed at the front door. Perhaps it had missed breakfast or been accidentally locked out.

Nobody came to the door, even as the cat's complaints increased in volume.

Something's not right.

It would only take a moment to tap on the door and ask if the cat lived there.

Closer, the cottage was a bit like a make-believe one from a story. It was tiny and perfect with beautiful flowers planted across the front and fresh paint. A bicycle with a woven basket at the front was at the end of the verandah. And on the lake, a wooden rowboat floated loose.

Sadie tapped on the door. 'Hello? Sorry to bother you.'

The cat added its own chorus.

She glanced back at the rowboat. Oars dipped into the water. Her heart was thudding and she tapped again, much harder.

The front door made a small 'click' and opened a bit and the cat sped inside.

'Is anyone home?'

Only the cat replied.

Pushing the door further open, Sadie stepped into the cottage. 'I'm so sorry to intrude, is anyone home? The cat insisted I come in.'

She was in a hallway with both walls covered in art and beneath the paintings, low shelving filled with books. With every step, Sadie was poised to run. It was ridiculous. She wasn't doing anything wrong, other than being in a stranger's home without permission.

The cat reappeared to deliver an annoyed growl before hightailing it back to the kitchen at the end of the hallway. Sadie had given up on finding anyone here but glanced into each room in case someone had fallen or who knows what. In the kitchen, the cat ran to a bowl on the ground and then to the fridge with an expression of desperation. 'I can't just poke around in someone's fridge.' Green eyes glowered at her. 'Fine then.' At this point she might as well feed the cat and get out of here. There was an open tin of tuna covered in foil and as soon as she tipped it into the bowl the cat devoured it.

There was a wooden table with chairs in the middle of the room and on it was an open handbag. Sadie didn't need to touch it to see a set of house keys on a large tag with a name in beautiful handwriting – Rebecca Meyers. Was there any chance the owner was just out for a walk? But without their keys?

The rowboat.

Sadie hurried from the kitchen, pulling her phone out as she headed for the front door. But something made her stop halfway down the hallway. One of the paintings had the signature *Becky M*. It was a sweeping oil painting of a lighthouse, with a wooden rowboat foundering in the middle of a savage storm.

The hairs rose on the back of Sadie's arms.

'Where are you, Rebecca Meyers?'

FOUR

62 YEARS AGO

Rain streaks the window pane as the removalist truck pulls away, its heavy tyres churning up mud and leaving huge dents in the driveway. My nose is cold, pressed against the glass, and I stare until the red tail lights disappear into the grey gloom.

It is done now. Too late to go back but all I want is for the truck to turn around and collect all our furniture again. Take it all home. Mine and Dad's and Charlie's home which is so far away now. If I stay here I'll never visit Mum again. Never take her flowers and sit on the ground and talk to her. Mum is all alone in that place with nobody to brighten up her grave.

My hands hurt and when I lean back and look at them, each is balled up so tightly that my knuckles are white. I force them to open and straighten my fingers before resting the palms on the window.

The rain hasn't stopped all day. When we arrived in Dad's car he'd had to carry Charlie in with me holding an umbrella over them and then I helped bring Charlie's wheelchair and our personal bags and pillows and bedding. It still fell when the truck arrived a bit later and had to back up to the door and lower a ramp. The men had carried in our sofa and beds and fridge and all the things from the apartment and they traipsed in mud and shook rain off their hair.

I'd started to clean up every time they left mud or pools of water behind but Dad said to leave it until they were done. So I helped direct the boxes and furniture into the right places. When the final item was inside and the men said goodbye and good luck and went to ready their truck for the drive back to Melbourne, I filled a bucket with hot water and mopped the timber floorboards until there was nothing left of the outside. And then I watched them leave.

Dad offered to help of course but I said I could manage and he should keep sorting the furniture out. Charlie was with him, likely sitting on the floor, chatting away like always.

And that is the only reason I don't run out onto the road and try to find my way home.

Charlie needs to be here until he gets a bit better.

None of it makes sense to me but Dad is sure being here in this odd little town in the Victorian countryside will help because there is a special school here. A teacher who will make a difference to Charlie and that is all that matters.

My stomach grumbles. If I'm hungry then so are Charlie and Dad. My hands are wet from the condensation inside the window and I wipe them on my pants and lift my chin. Mum always said to stand tall. That way, nobody knows what I am thinking.

The kitchen is so big. The fridge looks small in here and until it has run overnight and got cold again we can't open it. So I search through the boxes until finding one with Dad's writing.

Cold for meals.

Inside is enough food for tonight and breakfast and then we have to find somewhere to go shopping. Does the town even have a proper grocery shop? I pull the tape off the box and open the flaps. I'm not strong enough to lift out the big box inside. It keeps things cold but I can't remember what Dad calls it. The lid comes off so I can remove the dinner ingredients I'd packed before the truck arrived. Everything is still cold.

Another box says *Saucepans* and from there I take a big pot and put it on the stove. The biggest stove ever with four coils of electricity.

Charlie is laughing and a little bit of the lump in my chest lightens. I can't hear what Dad says but Charlie sounds happy.

Once I add water to the pot I work out how to turn the coil on. It heats up faster than our stove at home and as the water begins to bubble I add vegetables I'd chopped before we left. Dad had said we'd have a big, long day travelling and would need to have some food prepared. He suggested sandwiches which was silly. I knew we'd need a proper dinner so did potatoes and onions and green beans and carrots which all are fine to cut up ahead of time. Then I add some rice and herbs. I like herbs. No meat tonight because without proper cooling it might make us ill. Now it is bubbling away, I slice some bread and butter, a piece each, before carefully replacing anything cold into the cold box and closing the lid.

'Becky! Becky, come see!'

Charlie sounds excited and I turn off the coil and put a lid on the pot. I'm not sure what part of the house he's in but he keeps laughing and I go past my bedroom to his. Both rooms face the ocean – not that we've been able to see much with all the rain. But the rain must have stopped while I cooked and a late afternoon sun pushes enough of the cloud away to cast some light across a bay.

Dad is making Charlie's bed, tucking in the blankets with precision. The room is already almost set up with a bedside cupboard and lamp in place and his wheelchair out of the way in a corner. Charlie stands at the window, holding the edge of a deep window sill. With his callipers on his legs, he stands okay and walks a bit holding on to one of us but the wheelchair makes it easier for him to get around faster. He's pretty speedy in it. Now he is seven he hates the callipers and wants to be like other children.

'See out there?' He taps on the window pane and I go to look.

The back of the property slopes away so while the front of the house is level with the street, the back looks down. There are steps from the back door going to the small garden and there is a shed and no fence at the back. The ground disappears.

'Doesn't look safe.'

'We'll put a proper fence there if we need but let's worry about the house first, Becky,' Dad says. 'It isn't that steep though, the path to the beach.'

'Beach?' Charlie's mouth is a big 'o' and his eyes are wide as he turns to Dad. 'Our beach?'

Dad chuckles. 'Not just ours but it looks pretty quiet and safe. Becky, do you need me to help unpack anything?'

'Plates and stuff. And dinner is almost done.'

On his way out, Dad ruffles my hair with a quiet, 'Thanks.'

'Is that what you wanted me to see, Charlie? Are you hungry?'

'Hungry, yes. Further.' He points.

There are rocks in the water. Piled on top of each other like a column of stone.

'Light... lighthouse,' he says.

'Nah, those are just rocks. Coming to have dinner now?'

He shakes his head, eyes never leaving the rocks.

'Just yell when you want Dad to collect you.'

Charlie doesn't answer.

Dad has found the right box and is lifting plates and bowls out in the kitchen. I can't help grinning. 'Charlie thinks those rocks are a lighthouse.' I turn the coil back on. 'Is there a big serving spoon in there?'

'This one?'

'Thank you. We might eat out of the bowls. And then I'll wash up and start unpacking in the lounge room.'

Dad straightens but he makes a funny face as if his back hurts. 'After dinner you can unpack your room, if you really want, but leave the rest. I'll wash up. We're going to live here for a long time, Becky, so there's no rush to do it all in one day.'

My eyes are all misty and I stir dinner, blinking fast. If Dad thinks we will live here for a long time then won't we ever go home? Not even to visit Mum?

Charlie calls for Dad to get him and then I'm alone again so quickly wipe my eyes with the sleeve of my jumper. Charlie already likes it here and that has to be enough for now.

From the kitchen window I can't see the rocks. Maybe they weren't even real but a trick the light played on the water. Sometimes when everyone else was asleep at home I think I've seen Mum smiling from outside my window, but that was the moonlight playing tricks. Mum isn't here so I'm going to have to believe in what Charlie believes. In Charlie's lighthouse.

FIVE

NOW

Sadie burst out of the cottage, pulling her shoes off and tossing her phone and keys beside them on the grass at the side of the lake. Intending to swim to the rowboat, she noticed a narrow pier and ran along it. The timber was old and creaky but it was stable enough. It stretched out for twenty metres or so and every step brought her closer to the rowboat.

At the end, she dropped to her knees and grabbed a fine rope which was tied to a post. It was long and looped into the water but when she began pulling it in, the rowboat moved. She yanked harder and with barely a ripple the tiny boat drifted her way. As it closed in, she reached for it, one arm outstretched and the other holding the rope.

'Come here... argh.'

Another tug and it gently bumped against the end of the pier. She quickly stood and wrapped the rope around the post until most of the slack was taken up. There was no evidence a person had been in it. No towel or water bottle or shoes. Nothing. Other than the oars being in a rowing position.

Sadie kneeled again, peering into the water. It was impossible to judge how deep the lake was. Presumably here, with the pier built just over the surface, it wouldn't be terribly far to the bottom, but toward the middle the water was a deeper shade. She'd rather not be swimming around without any knowledge of what lurked down there. And had there been a tragedy then her diving in wasn't going to change the outcome.

Before the gloomy thoughts took hold, Sadie returned to firm ground, collected her phone and keys, and put her shoes back on. She'd left her water bottle in the kitchen when she'd fed the cat. The front door was wide open now and she slipped inside and hurried to retrieve the bottle. Surely this Rebecca person was just nearby. Perhaps visiting a neighbour?

Back outside she brought up a map program on her phone to see where she was in relation to home. It was only a couple of kilometres across country but the track she'd been aiming for – before the cat had stopped her – was a better option. Although a bit longer, it was mostly on flatter ground.

A warm, soft body curled around her ankles with a quiet meow.

'Feel better? Where's your human?'

The cat, tail high, trotted onto the grass and then glanced back.

'I think you should stay here.'

Letting it follow her into town would be a mistake. She caught up and carefully scooped the cat into her arms, hoping she didn't end up with a million scratches. 'Sorry, buddy. I'll make a deal. You stay inside and once I get to my car I'll come back and check on you.'

Short of phoning the police, what else could she do? And what would she say? She'd been trespassing, fed someone's cat, messed with their boat? And had a hunch something wasn't right? The cat complained loudly from the other side of the door when she closed it and again, Sadie hesitated. She dialled her mother's mobile which went to voicemail.

'Hi, Mum. Strange question... I went for a walk up in the

hills and came across a cottage... anyway, long story short, I have the strangest feeling that I need to find someone. I think her name is Rebecca Meyers. Might head to the police station and then I'll come and see you for lunch. Bye.'

Sadie set off along the track, heart heavy with misgivings.

In her life she was precise and organised. No messing around with decision-making. But here, now, she doubted herself. At the first bend she stopped and gazed back. Who would have a cottage here in the middle of nowhere? No fences. A rowboat with oars hanging off the sides. A cat who was accustomed to being fed indoors but couldn't get in. A handbag and keys but no sign of who owned it?

The sense of unease turned her stomach and she began retracing her steps.

Halfway to the cottage, the phone rang.

'She wandered off last year, about this time I think.' Pam jumped straight into the conversation. 'I remember it was a hot day and she became unwell. Best to call the police station. Probably will need the SES as well to cover more ground. And I'm sending Daniel.'

'Daniel?'

'He'll be there soon.'

'But Mum—'

Pam wasn't there.

As she walked, Sadie looked up the number for the local police station and called them. Another voicemail. Did nobody answer their phones these days? She left a message with her location and a curated version of the events. The cat continued to protest so she opened the door enough to release it, not expecting it to streak past her and run in the direction of some rocks at the base of one of the hills.

'As good a place as any to start looking.'

Sadie followed the cat. Again.

.   .   .

The cat settled onto a flat rock in the sunlight and ignored Sadie when she caught up.

A narrow stream trickled between the boulders from up the hill into the lake. She jumped across and then remembered the cat.

'Are you coming?'

The look she got was comical. The cat sat, tail flicking side to side, and then it decided to groom itself.

'Okay. I'm walking all the way around. Meet you back at the cottage.'

There were scattered clumps of reeds around the edge of the lake and the water level was almost as high as the soft grass surrounding it. The temptation to lie on her back and watch fluffy clouds float above almost undid her resolve to find Rebecca Meyers.

Whatever is going on with you, Sadie?

Rivers End was going on. How she'd missed the gentle life-style and tranquil environment.

A motor interrupted the peace as a vehicle approached. Sadie hurried to meet it, hoping it was the police. What pulled up wasn't a police vehicle but a large, dark blue four-wheel drive with white signwriting: Harrington Homes.

Whoever was driving sat inside for what seemed minutes. Sadie couldn't see in thanks to dark tinting and it was only when the door opened a crack that it became clear the driver was on a phone call. His voice was deep, but too muffled to hear a word. It was a bit awkward hanging around for whoever this was to make themselves known so she turned her back and stared at the lake. The cat was racing toward her.

And zipped straight past.

'Hey, Percy. Where's your mamma gone?'

The man had climbed out and was nursing the cat who was purring loudly.

Percy. Mamma? Who is this?

He glanced up with a smile. 'I'd shake your hand but... cat and all. I'm Dan Harrington.'

'Sadie Forest.'

'I know.'

'Oh. Someone else recognised me yesterday. It is still a weird feeling when that happens.'

'Recognised? Oh, from when you used to live here. Nah, Pam told me your name.'

Way to bring me back to reality.

Well, good. The fewer people who saw her as a television personality the better.

'I'm Rebecca's closest neighbour. Only neighbour really.' He nodded his head behind the cottage where the hills rose again. 'Other side of there. Sure she's not inside?'

'Unless there's a trapdoor...'

The man's eyes settled on her face in a long, serious stare. Probably no sense of humour. Often the case with good-looking men. Men with broad shoulders and a narrow waist and muscular thighs filling out their jeans—

'I've checked the lake as best as I could,' she managed.

He gently placed Percy onto the ground. 'Rebecca doesn't get in the boat. Not that I've ever seen. Let's take a look at the cottage.' Dan didn't wait for Sadie.

She watched him stride toward the cottage then gave herself a mental shake and followed. A really good mental shake.

The first thing he did was to remove his boots and then he tapped on the door. 'Rebecca? It's just Dan checking up on you. Can I come in?' He waited and repeated himself then glanced at Sadie as she joined him. 'Door was like this?'

'Not quite. The cat was frantic to get in and I knocked and called out and then it kind of clicked and opened.'

'You opened a stranger's door?'

'Yes.'

'I see.' Dan pushed the door wide and went inside.

Rather than answer any more pointed questions, Sadie waited on the verandah. The cat jumped onto the rocking chair and curled into a ball. Sitting here as the sun set would be so pretty as the sky changed the colour of the water and shadows crept over the grass.

'Did you look inside her handbag?'

Sadie jumped.

'Of course not!'

'She's done this before.'

'Mum said the same thing.'

Leaving the door partly open, Dan put on his boots. 'I can drop you at the inn. Or Pam's house.'

Get in the car with you? I don't think so.

The smallest smile touched his lips. 'Or you can walk back. Takes about thirty minutes along the track.'

'What about Rebecca?'

'I'm going to look for her.' And off he went again. The cat raised its head and blinked.

'And you like this man?' Sadie whispered to Percy.

'So, am I dropping you somewhere?'

SIX

Sadie clutched the grab handle for dear life as the four-wheel drive swung perilously close to the edge of the track, which was also the edge of a steep slope. She wasn't about to look down and dug deep to avoid telling Dan to take more care.

'All good over there?' He drove with one hand on the wheel while the other tapped on the navigation console in the dashboard.

'Sure.'

As they neared a sharp curve he touched the brakes and the vehicle slowed to a crawl. The console came to life with a map of Rivers End. Dan moved the map with a finger along the coastline past bays and inlets until it reached Warrnambool. The town was the largest in the region and between it and Rivers End were a dozen or so tiny villages, some little more than a convenience shop and petrol station with a handful of houses. He expanded the view to show both towns.

'Rebecca was found last time about here,' he pointed.

'Up past Willow Bay. Was she on foot?'

'Yes.'

'But that's a long walk from here.'

He put both hands on the steering wheel and accelerated. 'I got the feeling she was trying to get somewhere but she never said where. Think I'll follow the coast until I find her.'

'Can I help?'

Dan gave her a curious look. 'Why would you want to?'

'Because she's missing. Or lost. Does she have memory issues or—'

'Whoa. Don't jump to conclusions. There's nothing wrong with Rebecca other than slowing down with age and that'll happen to us all sooner or later.'

'People don't just wander off with no triggering factors,' Sadie said. She released the grab handle and turned a bit in her seat toward the driver's side. 'You seem concerned, certainly enough to go looking for her.'

'Her mind is good. And I'm pretty sure her mental health is fine. But she ended up in hospital with heatstroke last year and today is hotting up already.'

'Then why would she leave her handbag and keys inside an unlocked cottage? And her cat who clearly was hungry.'

Dan burst into laughter.

'How is this funny?'

His smile somehow stuck a pin in her ballooning outrage.

'Have you ever owned a cat? I guess not because out of all of Mother Nature's creatures, they are the ones who will lie to your face. Percy is a very well-loved and well-fed cat with a typical feline sense of entitlement.'

She'd never owned a cat. Or a dog. No pets despite living on several acres growing up.

I'd love a cat. And a dog.

But apartment living wasn't ideal for a pet, let alone her life-style. The hours she kept during filming were ridiculous and took her all over the country. If she had a flatmate or a partner it might be different but Sadie had long since resigned herself to a solitary life. It was best like that.

'Sadie?'

'Oh, sorry.'

'I asked if you really do want to help.'

They'd descended the final hill without her noticing and she recognised the road to the mountains ahead.

She wasn't here to go on a search for someone she'd never met.

Her mother was her priority.

'Yes. I'd like to help.'

'Okay then. Let's find her.'

Pam brushed off Sadie's apology when she called. 'You and Daniel are lovely to go looking. Best the old dear sees a friendly face rather than one of the rescue people she might not know.'

I have so many questions.

'Happy to have a bit of a drive?' Dan turned onto the road leading out of town. 'And a few stops?'

'Whatever it takes.'

He'd had a call from someone who was driving in the opposite direction toward the town of Green Bay.

'And the police? I left a message,' Sadie said.

'Yeah. Well.'

Rivers End had only ever had a one-person station as far as Sadie could recall. Now, with all the new growth, surely something had to change? Whoever was stationed here also lived here, in the house behind the old-fashioned station. And they had a large area to cover with farms and remote villages part of the territory.

'That good, huh?'

They drove past Palmerston House and Sadie craned her neck to look at the beautiful old home. She'd dreamed about living there as a child, with its grand foyer and expansive grounds. No wonder people chose it as accommodation over the inn. Who wouldn't?

'How do you know my mother, Dan?'

'I stayed at the inn for a few weeks when I moved here. Well, not moved here but came to work short-term for a local builder. Pam was always very kind. So was Ron.'

Sadie felt her mouth drop open and she spun her head to look out of the window.

Kind? Ronald Carson didn't have a kind bone in his entire body.

'I'm sorry for your loss,' Dan said.

She felt far from sorry but managed a curt, 'Thanks.'

'Keep an eye out in case Rebecca is sitting down or walking under the trees.'

'What does she look like?'

'Seventies. About your height – what are you, one-seventy centimetres? White hair. Fit as a fiddle.' He flicked an indicator on and slowed. 'Let's hope she's here.'

They turned onto a road between dense bushland. Sadie remembered it as being a dirt track but now it was sealed and wider. At the end, the previously small and dusty carpark had been redone with gravel and could fit boat trailers with a large turning circle and a ramp leading to the water.

Leaving the four-wheel drive in the shade they hurried to the beach. Half a dozen people lay on the sand or swam in the calm sea.

'Look at all those boats,' Sadie said.

'Soon enough a small marina will go in here. Has to, just to keep up with demand and overall it will protect the environment more than the current setup. I'm going to go ask these guys if they've seen anyone.' He jogged in the direction of the nearest sunbathers.

Sadie couldn't take her eyes off the water. At least two dozen yachts – including a few in the luxury class – shared a space better suited for half as many. How could she have thought nothing had changed in Rivers End? The Willow Bay of her youth was a quiet retreat from the world where it was more common to be the only visitor than not.

'No luck.' Dan returned. 'You okay, Sadie?'

'I'm just... surprised.' There was no point thinking too hard about this. In a few weeks she'd be gone again and whatever the residents of this region chose to do wasn't her business. Not anymore. 'Let's go.'

Next to Dan's four-wheel drive, a uniformed police officer leaned on the boot of a patrol car, smoking. Beside her, Dan tensed and Sadie could almost feel the disapproval emanate from him.

'She's not down there?'

'No, Mick. Which direction are you going to look for her?' Dan took his car keys out. 'And have you alerted the bus company?'

'Don't even know she's missing.'

Mick's eyes moved to Sadie and an unpleasant shiver went down her spine.

'Well, if it isn't little Sadie Carson, back from the big smoke. Paying your old mother a visit?'

'Hello, Mick. I left a message about Rebecca Meyers. You haven't called back.'

'Bit busy.' He dropped the butt onto the ground and stepped on it. 'Might go drive around the town for a bit. Stop and ask at some of the shops.'

'What about a press release? Emergency services being alerted? Airwing?'

With a snigger, Mick opened the driver's door. 'Been watching too many of those reality shows you make? The woman isn't missing. She's got a screw loose. But you two go right ahead and waste your time.'

As he slid into the patrol car Sadie stepped forward to tell him he needed to do his job but she was stopped by Dan's hand on her arm. Her eyes shot to his and he shook his head ever so slightly, lips tight. She had so much to say to the pathetic excuse for a man – who had no right to wear the badge of an honoured profession – and had the benefit of life experience to protect her from his bullying. He didn't scare her anymore. But Dan's expression said volumes and she climbed into the four-wheel drive without a word.

They followed the patrol car to the main road where it turned toward Rivers End.

Once Dan had accelerated in the opposite direction, Sadie exhaled slowly. 'When... how? Mick Hammond? A police officer?'

'He came back to live here a year after I did. Loves telling people he gave up a fast track to advancement in Melbourne because he knew Rivers End needed him. Reality is that he's here looking for an easy life.'

'His superiors should be told he's not doing his job.'

'Probably. But you'll need more than him lacking interest in Rebecca's whereabouts. What reality shows?'

The road headed inland for a couple of kilometres. Surely nobody would walk all this way? There was little to see apart from salt bushes and occasional gum trees peppering an other-wise bland landscape. If they followed this route they'd meet up with the Great Ocean Road in a few minutes. Instead, Dan turned off at a signpost to Driftwood Cove. The road dipped and then, from the next crest, the town came into view. On either side of it, steep hills with scattered, large houses rose to overlook a bay. The main shopping strip was opposite the beach.

'Are you on television?' Dan asked.

'Sometimes. This is a sweet little town.'

'Sure is. I've built three houses here so far.'

'We must be ten kilometres from Rivers End. Add on

another few walking from Rebecca's house and this heat, and I'm struggling to comprehend how she would get this far.'

'There's a bus which she probably caught. Still a hike though. I might park and check in with some of my crew. They're all out searching.'

How different could two men be? Dan was too busy finding a place to park to notice Sadie watching him. The police officer who should have cared enough about the wellbeing of an elderly person to mount a search was nowhere in sight but this man... he had a good heart. Rebecca was his neighbour. Not his relative. But he'd dropped whatever he was doing and sent his crew – who he was most likely paying for their time – to look for her.

Her heart warmed to him.

And that scared her.

She opened the door and when he glanced over, she gestured up one of the hills with a whispered, 'I'll look up there.'

There was a narrow park between the beach and the main street, complete with tall pine trees and a fountain, where a group of small children splashed around. The shops all had multicoloured awnings. A small supermarket. An ice-cream shop with umbrellas and seats outside. What looked like a gift shop, a pharmacy and a few others, ending with a café on the other corner.

From one end of the park, a wide footpath weaved up the hill, lined on the ocean side by a series of low logs strung together to form a fence of sorts, probably to remind walkers there was a drop. Although the hill was steep, there was no cliff edge but rather, a rugged slope back down to the sea.

The walk would be pleasant on a cooler day but she'd long since run out of water and with the sun directly overhead, was overheating. Perspiration dripped between her shoulder blades.

What kept her climbing was a bench up ahead. Or at least,

the person sitting on it. Sadie glanced back. Dan was out of the four-wheel drive, still on his phone and gazing around. She waved but wasn't certain he'd seen her over the distance so kept going.

The closer she got, the more her heart thumped. Not from the heat or the climb.

The person on the bench had long, white hair in a braid down her back. Sadie made sure the woman could see her as she approached, not wanting to startle her.

Beautiful, piercing blue eyes sized her up. The woman's face was etched with wrinkles. She sat straight-backed on the edge of the seat, a sunhat in her hands, head tilted in curiosity.

'Hello. I'm Sadie. Do you mind if I sit with you?'

There was no answer and Sadie perched on the very end.

'Are you Rebecca? Rebecca Meyers?'

With the heaviest of sighs the woman's shoulders slumped. She turned her face to the sea. 'Today, I am Becky.'

SEVEN

62 YEARS AGO

A week of unpacking and settling into a routine has made things a bit easier. A bit more normal. But this house is so large! Even after Dad set one bedroom up as a home office there are two spare. He joked about getting a lodger to help pay the rent but Charlie told him it would be better to make it into a room for a kitten to sleep in. Dad didn't seem to know how to answer and the subject was dropped but Charlie whispered to me that he'd wear Dad down.

After Dad gave me the go-ahead, I turned the smallest of the bedrooms into a place for Mum's belongings. When Dad told us we were moving, I made him promise we could bring everything of Mum's as well. Nothing was to be thrown or given away. I'd carefully packed Mum's clothes and shoes and locked diaries and photographs into especially sturdy boxes. And made a nest in the middle of Mum's softest jumper for the jewellery box. I do love the small box with its lavender pattern with gold metal around the edges and when it is opened, a darling little ballerina lifts up and slowly spins in a perpetual pirouette as music plays. As long as I wind it up first with the key on the back, the dancer always dances.

One day, maybe, I could be a dancer.

There's no bed in this room. Mum's dressing table with a mirror and middle drawer and two drawers on either side is on one wall and the only other furniture is an old wardrobe already in the room. I cleaned it from top to bottom and hung Mum's hanging clothes and folded the rest for the drawers. Her three pairs of shoes fit nicely on the bottom beneath the hangers.

'You know that your mother would have wanted you to have the dressing table in your room as your own.' Dad had stood in the doorway. 'Why not take the jewellery box at least?'

I can't speak. Mum's things belong together. Dad doesn't understand. But now he gives me a quick hug and reminds me we're going shopping.

'What are we going to get for dinner? Do we need a list?'

'I already did one, Charlie,' I glance over my shoulder from the front of the car. Charlie is in the seat Dad got made to special specifications to keep him secure. 'But you can tell me what meals you'd like this week. Any fancies?'

'Spaghetti on toast. Tomato soup with those yummy bread rolls you make. And ice cream.'

The only response is to laugh and I do.

'Is it funny?' Charlie frowns. 'Why?'

'Only because you would have that every single day if I let you.'

'And twice some days,' Dad adds.

Charlie slaps his hands more or less together. 'Ooh... twice a day. Ice cream for breakfast.'

The drive into the village nearby isn't long and in pleasant weather we'll probably just walk down. But the clouds are puffing along as if they want to spit rain everywhere and the climb back up to the house is too steep with a lot of shopping and the wheelchair. Earlier I wrote out a long list of staples as well as fresh food to buy. We used to visit the big market in Melbourne each week but Dad thinks there's nothing like it in the area. There isn't much in the area anyway, from what I've seen on our drives to explore.

My school is walking distance and I start next week. Butterflies tumble around in my tummy. New teachers and children. If only I was old enough to finish school and just look after Dad and Charlie. His new school is really just a house with some paddocks around it. I'm still confused what is special about it but Charlie is excited to start and keeps reminding me there is a pony there.

'Here we are.' Dad parks the car across the road from the shops, alongside a strip of grass lined with pine trees. On the other side of the trees is the beach. It isn't busy now but I've seen people swimming there another time.

I'd never swim in the sea. Who knew what was out there?

Charlie spies a set of swings under the trees. 'Can we? Please. Please.'

'Today is for shopping. And I reckon the rain will be here soon so why don't we come back when the weather is nice?' Dad has got the wheelchair out and lifts Charlie from the car. 'How do you think we can help Becky?'

'I can look for the things lower down.'

'Excellent. Will that be helpful, Becky?' Dad locks the car.

'Very helpful.'

The grocery store is so small. How will I fill the big pantry and the fridge? Dad did some shopping the second day we arrived and it was hard getting it to stretch. There are only four aisles and one big checkout and behind it is a stern-faced woman with horn-rimmed glasses and her hair pulled back in a tight bun and a striped apron over a black dress.

'Good morning!' Dad believes in being friendly and treating other people as you want to be treated. 'Bit of rain ahead?'

'Good morning. It is a grey old day.'

The woman stares at Charlie as Dad pushes him through the entry.

Charlie waves.

I glare at her. Why do people have to stare all the time? Would she like it?

Once I get a shopping trolley I follow the other two. Charlie keeps finding things which aren't on the list and I have to keep saying no, which makes him cross. Before long I'm even cross and then Dad stops pushing the wheelchair and squats in front of us.

'I have an idea. Because this is our first shopping trip together in our new town, why don't we each treat ourselves to one special thing we wouldn't normally have.'

'Like a chocolate bar?' Charlie asks.

'Yes. Or even those things you can freeze – Sunny Boys?' Dad grins. 'But you have to tell me another object which is also a tetrahedral shape like they are.'

Charlie rolls his eyes. 'Dad. Everyone knows they are just a frozen pyramid.'

'Except they aren't frozen yet. Are you getting those?' My mind fills with possibilities. We never get special stuff. Not like this. ''Cos I thought I might get a packet of Tim Tams.'

Dad and Charlie's mouths drop open and I giggle.

'What if we share everything?' Dad suggests.

Charlie and I looked at each other. 'Depends what you choose, Dad.'

'Becky, really? I'd share with you both.'

'But you might get something too grown up for us,' I search for something awful. 'Like... um, I don't know, stinky cheese.'

Dad bursts out laughing.

'No stinky cheese, Daddy, I think you should choose ice cream.' Charlie is serious.

'Let's see what we can find and I promise no stinky cheese.'

. . .

Dad and I unload the contents of the trolley onto the counter. There was more here to buy than I expected and we're going to visit the greengrocer and butcher further along the street next so at least we won't need to shop for a while.

The woman from before taps on the cash register and I pack into the boxes from a pile at the end. Dad is telling her way too much. Like about us moving from Melbourne. And how we only arrived a few days ago.

'There's a lighthouse outside my window!' Charlie announces.

'Shh. The lady doesn't need to know that.'

'But Becky—'

'Poor little mite. Whatever happened to him? Car accident?' The woman leans over the counter and slows her voice as if talking to a baby. 'What is your name, little man?'

'I'm Charlie Hamilton. What is your name?'

'Mrs McKenzie.' She straightens and finishes ringing up the sale. 'I bet your mother has her hands full looking after you two. How nice of you to let her have a break because it's not often I see a father shopping with his children.'

Nobody speaks. Dad shuffles his feet and gives me a look I understand. *Stay quiet.* Well why should I? What makes adults think they can say anything they want but I can't? Mrs McKenzie is rude to have said any of that. I put my hands on Charlie's shoulders and gently squeeze. He matters, not that woman.

Once the shopping is all packed up, Dad pays in a lot of pound notes. Mrs McKenzie suggests we borrow the trolley to wheel the boxes to the car.

'Greengrocer next?' Dad asks as he closes the boot.

He always acts like nothing has happened. Not even when people make fun of Charlie or poke their noses into our private business.

'Can you take the trolley back, Becky? Charlie and I will start looking for some vegetables.'

I'm fuming still and decide just to nod because if I open my mouth I'll say something mean about that woman. I wheel the trolley back inside the grocery store.

'Thank you, deary. I look forward to meeting your mother next time.'

Lift your chin. That way they'll never know you.

I stand as tall as I can and use my most grown-up voice. 'My mother is deceased. And Charlie was born with spastic palsy but is very smart and very *polite*.'

There is a certain satisfaction in seeing Mrs McKenzie's cheeks blush bright red but I'm not staying here a second longer. I spin around and run out of the store. Before the tears can start.

EIGHT

NOW

Sadie had no idea what to say. It was as if Rebecca pulled down an invisible barrier because she stared out at the ocean without moving and hadn't responded to Sadie asking if she was alright.

The bench was on a concrete slab just off the footpath which then changed direction to intersect with the road a dozen or so metres away. Between the bench and the first of the large, modern homes further along were a handful of abandoned old houses, weatherboard cottages in poor repair with overgrown grounds.

'They pull more down each year.'

Rebecca wasn't even looking at them or Sadie.

'Families lived there once. Children. All gone.'

Had she lived in one of those ruins? Perhaps her visit was simply to reminisce. But why walk here and without her handbag?

Fingers touched her arm and Rebecca stared intently at her. 'I need to find them. Will you help me?'

'Of course I will. Who are you looking for?'

An odd expression crossed the woman's face... a mix of sorrow and possibly fear, and then she shook her head.

'Ah, there you both are. I brought some cold water.'

Dan held out bottles and Rebecca looked up at him, blinking as the sun caught her eyes.

'Whatever are you doing out here, Daniel? Aren't you building a house somewhere?' Rebecca accepted the water. 'Or are you responsible for those monstrosities?' She gestured in the general direction of the new homes.

'Not those ones.' He squatted a few feet away and his eyes met Sadie's.

Eyes filled with relief.

Warm, brown eyes.

Sadie opened her bottle and gulped some water, almost spilling it in her haste.

'Have a drink, Rebecca. That sun is pretty fierce,' Dan said. 'Then I can drop you home. Both of you.'

Rebecca glanced at Sadie. 'Do I know you, young lady? I'm certain I'd remember.'

'I'm Pam Carson's daughter. She owns the inn in Rivers End, but I haven't visited in a few years. How long have you lived there?'

'Three years. So we've never met.' Losing interest, Rebecca removed the cap from the bottle and sipped, her eyes back on the ocean.

Only three years? The little cottage by the lake radiated the warmth and comfort which only came from a loving resident and it looked so... lived in. Although Sadie had only been inside briefly she'd noticed the little touches everywhere which made it into a home. A calm and happy place. Her own apartment of six years wasn't as inviting. Something strange tugged at her.

First you want a pet and now a cottage by a lake?

'Rebecca, would you like me to bring my car up? It's right down near the park.'

'Oh... we're leaving?' After plonking her sunhat on, Rebecca stood, swaying a little, and her hand reached toward Dan. He steadied her. 'I'm fine but may I lean on your arm while we walk?'

'You may.' Dan's smile was wide and genuine.

It was obvious he liked the woman and his kindness once again affected Sadie on some level she didn't want to examine too closely. She followed them down the footpath, confused at herself. Why *wouldn't* a person care about the wellbeing of their neighbour? Mind you, her father never had. He rarely had a nice word to say about anyone unless it was to the face of a guest. But she couldn't blame one man for her narrow view of the world. She worked with men a lot and some of them were decent blokes.

Some of them.

This new introspective Sadie was an unexpected – and frankly, unwanted – side effect of being back here. If she was going to worry about who was decent and who wasn't then she'd end up without a career. Her close-knit team were one thing and they all had each other's backs but creating a documentary series meant working with a wide range of people both in and outside the industry. Not all would be on her list of friends.

How many real friends do I have, anyway?

Oh, this had to stop!

Sadie pushed the weird thoughts away.

Dan was pointing out houses to Rebecca. 'Right in the middle over there... about fifty metres up the far hill? One of the loveliest houses I've had the pleasure of building. Everything about it is eco-friendly and it has perfect views of the bay.'

'Views aren't everything.'

'They are these days. People are all after the lifestyle of a functional but beautiful residence and the best aspect they can afford.'

'I'll settle for the view of Whisper Lake any day, watching the wildlife come down to drink.'

'Do you sit in the rocking chair watching the sun set?' Sadie asked.

Rebecca glanced over her shoulder. 'We've established we've never met, so how do you know about my rocking chair?'

Oops.

'Um... earlier today I accidentally went onto your property. I was walking in the hills and was drawn to the lake and had no idea there was a cottage there. Sorry.'

They were almost at the bottom of the hill and crossed onto the grass of the park.

'Did you meet Percy?' Rebecca asked.

Sadie couldn't help smiling and she snuck a look at Dan, who was oblivious to her memory of his cuddling the cat as if it was the most natural thing in the world to do. 'Green eyes? Black fur? Sure did.'

'Percy is particular. Did she like you?'

Tail aloft, curling around her legs. The softest sensation of fur against bare legs.

'Percy's a girl? Hard to tell what she was thinking but she talked to me a lot.'

Rebecca chuckled but said nothing more.

Who do you want me to help you find?

The moment didn't feel right to ask and then they reached Dan's four-wheel drive and he opened the front passenger door, offering his arm again as Rebecca climbed in. Sadie got into the back seat. A moment later the engine started and Dan nosed out of the parking spot.

'Daniel. Wait a minute?' Rebecca leaned forward, eyes on the shopping strip as Dan came to a stop again.

'Need something from the shops? We can get ice creams.'

Rebecca didn't speak. Her focus was on the gift shop and for a moment, Sadie was certain there was a glistening of her eyes. But the moment passed and Rebecca sat back and then they were on their way home.

All of Sadie's journalistic instincts were on high alert. There was a story here. A deep, important story of a woman who was so drawn to a place – possibly searching for someone – that she'd travelled by bus and foot in the heat of summer. What an interesting puzzle she'd stumbled across.

After a much-needed second shower and change of clothes, Sadie drove to the inn. Dan had dropped her home first and then he and Rebecca had left without a backward glance.

Pam was in one of the inn rooms, cleaning.

'Don't you have someone who does this?' Sadie stuck her head inside. The bed was stripped bare and her mother held a fresh fitted sheet. Leaving her shoes outside, Sadie gave her a hand.

'I do have someone to help but this is the third time they've not done a room properly. I only came in to put the fridge on and pop some milk and a jug of water into it and found the bed wasn't changed from the last guest nor the towels. Fold that corner a bit tighter, love.'

'Like this? Well, I'll help. Is it just this room?'

Pam straightened, rubbing the middle of her back. 'I hope so.'

'Leave this with me and you check them.'

Half an hour later they'd cleaned two other rooms and had everything back to the level the inn always kept. Despite its age and plainness, cleanliness was always a priority. The beds had been replaced since the last time Sadie set foot in the rooms and each unit had a comfortable armchair, small desk, and a fold-out table for meals. There were no cooking facilities apart from a toaster and kettle but guests could bring takeaway in from the restaurants which were a short walk away.

'Do you still provide those breakfasts I used to love so

much?' Sadie pushed the cleaning trolley toward the office. 'Remember how I wanted to become a guest just to have them?'

'A mini box of cereal, a fruit cup, piece of toast, and individually wrapped butter. I certainly do remember. I think you were about seven.'

'And juice, Mum. Pineapple and orange because it sounded very exotic.'

They laughed at the memory as Pam opened the door to the utility room and Sadie pushed the trolley.

'New washing machine and dryer? Nice.'

'Had to replace them. When we were a lot busier they'd be going several times a day and appliances wear out. People too.'

It was a throwaway comment and although her mother began shoving sheets into the washing machine, her face was set. Sadie had rarely seen her mother sit down. Take it easy. Relax. Last night was the first time she could recall seeing her in one spot for so long. The woman was always a whirlwind of activity whether here or at home and surely that must take its toll.

'What time are your guests arriving?' Sadie put the excess washing into a hamper and pulled the rubbish bag from the side of the trolley. 'Still up to lunch with me?'

'One couple arriving mid-afternoon. Another isn't here until this evening because they are driving a long distance and unsure of their timing. But before nine. I've told them to phone me when they get to Green Bay and then I'll meet them back here.' She turned on the machine, then straightened with a sigh. 'Lunch sounds nice.'

'Can you leave the office to come to a café? Or shall I duck across to the bakery?' Sadie rushed her words for the second suggestion. After her mother's reaction last night to going out to dinner, she didn't want to upset her again.

'Bakery, please. I do quite fancy one of Sylvia's cottage pies.'

The main street was quiet which wasn't really a surprise in

the heat, which was getting steamy. She'd be inside under air conditioning if she had the choice. Most of the shops' roofs extended over the footpath offering a brief respite from the sun and she slowed her steps a few times as she came across new businesses.

A beauty salon where once had been the town's only hairdresser. All the chairs inside were full and bright music filtered through the glass.

So not everyone is home today.

The dress shop she remembered from her childhood was now a cute boutique for kids' clothes and toys. And one shop was being renovated. She couldn't recall what used to be there. But the bakery was the same. Colourful umbrellas outside and a tempting window display of iced cakes.

She pushed the door open and almost moaned in delight with the mingled aromas of flour and apples and sugar and earthy savouries and bread. Her mouth watered. The clock behind the counter said it was almost two o'clock which accounted for her rumbling tummy and the almost empty shelves.

The original owner still worked here.

'Hello, Sylvia.'

Hair piled up in a bun, the older woman peered over the counter before a smile softened her otherwise stern expression.

'Sadie Carson? Is that you?'

'Sadie Forest these days. And yes it is.'

'Of course, I should remember the stage name... or married name? We've watched every documentary you've made.'

Relieved Sylvia hadn't dwelt on the marriage comment, Sadie smiled in return. 'I'm so happy to hear that.'

'Visiting Pam? She's had such a sad time and must be comforted you're home again. But you didn't come here to chat, so what can I get for you?'

'Mum had her heart set on a cottage pie but I can't see any today.'

'Just took a batch out of the oven. And what about for you? There's some curried vegetable pies, a couple of pasties, or I can make you a fresh salad and cheese roll?'

'Veggie pie thanks. And two apple turnovers.'

A childish giggle bubbled up and she caught it just in time. How long since she'd eaten anything so... delicious? And so naughty, with whipped cream layering the apple and caramelised sugar crystals baked into the top.

Sylvia slid everything into two small boxes. 'Staying for long? There's plenty of folk who'd love to say hello.'

'A few weeks. Just to help Mum sort out a few things. Thank you for these.' Sadie paid and took her leave.

She hadn't even been here for a full day but already Rivers End was inching its way back into her heart. A horn tooted and as she looked up, a hand waved from the window of a blue four-wheel drive as Dan drove by. If someone like him had lived here when she'd finished school, Sadie might never have left.

Good thing I have a life to return to.

NINE

As if she hadn't eaten in a week, Pam demolished the cottage pie and the apple turnover disappeared soon after. Finishing up the last crumbs she gazed at her daughter's amused face. 'What?'

'Nothing. Well, actually I'm wondering how someone can eat like that and stay so thin.'

'You're not exactly tubby yourself, child. Not on any of the new-fangled diets, are you?' Her mother was already back on her feet, heading for the kettle. 'More coffee is in order.'

'I walk just about every day. Usually along the beach. And no, I don't follow any diets and if anything, eat badly. Good genes, I guess.' Sadie cleaned up their lunch. 'But seriously, Mum, are you eating properly?'

'Since when do you worry yourself about such nonsense? Of course I eat properly.'

'But you have next to no food in the house—'

'Goodness' sake, Sadie. I'm fifty-five years old, manage a business, and raised a child. Though obviously not very well! Quite certainly I can feed myself. And make a bed. And deal with funeral homes and solicitors and real estate agents.

Damned vultures, each and every one of them!' She slammed down her cup and it shattered.

'Oh, Mum...' Sadie knelt to pick up pieces.

'No. No, Sadie, that is quite enough mothering for one day. I think you should go home.'

She kept collecting shards and the handle. 'Which home, Mum?' When there was no reply, Sadie sighed. 'I'm just picking these up, okay? I don't want to go home. Not to Sydney and not to the house.'

Mum's palms were flat on the counter and she stared ahead at nothing, lips pressed tight against each other. Sadie had never seen her so agitated, even when Dad was at his worst. A sliver of guilt cut deep. She should have come sooner. When she'd emptied the pieces into a bin, Pam was still rigid.

'You know what? I just realised that we are both suffering from a sugar high.'

Her mother didn't move but the corners of her mouth did. Ever so slightly.

'Sylvia has a lot to answer for with those apple turnovers. Sugar in the apple. Sugar in the pastry. Sugar all over the top. Then when innocent... *innocent* I say, and unsuspecting customers come along, they are ill prepared for the whammy that hits them.'

This time there were definite signs of a smile, even if it was fleeting.

Sadie wrapped her arms around her mother and leaned her head on her shoulder. 'You are right. You don't need mothering. I'm just a bit worried about you.'

'I really am fine.' The anger had gone.

No, you really are not. But I'll let it go for now.

'In that case, how about that coffee? That wasn't your favourite cup or anything, was it?' Sadie released her mother and opened an overhead cupboard, rummaging around at the back. 'This one is sweet, with the bowl of ice cream and fruit.'

'Oh my. I forgot I had that.'

'Do you still make ice cream?'

Pam filled the kettle. 'Not for a long time.'

'I noticed in the pantry that there wasn't much in the way of your preserved fruit or vegetables or jams. I guess you've had a busy year.'

'It was only me eating them most of the time so I stopped. Your father decided a few years ago he only want fresh.'

'But they are fresh.'

'According to what someone told him, there is a high risk of serious illness from home bottling. Actually accused me of trying to poison him.' Pam shrugged. 'So I made everything from scratch for every meal. And took to freezing what I could from the garden to reduce wastage because he refused to let me donate any or even sell it.'

Sadie noticed herself squeezing the milk container into a peculiar shape. She forced her muscles to unclench and managed to straighten the spout enough to pour milk into her mother's cup.

'I'm not sure if I can get the fruit trees right. The birds take everything and it's been years since I did more than trim back the worst of the overgrown branches.'

They took their coffees to the sofa.

'You taught me that most fruit trees are hardy so I bet they just need a bit of your love and attention, Mum. I saw a nice little orchard today... at Rebecca Meyers' property.'

'Oh, I never asked. Did you and Daniel find her?'

'We did. Do you know her well?'

'Only to say hello to these days. Haven't really talked at length to her since just after she moved to the town. But her fruit trees are thriving?' Pam took a sip of coffee then held the cup up with a small smile at the pattern.

'And a vegetable garden behind a white picket fence. She'd gone all the way to Driftwood Cove.'

'On her bicycle?'

'No, that was still at her cottage. On foot, and Dan thinks by bus as well.'

'*Dan*. Now, that's a nice young man.'

There was no chance Sadie was going to give her mother something to talk about. As it was, there was a twinkle in her eyes as she regarded her daughter over the coffee cup.

'What do you know about Rebecca? I'm genuinely interested in her background, if you know anything?'

Her mother made a strange tutting noise. 'Fine, let's change the subject for now. Rebecca appeared from nowhere about three or so years back. She stayed here for two nights after arriving on the bus from Melbourne. She paid cash, which you know I'm not keen on taking but she said she didn't have a credit card. A taxi collected her after she checked out and a bit later the same day a removalist truck went past here in the direction of where she now lives.'

Sadie stretched out her legs. They were pink from the earlier sun. 'But she definitely came from Melbourne? Not Driftwood Cove?'

'She came all the way from Mildura.'

'Right up on the Victorian border? Goodness, big change to come and live here near the sea. Although...'

The bell on the front counter dinged.

'That'll be the first guests. Be right back.' Pushing herself to her feet, Pam left the coffee cup on the counter and hurried out.

Why would anyone make such a sea change – assuming that was what Rebecca had done – to hide herself in a valley with a view only of a tiny lake? What had Rebecca called it? Whisper Lake? A quick search for the name wasn't helpful so Sadie opened an app on her phone she used for notes.

- *What is the history of the cottage by the lake?*
  (*Whisper Lake*)

- *Who is Rebecca?*
- *Why has she wandered from home at least twice?*
- *Who does she want me to help her find?*
- *Am I just being curious for no reason?*

She deleted the last line. She was always curious. It came with the territory. After putting the phone away she washed out the cups, yawning a few times. This morning's adventures were catching up with her. But what she'd said to her mother was true. There was almost no food in the house and if Pam had to hang around here late then Sadie would refill the pantry and fridge. If anything it was better she did so before her mother got home because she was already tired of watching what she said. Pam had never been so reactive and Sadie had no idea how to handle it.

* * *

Tears streamed down Pam's face.

She was wringing her hands, shoulders slumped, face contorted. Sadie's heart raced and her stomach churned.

It was just after seven that evening.

The second lot of guests had arrived earlier than expected and Pam had insisted on walking home once she settled them in rather than letting Sadie collect her. But that gave Sadie time to prepare dinner. She had everything almost ready when her mother had wandered in.

And started crying.

Sadie grabbed a box of tissues and held them out. 'Hey, stop that. I'm really sorry, Mum, I didn't mean to overstep. I just wanted to—'

Suddenly, Sadie was enveloped in a hug and Pam sobbed against her shoulder. Sadie's heart was breaking. How had she messed up again? Her mother was so proud, so determined to be in control of her life now. And Sadie had taken it upon herself to shop and cook without consulting her.

What was I thinking?

'Oh, sweetheart,' Pam said, stepping back and taking a handful of tissues. 'You are the most thoughtful person I know. You didn't overstep at all.' She gazed at the kitchen bench, where Sadie had made a salad and had plates waiting for the lasagne in the oven. 'Everything looks lovely and more importantly, it smells divine. You kind, clever girl.'

Silly tears welled up in Sadie's eyes and she blinked fast to avoid having them fall. She quickly headed for the fridge. 'Okay. I have a lovely bottle of white wine chilling, if you would care for a glass?'

Pam was busy drying her face but nodded.

'Excellent. It is one of my favourites from the Hunter Valley. I've driven there a few times and stayed at a friend's winery.' Sadie collected the bottle, closed the fridge, and put a big smile on her face. 'I also buy their reds but thought white might be better to start you off. This is dry but not too dry, so for a sherry drinker, it isn't a big leap. I have a few dozen mixed of these at my apartment.'

'Do you have photographs?'

Sadie opened the bottle and began pouring into two wine glasses she'd bought at one of the bottle shops today. There'd been none in the entire house.

'Of the winery? I do.'

'No, love. Of your apartment.'

'But I've sent you some. A lot actually. In emails.'

'I think I've only had two or three emails from you in the last few years and none with photographs.'

That couldn't be right. Pam must have forgotten.

'Let's have dinner and afterwards I'll open my laptop and show you some. Take a sip and tell me what you think. Cheers.' Sadie handed over a glass and tapped it with hers.

'Cheers.'

The oven dinged and Sadie busied herself with the lasagne while her mother set the table in the dining room. When they sat, their eyes met and both smiled.

'This looks and smells wonderful, Sadie. Did you shop in town?'

Sadie began filling their plates. 'I did. The supermarket has had a refit and looks great. And I was stopped twice by people who recognised me.'

'Well, you did grow up here.'

'No, from television. Would you like some salad?'

'Please. Well how funny is that?' Picking up her wine glass, Pam grinned. 'To my daughter, the TV star.'

'Aw... not really, but thanks.'

'Our little town is lucky. You. And the lass who owns the beauty salon used to be a Hollywood make-up artist. Worked on a lot of the big films. And we've got a couple of the best artists in the region, if not the state. Lots of talent.'

Sadie slid some lasagne onto her fork. 'I noticed the salon earlier. Busy and looked like everyone was having a good time. I might need to check it out while I'm here. But for now, I am starving!'

'These are the newest photos of the apartment. I'd just repainted and put in some new rugs and was sure I sent these,' Sadie said. 'Perhaps I forgot.'

She'd opened her laptop on the dining room table after the remains of the lasagne and salad were put in the fridge and the plates washed up. Pam peered at the screen as Sadie clicked on a folder named 'Apartment photos for Mum'.

'This is the entry, actually, you can tell that. You walk in and there's the coat stand and a shoe rack.'

'What are those slippers all doing there?'

'I keep them for visitors. They slip on easily and are comfier than walking around in socks.'

Pam's mouth opened and closed. She had that look Sadie knew from a lifetime of her mother wanting to speak and deciding against it and it was time she stopped. Dad wasn't here to yell at her for saying the wrong thing.

'What are you thinking, Mum?'

'Well...' and a shake of her head.

Sadie let it go for the moment and clicked on another image. 'At the end of the hallway there's the open doorway to the right, which doubles back behind the wall to two bedrooms and a bathroom.'

'This is an apartment, though? Not a house? It looks so big.'

'I guess it is, but I like having the extra rooms. I always hoped—'

'Any of the lovely wine left?'

Sadie poured two more glasses as her mother continued.

'You hoped for a family? Or visitors?'

'One visitor, Mum. Just you, and yet I know it was impossible for you to visit. I really do understand but there was always a nice bedroom there if you wanted it. There still is.' Keeping herself from blaming her father for stopping her mother from ever going anywhere without him took all of Sadie's resolve. 'You will visit one day?'

'I've never been to Sydney. Always wanted to see the Opera House.' Pam reached out a hand and gripped Sadie's. 'So, what about a family?'

'Mother!'

They both laughed and the tension evaporated.

'Families need big gardens, not a little balcony. But honestly, the time for a family passed me by and I'm fine with my life.'

Liar.

'Show me your kitchen, love. That is the heart of any home.'

TEN

62 YEARS AGO

The endlessly rainy and gloomy weather is finally replaced with longer days of sunshine and warmth. School is an annoying interference. Charlie is less concerned. After all, he is learning to ride that pony at his new school and does a heap of fun activities, unlike any classes I have.

Dad is working again. He is a clever and well-educated man and has special letters he uses after his name. He writes scientific papers for universities and big businesses and does almost all his work at home. When we still lived in the city he would go to meetings sometimes but he's promised not to go anywhere for a few months. Until everyone is settled in. I doubt I'll ever feel settled. Not in the town and definitely not at school where I'm already being teased for being too quiet, too studious, too unfriendly. It doesn't matter. I'm used to bullies.

I fill an empty cordial bottle with water from a jug in the fridge and collect two thick plastic cups from the cupboard. 'Do you have your sunhat, Charlie?'

'On my head.'

Two cupcakes from a batch I made earlier go into a little container and then inside a carry bag and I zip it up. In the bottom are towels and a plastic bucket and shovel. This is our third visit to the beach and I'm getting more ideas of things to take each time.

'Let's go, Becky. Let's go, let's go!' Charlie is almost bouncing out of his wheelchair near the back door.

'Almost ready. Just going to let Dad know.'

I dash up to Dad's study and tap on the part-open door. Since he's started working again, he is preoccupied a lot and more serious than when we first got here.

'Heading down to the beach, sweetie?' Dad turns in his chair. There are books open all over his big desk and his type-writer has a fresh piece of paper waiting for him to start typing. 'Would you like me to carry Charlie down?'

'We're going to try something new. We have a plan but if it doesn't work I'll run back.'

'I'll be an hour or so then come and join you two. Have fun.'

'See you later, alligator.'

'In a while, Crocodylidae.' Dad tousles my hair and I giggle, as always, at his insistence on using the scientific name for the creature. 'Off you both go.'

I sprint to Charlie. 'Think we can do this?'

He grins broadly and nods, and when I open the back door, bag in hand, he wheels onto the timber deck. There are a dozen steps in one direction but one of the first things Dad did when we moved in was build a timber ramp off the side. Charlie is getting good at using it.

'Not too fast, buster.' I have to walk quickly to keep up.

'Why am I buster?'

'If you go too fast you might fall out and buster your arm.'

Charlie slows right down. 'Isn't it *bust* your arm?'

'Yes, but it's funnier how I say it.'

'Not funny, Becky. If I buster my arm how will I eater those cupcakes?'

He is worse than Dad because at least his jokes are obviously silly, but Charlie has a deadpan face when he delivers a line.

'Then I'll have to eater them both.'

'Becky!'

At the bottom we continue along a concrete path to a small shed at the back of the garden. I plonk the bag onto Charlie's lap as he stops. 'I hope this works.'

Inside the shed, along with some old gardening stuff, is a surfboard and a funny-looking sled made from wood. Dad said someone left them behind. I haul the sled out and lay it on the grass at the edge of the track leading to the beach. There's a rope attached to one end and runners underneath.

'You'll have to hold on very tight, Charlie.' I take the bag from him and drop it onto the front of the sled. 'I'll carry you to it.'

'I can walk.'

'Save your energy for the beach.'

He is getting a bit too heavy for me but I manage the short distance and lower him as carefully as I can.

'Do you want to lie on your tummy or sit?'

'Sit. Let's go!'

'Just yell if you want me to stop.'

I grab the rope and walk backwards so I can keep an eye on Charlie as the sled moves. It's lots harder to get going than I expect so I unravel a bit more rope and pull from further away. That's a bit easier and once the sled is on the sandy track it moves better. Charlie clutches the sides, his eyes wide with excitement as, bumping and zigzagging, we make our way down the steep slope.

We stop a few times to adjust the bag but Charlie doesn't let go of the sled for one second. He must be getting stronger from doing different physical therapy than the exercises Dad and I have done with him over the years and if just a few weeks makes such a difference then living here is worth it.

At the bottom, the sled kind of bumps to a halt and refuses to budge in the soft, deep sand so I sling the bag over a shoulder and help Charlie onto his feet. Normally he'd wear callipers to help keep his legs straight but they would get filled with sand and ruined. 'Need a lift?'

'I'll hang on to you.'

After a few steps, he shakes his head. 'Need a lift, Becky.'

Carrying both is too much so I leave the bag and pick up Charlie. 'What if we go near that little cave so we can sit in the shade if it gets too hot?'

'Good. And I like the lake.'

'What lake?'

Walking through the sand is hard going. Thank goodness it isn't far. With a sigh of relief, I sit him onto the sand. 'Be right back.' A minute later I have the bag and in no time we are sitting on spread-out towels and munching on cupcakes.

'There are fishies in the lake.' Charlie has pushed himself on his bottom from the village of sandcastles we've built. Now he is close to a pool of water.

'Ah. No, its called a lagoon, not a lake.'

'Nah. Lake. See them?' He points at the middle, where a school of tiny fish dart in one direction then another. 'Blue. And now silver. Watch them, Becky.'

'I am. They are very sweet.'

'Do you think they bite?'

'Not a chance. Not those fish. Shall we sit in the water with them and see if they come closer?'

Charlie almost overbalances in his excitement and I ease him into the water until he sits on the bottom. Then I climb in. The water only comes to our waists and is warm and clear and feels sort of velvety against my skin. Much nicer than the sea with its bitter, salty waves and relentless motion. Underneath, the sand is firm and darker than the golden-white beach and there are no shells to stand on or icky seaweed touching me.

With a shriek which makes me jump, Charlie's hands fly out of the water to clap in the way he does. A bit hit and miss but always, always because he is so happy he can't form the words at the time. The fish are around his legs. And mine. I draw in a breath and force myself to stay still. They won't hurt me.

Just as quickly they are gone, flitting to the other side of the lagoon, their colour changing as the sun dances on the water.

He laughs with his mouth wide open and his hands whacking the top of the water with his open palms. Charlie is a wonder. So much joy locked inside his poor body. Tears scorch my eyes and fall down my cheeks and all of a sudden, Charlie isn't laughing. He leans closer and one of his hands waves around for a moment then touches my face. 'Don't cry.'

My perfect little baby brother isn't perfect. Not in the eyes of doctors and definitely not in the minds of people who judge and scoff. His legs and arms might not always work very well and walking is hard but never once, not ever, has Charlie complained. He loves everyone and everything and is smart and funny.

'Becky. No crying! You scared away the fishies.'

Silly laughter comes from nowhere and I splutter a bit.

'And no drinking sea water,' Charlie says sternly. Like Dad would.

And then we are both laughing and I wipe the tears and put an arm around Charlie's shoulders.

'See. It is a lake. A magic lake which makes people laugh,' he says. 'And when we sit in our magic lake we can whisper secrets to each other. Whimsical whispering water. With fish.'

Since when did Charlie become a poet?

'Hey there, anyone fancy a swim?'

Dad is in bathers with a towel wrapped around his shoulders as he carries the old surfboard beneath an arm.

'Me, Dad.'

'Oh, Charlie no, you don't want to go in the ocean?' My heart races. 'We can sit in here with the fishies.'

'Of course he does. What about you? Care to try out the surfboard?' Dad tosses the towel down. 'I'll be with you so you'll be safe.'

'No. Dad, you know I would never... and Charlie shouldn't. And you shouldn't either.'

'Well you can sit in there and Charlie and I will have a paddle in the surf. Come on, kid.' With his spare arm Dad scoops Charlie out of the lagoon and before I can find the right words to stop them, they are at the edge of the sea.

Dad drops the surfboard into the water and adjusts Charlie against himself so he is upright and can hold on to Dad's neck as they wade in. Small waves rock the surfboard up and down and Charlie squeals in delight as sea spray tickles his feet.

I have to stop them before they go any further. Everybody knows how dangerous the ocean is. Everybody. I scramble out of the lagoon and my legs are so heavy running across the sand. My words aren't working at all and when I finally stand on the hard, wet sand near the tideline there is no point even trying.

Charlie sits at the front of the surfboard with his legs dangling either side while Dad has a hand on his back to keep him upright. They are on the other side of the small waves and the water comes right up to Dad's chest.

My legs give out and I flop onto my bottom.

They're going to drown. They will drown just like Mum.

I'll be all alone in the world.

I curl into a ball and close my eyes.

ELEVEN

NOW

How had she forgotten the joy of swimming before dawn at Rivers End beach?

On her way down from the car she'd noticed new signage about safety – swimming with others, avoiding dusk and dawn, and keeping between the flags when there was a lifesaver on the beach. Growing up that wasn't a thing and she'd survived.

Rule-breaker.

She was a hundred metres or so out from the beach and treading water. The first rays of light peeked over the horizon and soon the precious bubble of sanctuary would burst. Others would come down to surf or run their dogs and these blissful moments would evaporate. Against the lightening sky, the long, curving cliff which separated the beach from the town might well be the walls of a fortress. On either end were buttresses, tall and resolute against the ravages of the weather and the relentless Southern Ocean. Daylight might erase the illusion but for now, it was a fantasy world and she was a warrior mermaid.

Memories were strong. Swimming with friends, or, like now, with nobody. Late-night campfires on the beach with other teens, always without their parents' knowledge. Hiding in the cave near the stone steps during a thunderstorm. Her first kiss was there.

Sadie drew in a breath and dived, unwilling to revisit that embarrassing moment.

Beneath the surface anything might lurk yet not once had she feared the depths. There was a slightly increased risk of shark activity at this time of day but no attack had even been recorded along this piece of coastline. And although it wasn't an exact science, there were certain conditions more likely to attract the predators and she'd learned young how to read them.

Because Dad taught me how.

Air bubbled through her nose until nothing was left in her lungs and she kicked her way to the surface, gasping for oxygen when she breached it.

Where the heck had that come from? She turned onto her back and floated, forcing her shoulders to drop deeper in the water and visualising the sudden anxiety seeping from her fingers and toes to disappear with the current. The snippet of a memory hammered away and with a groan, she followed the mental path over barricades and side-trips to a crystal clear moment as a child.

'Watch the water. Always spend a few minutes observing before you swim. If there are fish in the waves observe more closely. Are they panicked and seeking escape? Are seabirds diving in large groups? Then that is rule two of avoiding the surf.'

'And what is rule one, Daddy?'

'What do you think? Use that sharp intelligence, Sadie.'

'I know. Rule one is to look for a tell-tale fin.'

'Good girl. Knew you were smart.'

Sadie waited for a wave and body-surfed to the shallows. Then she waded to the old jetty and walked all the way to the sea end, dropping onto the creaky boards, her toes dangling in the swell.

She'd been here with her father many times. He'd taught her to dive off the end and be safe doing so. Shown her how to identify fish species and tell the difference between juvenile and adult King George whiting. And scolded her for refusing to come out of the water one day but then hugging her when she'd cried.

'Why did everything change, Dad?'

Her words were meaningless. *He* had changed and what once was good turned bad almost overnight. Living through those terrible years with his powder-keg temper and judgemental, unkind parenting overshadowed any closeness and love they once shared. This was the first time Sadie had remembered a time when they were happy together.

In the distance a dog barked.

Back on her feet, Sadie stretched. The dog was a golden retriever running in and out of the waves close to the far cliff. A man with a surfboard followed.

There goes my bubble.

She was parked in the other direction at the top of the stone steps. As she ran up them the first real rays of sun lit the sky and Sadie tried to shake off the melancholy. There was too much going on today to wallow in the past – there'd be enough of that later thanks to a meeting with Pam's solicitor and then a real estate agent. It was a week since she'd stopped here on her way to the house and Pam had only just agreed to talk about the future and only because of these meetings.

There was a tap at the top and she rinsed her feet and slid them into sandals from the bag she'd left on the sand before her swim. One last look at the sea as it changed from black to hues of blue and then she climbed into the car.

* * *

Sadie had dealt with solicitors often enough to lead the discussion in Mr Appleby's office. Her mother was a bundle of nerves and made no effort to ask questions or read the paperwork which was prepared for her to sign, almost as if afraid the news would be all bad.

'Just to be clear, Mum now owns the inn and the house outright. There's no money owing on either thanks to Dad's life insurance?'

'Exactly. Mrs Carson, finalisation is still a few weeks away but you are debt-free and have two valuable assets.' Mr Appleby gently pushed the papers a little closer to Pam. 'Just your signature on the pages which are marked if you don't mind. I can lodge them with the relevant authorities and then you won't need to see me again in a hurry.' He smiled and Pam nodded. He'd been the family solicitor for years as well as a volunteer firefighter and local councillor and was well liked in the community.

Pam leaned forward to find the places to sign and did so with her neat, legible signature. When she straightened, she discreetly dabbed her eyes with a handkerchief and Sadie rubbed her back.

'Lovely, thank you. Before you leave, there are two more matters to discuss.'

'I don't understand.' Pam finally spoke. 'Wasn't everything covered already?'

'Not quite. One is the van which is registered solely under your husband's name. There is a fee to transfer it unfortunately but—'

'No! I don't want the van. Can it be disposed of?'

'Mum?'

Mr Appleby clasped his hands together on the desk. 'As you are the main recipient of the contents of the will I recommend you do the transfer and then sell it.'

'Can't someone just come and remove it? I don't want a cent for it.'

'I need to make some enquiries if that is your preference. There may be a way to transfer the registration directly to a third party but the cost will still need to come from the estate.'

Pam pushed herself to her feet. 'Please do whatever is necessary. May we leave now?'

'There's just the matter of Sadie's inheritance.'

'What?' Sadie's head swung from looking at her mother to staring at Mr Appleby and Pam sat again. 'Inheritance?' She flattened her palms against her legs. Was this a joke? Probably. Knowing him it was a copy of one of his new-age-religion books with lots of red underlining of text.

'Mr Appleby, what on earth was left to leave Sadie?' Confusion filled Pam's face.

'A number of years ago, Ron had me open a trust account. You would recall he'd received close on half a million dollars from his mother's estate which he deposited into the trust. It's collected a reasonable amount of interest and he continued to add to it over the years. The other thing is... he had a second life insurance policy to protect the trust.'

'A trust?' This meeting was getting stranger by the moment.

'Its purpose is to offer scholarships – to students in need of extra help, or older folk wanting to study to learn new skills. That kind of thing... To date, none have been given because he wanted nothing to do with it, other than contributing to the financial side. On his death, the trust was to be taken over by you, Sadie.'

'You do mean *my* Ron? I know nothing about an inheritance from his mother! Why is this the first I'm hearing about it, as his widow?'

'Regrettably, I cannot answer that. He was specific with his instructions. It was a secret trust which was only to be revealed when he was ready to tell you himself, Sadie. As well, there were many conditions and I do have a brief for you to take today to familiarise yourself.' Mr Appleby picked up a thick, spiral-bound A4 book. 'Once you've read it, come back with any questions.'

Sadie took it, turning it to read the title under the heavy, clear plastic top page.

Sadie Carson Trust: Invisible Years.

With an audible gasp, Sadie dropped the book onto her lap.

'What is it?'

Pam read the title and her mouth fell open.

Mr Appleby smiled again. 'He told me that you have a special interest in helping the elderly who would otherwise fall through the cracks in the system.'

'What is the catch, Mr Appleby?'

'Sadie!'

'Sorry, Mum. But as wonderful as this looks on the surface, there has to be more to it.'

'Everything is there inside, all the fine print, and the majority of it is straightforward.'

'But?' she pressed. The first few seconds of amazement had already turned to suspicion because the Ron Carson she'd come to know wouldn't give money away. There had to be a motive.

'There's a clause, though I wouldn't call it a catch. Your name must be left as it is on the trust. He must always be acknowledged as your father and the person who set this up. You must administer it for ten years before any changes to his conditions can take place and after that time it is yours to do with as you wish.'

The book ended up on the floor as Sadie leapt to her feet.

'I want none of it. None.'

'Well, we are a fine pair.' Pam tipped an uncharacteristic second packet of sugar into her coffee. 'Mr Appleby must consider us quite ungrateful.'

Sadie swallowed too-hot coffee too fast rather than answer.

The minute they left the solicitor's office Pam announced she'd like to go for a drive somewhere away from the town and Sadie hadn't hesitated to drive her. They'd found themselves in Driftwood Cove, bought takeaway drinks, and settled at a table and bench in the park near the beach. With the beautiful weather today – not too hot but warm enough for swimming – the beach was alive with movement as people tossed big inflatable balls around and children squealed in the waves.

'I don't understand your father at all.'

'Makes two of us, Mum.'

'For our entire marriage he held on to money as if it was his life-blood. Never spent a thing if he didn't have to and kept a close eye on the household expenses. I always thought he was a... tight-arse.'

Sadie spluttered out a mouthful of coffee.

'Swallow first, love. Here's a napkin.' Pam handed one over and used another to pat a few spots on the table. 'But he was.'

'I agree. I've just never heard you say a word like that.'

'There's a few new things I'm trying on for size,' Pam said with that little glint of humour in her eyes. 'And now money isn't an issue, I have some serious thinking to do.'

'About your future? The inn and the house?'

'Yes. I guess. And I know we've got yet another property agent or whatever they call themselves coming in a couple of hours but quite honestly, Sadie, the whole idea of selling the inn frightens me, and if the mortgage has been taken care of, perhaps I don't need to anymore. Being involved in the running of the place is all I know. I don't have a degree or any real expertise that an employer would want.'

After putting down the coffee cup, Sadie reached for Pam's

hand. 'Okay, first of all, nobody is going to rush you into any decisions. Certainly not me. But you don't need to work anymore. Not to support yourself financially if you sell the inn as well.'

'I'm not old enough to retire! What on earth would I do to keep busy?'

Sadie had to smile. 'Work in your garden. Buy lots of books and read whenever you want. Go for walks. Make friends, Mum.'

'I have friends.'

'Then spend time with them. Come and visit me. Travel the world.'

Pam laughed without much conviction and withdrew her hand to pick up her cup. 'I'll come and see you. But I need to be doing more.'

'Then follow your passions. Think about the things you wanted to do for all these years but couldn't. There will be something you long for. A dream to make true.'

'*You* did. And I'm proud of you.'

Her mother had never said that before. A lump formed in Sadie's throat and she swallowed hard to push down the sudden urge to sob. This recent desire to cry at the drop of a hat was annoying. It was just a reaction to the events of the last hour. Surely.

Pam didn't seem to have noticed her discomfort. 'This trust your father set up. Why would he call it Invisible Years? The name rings a bell but I don't know why.'

'I guess you didn't get to see it. While I was still studying journalism I wrote a piece called Invisible Years and it was published in a major newspaper. Something about it got the attention of a documentary producer who was creating a series about elder abuse and she gave me my first job in front of the cameras.'

'I read that article! You know, I think I still have it somewhere.'

A beach ball bounced across the park in high, jubilant curves and Sadie ran across to capture it before it reached the road. She tossed it back to a kid who was puffing after his chase. 'It tried to escape,' she said with a grin.

Pam had an odd expression when she returned, part amusement and part... sadness? Was that even possible? Perhaps her mother was reminded of Sadie's childhood.

'Where was I? Oh, I'm so happy you read that. It never left my mind, talking to older people – some in their nineties – who had nothing apart from a meagre pension which barely covered their housing, let alone utilities and food. They'd worked their whole lives and were ending them asking for handouts and charity.'

'Does this mean you'll accept the trust fund?'

'I don't know, Mum. Once I've read the documents I'll make a decision, but I have to say that Dad has made this difficult for me.'

Which was the point. He had put her into an impossible position and was probably laughing at her from beyond the grave.

TWELVE

Sadie tended to a guest who was checking in while Pam showed the real estate agent through the inn. She remembered the process – down to how to work the antiquated computer – even though it must have been fifteen years since she'd last done so. Her parents had never upgraded their booking system. Once she'd finished, she followed the sound of her mother's voice. It wasn't a happy voice.

'You do know there have already been several agents here. They said what you just did and I disagree with the lot of you.'

Sadie stuck her head around the doorway of the last guest room. 'Hi, Mum. Hi...'

Wearing a suit and a pained expression, the young man clutching a clipboard looked ready to escape. He thrust a hand out. 'Zac, Zac Bolan.'

'Nice to meet you, Zac. I'm Sadie.'

'You are Mrs Carson's daughter? Aren't you on television?'

'She is. Zac wants to buy the land to develop.' Pam stalked past Sadie. 'Nobody wants to keep the inn the way it is.'

'What if we go to the office? Come on, Zac, we can have a chat there.'

Pam huffed a bit but led the way and by the time Sadie and Zac arrived was behind the counter, the door to the back room closed. She waited, hands held together in front of herself and no sign that she wanted to chat.

Zac held out a business card to Pam who ignored it. He placed it on the counter and Sadie peered at the name.

'Green Bay Developments. So you knew in advance you would knock the place down?' Sadie smiled to take the bluntness from the question. 'Did you mention that to Mum when you made the appointment?'

He shrugged. 'Thought it was obvious.' His eyes roamed the office with its aged curtains and prehistoric wallpaper. 'Rivers End needs a new inn, probably two, so why not take advantage of an existing business? There's room here for a two-floor complex and a pool but really, nobody wants to stay in these old-style places.'

Sensing her mother's escalating anger, Sadie winked at her.

'And what kind of offer do you have in mind, Zac?'

He opened his clipboard and extracted a thin folder with the company name in big, gold print. 'I can leave this with you to peruse at your leisure. If you have any questions, then just call. My card is inside as well. Day or night.'

'We'll let you get going, Zac. Lovely to meet you.' Sadie opened the door and he shot out without a backward glance at Pam. As soon as he was out, she closed the door and burst into laughter.

'Not sure why you are laughing. He wants to turn this place into rubble.'

'Take a look at the offer,' Sadie said.

'I'd rather not.'

Sadie opened the folder that he'd left on the counter. Then closed it, well aware Pam watched her like a hawk.

'Not even worth a look then, Sadie?'

'Not unless you want to add several million to your retirement fund.'

'Several... Stop teasing me, child.'

'Okay, Mum. So, what would you like for dinner?' Sadie was having far too much fun with this. Her mother needed a nudge. A big one. But selling made sense, so why not get the best price possible? 'I fancy Mexican.'

'Sounds good.' Pam touched the folder. 'I don't think I've tried Mexican food.'

'You are kidding me. Oh, Mum. When you come to Sydney we are going to go to all the fun places.'

'Sounds good.'

Pam opened the folder. And gasped. Then closed it again and glared at Sadie.

'Why didn't you tell me?'

'I did.'

'No, you joked about it. But it is millions. Oh my.'

With that, Pam sank onto her chair.

'Millions.'

* * *

'I would never have thought to try this but now I'm going to eat it every single day.' Pam turned her second taco sideways and bit into it with a satisfying crunch. Little crumbs dropped onto her plate along with a dribble of sour cream.

Sadie shook her head but couldn't stop smiling. She'd never seen her mother eat with such enjoyment... and mess. 'You don't mind it being the vegetarian option?'

'Mm... no. Delicious.'

'I like using the black beans. And not too spicy?'

There was no point asking questions requiring words. Pam took another bite and Sadie joined in. She'd made guacamole and the bean mix from scratch but the shells were store-bought.

Even so, this was a quick and easy meal and ticked all of her boxes for comfort food.

When all the food was gone and Pam had stopped trying to extract one last teaspoon of guacamole from its bowl, Sadie poured two glasses of wine. 'I'll wash up later. Have you given any more thought to the offer on the inn?'

They moved into the living room, Sadie bringing Zac's folder.

Pam settled onto her armchair. 'Your father would be shocked.'

'At the amount? Or that you are selling?'

'I haven't decided to sell. Not yet. But yes, he would be upset to think I'd even consider moving the business on. We both poured our hearts into building it up and keeping it running, even through the difficult times when people weren't travelling. It was the one thing we both loved equally. Apart from you. Somehow it doesn't seem right. I feel... well, I feel as if it is a betrayal.'

Keeping her opinion to herself tested Sadie. The betrayal was from Dad. For all the years he put the business first, ahead of Pam. Ahead of their family. And his insistence on controlling every little detail, not only at work but in almost every part of their lives.

'You can't work forever, Mummy,' Sadie said. 'The time will come you will sell but whether it is now or in ten or twenty years it still isn't a betrayal.'

'There are alternatives to consider.'

'Like which offer to accept?' Sadie smiled, knowing full well that wasn't what her mother meant.

'Did you ever wonder how I was able to send Daniel to meet you so quickly that day? When you were at Rebecca's cottage?'

Dan Harrington had crossed her mind more than once... and Rebecca. But not in the same thought. She felt heat rising up her neck and turned away to put her wine glass onto a coffee table, hoping her mother hadn't noticed. 'I thought you must have phoned him.'

'He was at the inn taking some photographs and measurements. And when I told him about Rebecca he left immediately to help. But he returned later and is going to give me some options.'

'Options? Do you mean renovating the inn?'

'He said it is possible. I don't really know why I asked him for an opinion before seeing what the state of my finances was but I felt I had to do more than just listen to developers and the like. As it turns out, there's a lot more money than I dreamed there'd be. Dan suggests expanding to a second row of rooms and upgrading the existing ones. In addition, he'd put in a small swimming pool with a spa and outdoor play area for children.' Clearly proud of herself, Pam leaned back in the chair, waiting for Sadie's response.

There was merit in the idea. And nothing to stop her selling in a few years when she was ready. This way she could make the inn hers.

'Interesting. When is Dan expecting to give you some firm quotes and concepts?'

'Tomorrow. I invited him over for dinner to talk it through.'

'O-kay.'

'I'll cook. I don't expect you to have to worry about feeding guests. As it is, you've cooked non-stop since arriving.'

That isn't the problem.

Pam tilted her head. 'Did you not like Daniel?'

Retrieving her glass, Sadie forced a smile. 'I hardly know him, Mum. We were kind of busy looking for a lost lady.'

There was a knowing glint in her mother's eyes which was both amusing and alarming and it was time to distract her. 'Earlier, you said alternatives. What else did you have in mind for the inn?'

'I'd rather talk about Daniel, but alright, back to the inn. Whether or not I go ahead with renovations I'd like to take some time away from the business. A proper chance to visit you, for one thing. With the financial situation being so vastly improved for me, I might be able to afford a part-time manager. Someone to look after things if I'm away.'

Who are you in my mother's body?

It wasn't the first time Sadie had thought that. Beneath the familiar exterior of a quiet, even meek woman was a sharp mind and business smarts. Dad must have known it so why not encourage his wife to contribute more than running the office? Yet, she'd just said they both loved the inn equally.

What am I missing?

'Oh. Not a good idea?'

Sadie leaned across and touched her mother's arm. 'Sorry, no... I mean, yes. It is a very good idea. And you need to find a cleaner again.'

'Well, that can be tomorrow's job. If you don't mind, I might go to bed. Today is catching up.'

After a hug, Pam headed upstairs and Sadie took the glasses into the kitchen. Washing up done, she made a cup of herbal tea and turned off the lights on the lower floor. Although tired, her mind wasn't going to let her rest so early and the garden was a good place to sit for a while. There was a bench surrounded by roses and although they were in dire need of pruning, each was covered in blooms sending heavenly scents into the air.

The peacefulness settled on Sadie. Overhead the constellations were easy to pick out in the night sky. The Southern Cross. Vela. Carina. Nothing like over Sydney, not even on the clearest night thanks to the mix of lights from thousands of homes and businesses, and the ever-present air pollution. No, this was magical.

The money coming to her mother was a huge relief. Sadie would always have cared for her but so much better to be self-sufficient. Too many people worked their entire lives for little and when they were too old to work, they had nothing. Like the people she'd interviewed for the documentary. And the people she might be in a position to help thanks to the trust fund. Yet how could she accept it?

Dropping her eyes from the vista above, Sadie sighed. Maybe she should follow her mother's lead and hire someone to manage the trust. Only do enough to fulfil whatever terms were attached to it and wait out the ten years – except people who needed scholarships would miss out.

Her phone vibrated in her pocket and she wiggled it out, careful not to spill any of the tea.

The message was from Lina, the closest person she had to a best friend. Lina was a brilliant researcher who often worked on the same projects. She also was apartment-sitting for Sadie.

> The tomato plant is mounting an escape over
> the railing. Send help.

A photograph appeared of the offending plant which had doubled in size since she left. Some of its branches were dangling over the edge.

> There are thin stakes and plant tape
> underneath the planter. Stick a couple near the
> existing stake, haul the escapees back, and tie
> them up with the tape. You can trim them if you
> need to.

How funny. Sadie had found a sad, underwatered seedling at a garden centre which was closing down and planted it in the hope it might eventually grow. Her sunny balcony and plenty of care had more than encouraged it and she'd probably have ripe tomatoes when she returned. It just showed what a bit of love could do.

A few minutes later another photo arrived. Three stakes formed a triangular prison with branches secured to each one.

> Good work. Are you going alright?

> Busy. I hear a rumour there's going to be a call out soon for a film-length doco about the housing crisis so will let you know if anything comes of it. How is your hometown?

Sadie tossed her now-cold tea onto the nearest rose bush.

> The same yet different. I'll have a lot to tell you in a couple of weeks.

> Don't hurry back. In fact, take a year off if you like. I can force myself to stay here if I must.

Sadie laughed. Lina lived in a shared house and hated it but wasn't good at changing her life around. Staying at Sadie's place was a step forward.

> I appreciate your willingness to sacrifice yourself. Night. ☺

She went inside, locking the door and checking it. Rivers End was low crime but it was force of habit from years of city living. At the bottom of the stairs she paused. There was a lifetime of memories here. She'd run from the bad ones for a long time but there were no more reasons to escape. This was just a house. Rivers End was just a town. And soon enough, she'd be back in her own home.

We are in our apartment in Melbourne and it is night. Everyone is asleep. Dad, Charlie, and Mum. At least, I thought Mum was sleeping but when I look out of my bedroom window she is across the road. I wave but she doesn't notice and begins walking along the footpath. Her feet are bare and she wears her swimsuit with the green and orange sarong she loves wrapped around her waist. Before she can get out of sight I run downstairs and follow. She turns the corner but when I reach it, running to catch up, she is a long way away, standing in the distance on a beach. My legs are so heavy as I try to get to her because I know something terrible is about to happen. I call out but no words leave my mouth. And then she undoes her sarong and as it drops to the sand she sees me and smiles.

Everything is okay again.

She is alive and safe and I'll get to her in a minute and hug her and then our lives will be normal.

But the waves get bigger and Mum walks into them, her arms outstretched, and even as I try to scream she is swept away from my sight. And my legs work properly again but now I am standing where she was except the beach has gone.

I'm in the cemetery.

With an awful jolt I wake up. There is a roaring in my ears and my heart is thumping and tears flow down my face and I don't know which part is real but then I hear the endless rushing of waves down at the beach and remember.

Mum is dead.

We live here now.

Without her.

Did I wake Dad or Charlie? I force myself to listen as the sound in my ears slowly fades. All is quiet in the house. I climb out of bed and go to the kitchen, careful not to tread on the couple of floorboards which creak, then turn the tap very slowly to fill a glass. Sometimes it squeaks. I don't want to disturb the others. I don't want company.

I sip slowly and the dreadful knot in my stomach begins to untie itself.

It isn't the first time I've dreamed about Mum but the beach was never part of it before. How will I ever find peace with this? Charlie and Dad love the ocean and even after me being so upset the other day when they were using the surfboard they keep going in to swim.

Dad talks to me about it. That what happened to Mum was a freak accident. He explains he'd never put Charlie in danger. That the water is really calm and shallow when they go in. And that Charlie is swimming well.

And I should learn to swim properly instead of the few lessons he made me take.

I never will.

Swimming makes people drown.

School is another pain. Final year of primary school and I dread being here every day but dread missing any, because I have to do well in the exams to show Charlie how important education is. Learning isn't the problem. I already know most of it. I was in an advanced class at my school at home but here, it is old news. So I listen and repeat some of the lessons I've done but make sure there's nothing different in this class to trip me up.

But Charlie's school is a whole other thing and he can't wait to go each morning.

His teacher just dropped him home after classes because Dad is getting ready for an important phone call about his work. She's nice, Miss Carlisle. Her hair is curly and cut very short, a bit like a boy, and she has a big booming voice and a soft gentle one and Charlie loves her. There are only five pupils and every student has different needs, although an older girl also has spastic palsy like Charlie, only worse. Miss Carlisle told me I am welcome to come and ride the pony outside school hours but I'm afraid to even try. Charlie says I'm silly and it is fun. Just about everything is fun for Charlie and when he laughs, it always cheers me up.

'Why don't we give the beach a miss today?' I still feel fragile about the horrible dream.

Dad is in the kitchen making a pot of tea. 'The weather will turn to rain tomorrow so go and enjoy it today.' He puts some biscuits onto a plate. 'Besides, I really could use a quiet house for this phone call.'

'We can be quiet.'

'Come on! Let's go go go!' Charlie shouts and then lets out a whoop of laughter as he wheels his chair to the door.

'I rest my case.' Dad carries his tea and biscuits to his study. 'Have fun.'

By the time I finish packing the bag Charlie is already at the bottom of the ramp. His confidence and strength grows every day.

'Did you bring water?' he asks.

'Yes.'

'And cupcakes?'

'Nope.'

His expression is priceless and it is hard to keep my face straight. 'I was going to bake some this afternoon but instead we're off to the beach again. There won't be time once we get back.'

Charlie hesitates, glancing up at the house.

I fold. 'So I packed some of those biscuits instead.'

'Becky, you are mean to tease me.'

'I might be too mean to go to the beach.'

This time he giggles and we get going.

Instead of making sandcastles straight away, Charlie asks if we can look at the rock pools. The tide is out and the rocks near the cliff are exposed so we step carefully on the flattest ones. He holds my arm with both his hands and it takes a while but we find a little pool filled with more of the fish from the other day.

'They're trapped,' he says.

We sit beside the pool and I keep my arm around him as he puts his face close to the water.

'Will they be okay?'

'See the end bit?' I point. 'It is a narrow channel going to the next pool and there's probably more. They have a lot of water to swim in and once it is high tide they can return to the ocean.'

'Good. Else we'd need to rescue them.'

After a bit we get up to go and eat our biscuits but Charlie gasps and when I look down, there's blood on his foot. I lift him into my arms and get him over to where our towels are spread out. After splashing some water from our cordial bottle onto his foot I see a cut under his big toe.

'We should go back.'

'Uh uh. Doesn't hurt.'

'But it is bleeding, Charlie.'

'Need a plaster. Can you go?'

I glance up the steep hill. I've only had to pull the sled up once and it was really difficult. Dad is busy now but he'd said earlier he'd join us once his phone call finishes.

'Okay. But I need you to promise to stay on the towel.'

'Biscuit first.'

After unzipping the bag and putting it next to Charlie I climb up the track, going a lot faster on my own and being able to keep to the sides, which are a bit grassy and easier to walk on than the sand. I am panting when I reach the house and stop for a second to catch my breath.

I tiptoe inside so as not to interrupt Dad or make him worry and once I find some plasters I hurry out again and then run down to the beach.

But Charlie is gone.

The bag is still there and the towels but he's vanished.

I race to the lagoon. What if he fell in?

'Charlie! Charlie, where are you?'

He's not in the water.

A terrifying shriek comes from the direction of the cave.

'Charlie!'

I've never gone inside the cave.

I don't like enclosed spaces.

But Charlie is moaning and making other noises I've never heard. My chest is about to explode in fear. There's lots of space inside. Firm sand. And I can stand up easily.

In the middle Charlie sits on a rock. He has something over his head. A towel, but not ours. And someone is kneeling near him, holding his foot.

'Get away from him!' I scream and with all my force I shove at the person's shoulders.

They fall onto their behind. It's another kid. A boy who looks a bit older than me.

Charlie pulls the towel off his head and he looks from me to the boy. 'I was being a ghost, Becky.'

'A what? Why?'

The boy is glaring at me.

'Tim is fixing my toe.'

My eyes go to Charlie's foot. There is a strip of something around his foot like a bandage. It is the same colour as the towel. 'Oh.'

'This is Becky,' Charlie announces. 'She's my sister.'

'Lucky you.'

Still glaring, Tim stands and he is quite a bit taller than me. I can't believe I pushed him over.

'Um, sorry. But I thought you were hurting him.'

'I'd never hurt anyone. You shouldn't have left him alone. His foot was bleeding everywhere.'

Tim is annoying and I crouch to check the towel bandage. There is some blood seeping through. 'We're going home, Charlie.'

Before I can even work out how to get him out of the cave, Tim lifts Charlie and leaves. I want to yell at him again. Tell him to leave my brother for me to care about. But they've gone and when I get outside, they are already on their way up the hill.

I grab the bag and toss that and our towels onto the sled and drag it behind me. I am fuming with anger. How dare this stranger move Charlie? I was only gone a few minutes and Charlie had promised not to move from the towel. Why didn't I do what I wanted from the beginning and pull Charlie up instead of leaving him? It might have taken a bit longer but I'm strong enough.

Why did I leave him alone?

Something bad might have happened.

Charlie is sitting in his wheelchair now and Tim pushes

him to the bottom of the ramp. I abandon the sled and run the rest of the way. I can't let Tim interrupt Dad.

'I can manage.'

'Are you sure?' Tim grins at Charlie. 'Once your foot is good we'll have a swim.'

'Yay!'

'No you will not.'

Tim leans down close to Charlie and says something I can't hear but my brother thinks is funny. He is still laughing when Tim waves and runs back toward the beach. I just want to cry. They were laughing at me and Charlie is hurt and I didn't look out for him.

I'm an awful sister.

FOURTEEN

NOW

Sadie found herself driving along the road to Rebecca's house.

It wasn't on purpose but not entirely by accident. Well, it probably was on purpose considering she had a container of freshly baked goodies beside her, but she might have been taking those anywhere.

Today was cooler and heavy rain clouds scudded across the sky. As Sadie nosed the car into the small valley, the lake reflected the sky. Grey and dismal.

No sooner than she'd retrieved the goodies from the passenger seat, a meow advised her she wasn't alone. She set the container on the ground and squatted as Percy trotted in her direction, tail high in welcome. The cat stood on her hind legs and touched her nose to Sadie's in a gesture which flipped her heart upside-down.

'She does like you.' Rebecca carried an empty washing basket and was walking toward the back of the cottage. 'Rain is almost here.'

She disappeared around the corner of the building.

'Do I follow?' Sadie whispered to the cat.

Percy took off after her owner.

'Guess so.'

As Sadie reached the back of the cottage the first drops of rain began so she left the container on the verandah and joined Rebecca at the clothes line.

'You don't need to help me.'

'I hear that from my mother a lot.'

Taking the lead from Rebecca, Sadie unpegged towels and sheets, folding as she went and putting the pegs into a little bag clipped onto the side of the rattan washing basket. As the rain increased, and the final pillowcase made its way to the basket, Sadie picked it up with a grin. 'Where to?'

Rebecca didn't argue, hurrying to the back of the cottage. This was as picturesque as the front. On the verandah was a table with two chairs, and lots of hanging baskets filled with colourful blooms. The back door was propped open and Rebecca – followed by Percy – went inside.

Sadie scooped up her container and followed.

'The laundry is to your right. Please leave the basket on the counter.'

It was a small but functional room with modern appliances. The basket went onto the counter and Sadie returned to the hallway. Across was a bathroom. To her right was the kitchen, where Percy sat on the floor watching Rebecca fill an old-fashioned kettle with water.

'Come in, child. Do you like tea?'

Sadie stopped just inside the kitchen. 'I love it. Thank you. Should I remove my shoes?'

'If you don't mind.'

Retreating to the back door Sadie took off her shoes where three pairs rested on a shoe rack. She padded into the kitchen. 'Mum and I were baking earlier and made too much. I wondered if... well, would you like some?'

'That is generous.'

Rebecca was preparing tea in an exquisite porcelain teapot

painted in vivid, swirling colours. Two matching cups and saucers joined it from a cupboard.

'There are apricot scrolls with fruit from Mum's garden, and some crusty bread rolls. For some reason, my mother has invited your neighbour, Dan, to dinner tonight and went on a baking spree this morning.' Sadie placed the container on the timber table in the centre of the room and gazed around. It was a beautiful kitchen with top-end appliances including a double width oven in an old-fashioned style complete with gas cooktop. 'You must love to cook.'

'Not so many reasons these days, with just the two of us, and Percy prefers hers raw wherever possible.' Rebecca shot a questioning look at Sadie. 'Was it you who fed her the tuna?'

'Yes. And that's one of the reasons for my visit. To apologise for coming into the cottage. I would normally never dream of intruding that way.'

'Yet, you did.'

'I did.'

'Hmm.'

Rebecca carried the teapot and cups to the table and sat.

'You'd better join me at the table if you want tea.'

Sadie sat quickly, feeling like she was in the presence of a school principal.

'I'm curious why you did come inside if my front door was closed.'

'Your cat made it clear that I had to let her in. Well, at least knock, which I did, and the door opened a crack. And when there was no answer I tried to leave but Percy became agitated and loud and insistent.'

The smallest flicker of a smile touched Rebecca's lips. 'My cat is a con-artist.'

'Perhaps. But I didn't know if someone was inside, perhaps needing help. Cats know this kind of thing.'

'Would you like sugar and milk?'

'No, black is fine, thank you.'

As she poured the tea, Rebecca's hands shook a little and her eyes were focused on the job at hand. Sadie thought her to be in her mid-seventies but her physical fitness and lovely skin and mental acumen made her seem younger. Living out here alone, apart from a demanding feline, meant she had to be capable of looking after herself. Sadly, that wasn't always the case in Sadie's experience.

'There you are, Sadie. I remembered your name correctly?' Rebecca passed the tea.

'You did. And thank you.'

'Just so you don't think badly of my feline supervision skills, the back door has a cat flap and in the bathroom there is a self-feeder which always contains fresh dry food for emergencies. And Percy catches rodents all day so she truly wasn't starving.'

As mild as Rebecca's tone was, Sadie was left with no illusion she shouldn't have opened the front door. She wasn't going to keep saying sorry. If she hadn't gone looking for Rebecca with Dan then who knows what might have happened to her. So Sadie plastered a smile on her face and then took a sip of the tea.

Percy jumped onto one of the spare chairs, her eyes huge under the single light above the table.

'She's a lovely cat. And followed me all the way around Whisper Lake.'

'Is there anywhere you *didn't* go?'

'Yes. I saw your orchard and vegetable garden but only from a distance.'

Rebecca chuckled softly.

'My mother has a similar garden, except it is all sadly in need of attention. I'm helping her get it back into shape while I stay because she has a great love of bottling and relishes and jam making and the like.'

'Your mother runs the inn on her own now. Time consuming.'

'It is. But even when my father was alive she had stopped following her passion. He wasn't very... encouraging.'

And you cannot speak to a stranger about these things.

Cup halfway to her mouth, Rebecca paused. 'She stopped bottling?'

Sadie nodded. 'I'm sure once the garden is sorted she'll go back to it. At least, I hope she will. I always thought she should make them to sell because she's very good.'

Returning the cup to the saucer, Rebecca stood and went to a tall, narrow cupboard. Inside were dozens of bottles all filled with different produce. 'Is there something she particularly likes?'

'Anything really. Mixed pickled vegetables are a favourite.'

'Perhaps she'll enjoy these.' Rebecca returned with two slender bottles. 'One is chillies of several varieties. The other is pickled carrots, gherkin, and onion.'

'These are beautiful, Rebecca. Better than those in a supermarket.'

For the first time since she'd met her, Rebecca really smiled. She sat again and nodded. 'Thank you. I'm making a batch of mustard relish soon and she is most welcome to have a jar. I learn something about flavours when tasting someone else's wares so perhaps it will encourage her. And I look forward to trying the baked goods.'

The rain intensified on the metal roof and Sadie glanced up. 'Oh dear.'

'It will pass. Have some more tea.'

For a while they sat, mostly in silence, sipping tea and listening to the rain. Sadie longed to ask questions. Ask to be allowed to wander around the cottage. But as polite as Rebecca was, she barely knew Sadie and might very well take offence at such boldness.

'Your mother was kind to me when I arrived in Rivers End.'

Oh, I am all ears!

Percy jumped onto Rebecca's lap and began purring. 'I hadn't been to the cottage at all so was taking rather a big leap of faith buying it without a personal inspection; and quite frankly, I knew nobody in Rivers End. My belongings were a few days behind me and I wasn't keen to move in without even a bed to sleep on.'

Sadie knew that feeling. 'I moved to Sydney when I was eighteen without a place to stay or a job. I remember feeling alone and a bit lost at first.'

'You were very brave. So young.'

'Too young, but not brave. More... bravado.' Sadie grinned. 'I bluffed my way into a job in a hotel which offered accommodation as part of the pay.'

That amused Rebecca and the lines around her eyes crinkled up. 'Resourceful.'

'But talk about brave... you bought this without even seeing it?' Sadie gazed around. 'It is just gorgeous, but what if it had been falling down?'

'Then I would have repaired it. Don't look surprised, Sadie. I'm almost seventy-five but I know my way around a hammer and nails and am capable of hiring people to do what I cannot. Electricians and the like. But the cottage needed only minor work and painting. The roof was the worst of it and Dan replaced it.'

Above them the rain pattered with less intensity and Sadie knew she had to get going. There was a lot to do at home and she didn't wish to outwear her welcome here. But one more question wouldn't hurt. Or rather, a carefully worded throwaway line.

'It almost sounds as though you were a carpenter before retiring.'

There was a subtle change in Rebecca's face. Something

switched in her eyes although she barely moved. 'Goodness no. I was a teacher and a chef. A cook who taught. Nothing interesting.' With that, she relocated Percy to the other chair and got to her feet. 'The rain is clearing so you might make it to your car without being drenched. Don't forget the bottles.'

'Thank you again, and for the lovely tea.'

Rebecca followed Sadie to the back door. Shoes back on her feet, Sadie stepped out into the cool air.

'I should get your container.'

'No, no. Please keep it and I'll collect it another time. If you don't mind me dropping in before I return to Sydney?'

For a moment, one which dragged, Rebecca said nothing, her eyes darting inside then back to Sadie.

'And I meant to ask... the other day you asked me to help you find someone. I'm happy to do that if you can tell me who and how.'

With a sharp intake of air, Rebecca shook her head. 'Not necessary. Thank you.'

She closed the door. She'd dismissed Sadie. There was no other word for it. And all it did was make Sadie more determined to uncover the story of this reclusive and interesting woman.

FIFTEEN

Sadie couldn't remember her mother ever being so nervous about having a guest over for dinner. She'd fussed about the menu, worried about the crockery, and then didn't know what to wear. Was the renovation of the inn so important?

'Do you recall the last dinner party we had?' Pam had finally settled on a pair of smart black pants and blue blouse. 'I'm sure it was those people... Dad's new "friends".' She used her fingers to emphasise the word. 'Three men who all ignored me even when I served them a lovely meal. Not one word of thanks, which I think annoyed your father because he thanked me several times as if to make up for their poor manners. And the conversation was about the dangers of modern science and the importance of controlling every aspect of one's life. And by that I mean his family.'

'Seriously? I had no idea, Mum. When was this?'

Pam frowned as she thought about it. 'You were here. Not at the table. No, Ron forbade that because it was a conversation for adults. I brought a plate of dinner to your room and you were studying. I think you were about eleven or twelve so no wonder you don't have a memory of it.'

Except... there was a glimmer of something in the back of Sadie's mind.

'You cooked a roast dinner.'

'Oh my goodness, love. How do you remember so long ago?'

More to the point, how had she forgotten?

'Were these men part of the cult he ended up following?'

'Not a cult. More the peculiar religion which he'd been raised in.'

'Huh?'

'Oh, you wouldn't know about it all. I'm so sorry, Sadie, there's a whole history you are probably unaware of and now isn't the time, but basically, your father left the religion when we met but went back to it.'

The timer beeped on the oven and they both hurried to the kitchen. It was only a few minutes until Dan was expected and timing was everything with the feast Pam had made.

'This looks done. I'll turn the oven off and let everything rest for a bit.'

'How about I open a bottle of wine, Mum?'

'Shouldn't we wait?'

'Nope. There's plenty of wine and I need a glass. And I think you do.'

Without waiting for an argument – or approval – Sadie pulled a chilled bottle from the fridge and poured two glasses. She offered one to Pam. 'Go on, a mouthful will help you relax a bit. Not that you need to be so worked up because everything is fabulous.'

She meant it. For once, Pam had let her manage things at the inn after her visit to Rebecca. Her mother's joy in cooking was evident with the menu and the aromas in the kitchen were mouth-watering. 'Dan isn't going to know what's hit him, Mum. Although, shouldn't you also have invited his wife... or partner?'

Pam held up her glass. 'Cheers, love. To single men who have a good job and are nice and on top of that, are easy on the eye.' She didn't wait for Sadie to tap her glass but swallowed a large mouthful.

So, Dan wasn't married. Presumably then, no partner. And Mum-approved.

Crap.

No wonder Pam was nervous. She was son-in-law hunting.

'Does he know I'm here?'

'Well, of course he does. I mentioned I'd like your opinion of whatever he's come up with for the inn.'

'And he didn't mind?'

'Mind? I think he jumped at the chance. And that dress is pretty with its little straps and swirly skirt.'

It was so much worse than Sadie had imagined. This poor man was being set up by Pam to spend time with someone he barely knew. How embarrassing could one parent be? She fingered one of the 'little straps'. Was there time to change into jeans and T-shirt?

'I'm going to put the finishing touches to dessert so would you mind taking the bread rolls into the dining room?'

Pam hummed as she slid a tray of mini cheesecakes from the fridge to the table.

She never hums.

Sadie stared at the basket of bread rolls.

'Not going to carry itself, love.'

Snatching the basket, Sadie stalked out.

Halfway to the dining room, there was a tap on the front door and a shadow moved on the other side of the narrow window.

'Would you get that please?'

She really didn't want to. But Sadie had good manners and this was only for a short time. An hour or two at the most. Over the years in her career she'd attended many functions and rubbed shoulders with more than a fair share of people who were rude, unpleasant, or boring. Dan Harrington was none of those so, with a sigh, Sadie opened the door.

He was taller than she remembered. But that smile was the same. And Dan looked nice in casual pants and a checked shirt with its top button undone and sleeves rolled up. There was a satchel over one shoulder.

His smile widened as the seconds ticked by and that wasn't helping her find an appropriate greeting at all.

'Are the bread rolls for me?' Dan asked. 'They smell delicious so would you care to swap for this?' He held out a bottle of wine.

Her eyes dropped to it then back to his face.

'Or I could come in?'

With an almighty mental kick, Sadie lifted her chin and the corners of her lips. 'Please come in. You didn't need to bring wine.'

He stepped inside and the hallway shrank around her.

'I'll leave these in the dining room. Mum is at the end of the hallway in the kitchen if you'd like to go through.' Closing the door behind him, she let him go ahead, ducking into the dining room in the hope of a moment to gather herself. She placed the basket to one side so that there was ample room for the starters and then turned around.

And almost ran into Dan's chest.

'Whoops, sorry about that.' He didn't look sorry. 'Before seeing Pam I wanted to say something but if I'm wrong, please set me right.'

If this was about the inn, then she was the wrong person to ask. And anyway, this was his arrangement with her mother and it was quite clear the two of them had already had several discussions.

He looked away for a second then back at Sadie, those warm eyes burning into hers. 'No offence, but I get the feeling your mother is playing matchmaker.'

She couldn't help it. Sadie laughed and as she did, the tension she'd not even realised she was carrying melted away. He got it. He'd already worked her mother out and now she didn't need to worry about how she spoke and what she said. 'You are correct. And I am so sorry. Since I've been home I'm noticing a lot of small changes in her and most of them are good. Not so much this one.'

'Hmm. I dunno. It shows how much she cares about you.'

'I would prefer she shows it in other ways. Shall we go and see her before she gets the wrong idea?'

Sadie made to step past but there wasn't quite enough room and she paused and looked at his face, acutely aware that this close to the warmth of his body, the earthy scent of him was sending her senses into overdrive. She'd never been attracted to a man so fast and it was just as well they both knew this was nothing more than a business dinner.

He moved to let her pass and she slid between him and the doorway without them touching.

'Well there you both are.' Pam was putting the finishing touches to a platter of antipasti. 'So nice to see you, Daniel.'

'Thank you for the invitation.' He leaned down and kissed Pam's cheek. 'This looks delicious.'

Pam blushed. She'd never been great with compliments – not that Sadie recalled hearing her get too many from Dad – but instead of brushing this off, she smiled, eyes alight. 'I've really enjoyed cooking today. Would you like a glass of wine, or something non-alcoholic?'

'Wine, please. With the rain disappearing I decided to walk.'

'How far is it, Daniel?'

'About three kilometres. Good to stretch the legs.'

'White or shall we open your red?' Sadie asked, holding both bottles up.

'White, please.'

She filled his, refilled hers and Pam's and then all three tapped the edges together with a collective 'Cheers.'

'Now, would you prefer to nibble on the antipasti in the dining room? I just have a few more things to do but am happy to join you both shortly.' Pam's expression was pure innocence and when Dan and Sadie exchange the quickest of glances it was as though they shared a secret.

Dan pulled out a chair and sat. 'I love country kitchens.'

Pam's lips pursed for a moment but then she passed him a small plate. 'Please, help yourself.'

'How long would it take to obtain the necessary permits for this design?' Pam had control of Dan's iPad and was peering at a drawing of what the inn might become. There were three designs but this was the best.

'Anything from six weeks to six months, depending upon the backlog of applications at the council offices through to whether there are any objections from neighbouring businesses. I wouldn't imagine any, not with the pub next door having recently upgraded their drive-through.'

Pam nodded. 'I received a letter about it and had no problem with their proposals. If it helps their business then why would I object.'

'But not everyone feels the same way so just be aware it is possible. This kind of plan is the least likely – in my experience – to attract objections or council issues because we're staying on one level and making better use of space currently being wasted. Adding another floor of units might be problematic.'

'Yet that is what the last developer wants to do.' Pam pushed the iPad to Dan. 'I like this.'

Once dessert was finished they'd moved back into the kitchen and had coffee while Dan shared his concepts. Pam asked a lot of questions, things Sadie wouldn't have considered, and Dan patiently answered, sometimes going back over a point until Pam was satisfied.

'What is the next step, Daniel?'

'Oh, Mum... don't you want a little time to think it through?'

Dan slid his iPad into the satchel, then sat back in his chair, hands cradling the almost empty coffee cup. Their eyes met but his were unreadable. Was he concerned Sadie would interfere with what would be a profitable job?

'I have, love. Selling to some developer doesn't sit well with me and I'm not ready to retire. As the inn stands today, I'm losing business from families and those who want a better standard of accommodation and although Daniel isn't building me a resort, it is the next best thing. More coffee?' Pam got to her feet. Discussion over.

The corner of Dan's mouth lifted and then he stood. 'I might head off. Tonight has been a delight both with the food and company.' He washed his coffee cup and then smiled at Pam. 'Sleep on it, okay? And if you come up with more questions just shoot me an email.'

Pam hugged him and despite her concerns, Sadie had to admit there was a strong connection between the two which was genuine. But she'd seen too many people lose everything thanks to poor business or personal decisions and wasn't going to let things rest.

'Mum, why don't you go and put your feet up and I'll see Dan out and then take care of the kitchen.'

'Go on with you both. Don't rush back in, Sadie.'

Pam's matchmaker expression was back and Sadie would have had to laugh except... she was worried. She led the way to the front door and was outside before Dan was halfway along the hallway.

'Close it?' he asked.

'Please.'

When he caught up with her along the driveway, she

slowed and then stopped near the gate. The night sky was clear. Not a sign of the earlier rain and even the air was warmer now than this morning.

'Making sure I leave the property?'

Oh my lord, I am so rude.

Yet, despite his teasing tone, Sadie couldn't muster a smile.

After dropping his satchel onto the ground, Dan leaned against the gatepost. 'Pam is safe with me, Sadie. I have great respect for her and would rather she spends a few days taking a good look at the concept and deciding whether this is the best decision for her. I'm not in the habit of ripping people off.'

The last few words were delivered mildly yet underneath was a steely edge.

Sadie lifted her chin. 'Did she tell you that Dad left a size-able amount of money? And no debt? But to do this upgrade she will need to borrow and that puts her back into the same situation she's been for most of her adult life.'

His eyes never left her face. There was something about him, something... compelling, which burned like embers waiting for her to fan it to a flame. See what happened. Be daring for once. But she was leaving in a matter of weeks and his life was here so anything which occurred would be purely physical. And she wasn't the love them and leave them type.

'Would you let me show you a project I'm working on? I'll spin by in the morning and collect you,' he said.

'Do you not actually need to saw or hammer something sometime? I've never seen you do anything other than drive around or socialise.'

He threw back his head and laughed and her heart light-ened. Once he stopped laughing, he touched her cheek with the tips of his fingers and electricity sparked through her body. She didn't move. Couldn't move.

'I'm a carpenter, yes. But mostly a project manager now. So, eight in the morning?'

'Sure.'

Dan dropped his hand and used it to scoop up his satchel. 'That antipasti platter was divine. And I think I recognised some of the pickles. Rebecca's?'

'Are you sure you aren't a food critic in disguise? Yes. I visited her today and she sent a couple of bottles back for Mum.'

Dan took a few steps then turned. 'She likes you then. Just like her cat, Rebecca doesn't take to people easily. Something in her past has hurt her and I'd never pry, but I am happy seeing her accept you into her small world. Goodnight.'

'Night.'

Sadie watched him until he disappeared into the darkness, yet still she didn't move. Something in Rebecca's past had hurt her. Shaped her. And there wasn't a chance on earth Sadie was going to go home to Sydney without finding out what.

SIXTEEN

62 YEARS AGO

Maybe I'm not such a bad sister after all.

Charlie's toe is healing well. Dad knew exactly what to do with the cut and although poor Charlie needed a tetanus shot (which he told me hurts!), it is almost better a few days later. I've made sure Charlie has everything he wants which means lots of tomato soup, spaghetti on toast, and ice cream but I don't mind.

'Becky... need more cupcakes,' Charlie calls from the living room where he is watching television. Outside, the weather is awful as a big storm thunders away.

It is Saturday and I am in the middle of getting dinner ready. Does he really want cupcakes an hour before our main meal? As I'm about to wash my hands after handling the chicken, Dad wanders in.

'One more cupcake and that child will be on a sugar high all night. No more. And sweetie, stop letting your brother take advantage of your kind heart.'

This is unexpected. Until now, Dad hasn't said a word about Charlie asking and asking and even demanding I run around after him even more than usual. 'But if I'd taken better care of him, he wouldn't be hurt.'

Dad frowns. He looks at the chopping board with the chicken almost ready to put in a big pot for a stew. I'll brown it first in a frying pan then it can join the vegetables which are already simmering. 'I'm sorry, Becky. I promised to cook today and got caught up finishing off the research paper to send on Monday.'

'I don't mind.' I do. But not a lot. Cooking is something I am good at and I feel useful being able to feed us all most days. Sometimes though it would be nice to do it a bit less.

'Can I help now?' Dad picks up a spoon. 'I can stir.'

'Becky! Cupcakes!'

Charlie sounds cross now and it makes me giggle. Not because he is cross but because I know Dad has my back. 'I'm fine with dinner but could you entertain Charlie? Take his mind off cupcakes?'

'If it will give you a bit of peace and quiet then it will be my pleasure.'

For the next half hour all I hear from the other room is laughing, mostly Charlie, but sometimes Dad. Then there is a long stretch of quiet and I wonder if they fell asleep in there. But when I go a bit closer and listen carefully I hear them talking softly. I even hear my name but the pot starts bubbling over before I can discover why I'm part of their conversation.

It is worse than I could imagine.

'Charlie and I were talking about how much you do for us, Becky. Most of the cooking, lots of cleaning and laundry. Coming up with ideas for meals and shopping. We really appreciate everything you do.' Dad is holding his fork over his plate as if deciding what to spear with it.

'We sure do app... um... I don't know that word.' Charlie stops and gazes at Dad.

For a minute or two, Dad talks him through 'appreciate' until Charlie manages to say it clearly. Dad believes it is important to understand how to say a word and what it means and he has always worked patiently with Charlie, even when other people said kids like him are speech-impaired. Well, those silly people need to learn new words and better manners because Charlie is only seven and says big words all the time.

'Part of our conversation was about helping you out a bit more.' Dad points at the big bowl of stew. 'Weekends are your time to relax as well, sweetie.'

'I really love doing stuff for us all. And weekends are easier for me because I don't have stupid school interfering with my time.' Something about the way Dad looks at me has me concerned. 'Am I not doing a good enough job, Daddy?'

'You do a great job. An incredible job. But you are sacrificing your own needs and time to take on so much, whether you enjoy it or not. I wish you were making friends and doing stuff for yourself so I'm thinking of hiring someone... a housekeeper.'

'A what!' I can't believe he'd even suggest such a thing.

'A housekeeper, Becky.' Charlie's brow is all wrinkled up.

'I heard him, Charlie!'

I know he doesn't understand why I'm upset, but I am. After Mum died, we had help. And it was horrible. I don't even remember her name because the person who would appear three times a week to clean and cook was a thief. I caught her stealing from Dad's office and she screamed at me and then told Dad I was lying. But he believed me and she left and I decided never to think about her again.

He holds my hand and I look at him. Dad understands. Kind of. 'I know what you're thinking. I know who you are thinking about but this time will be different. You can help choose the person, okay?'

'But we don't need help. I'm managing and if you want some different meals then I'll go through our recipe books and find some. We could write up our favourites and each week we can get together and plan the meals and the shopping list.' Even to me, I'm sounding ready to cry. 'And if you don't mind cooking twice a week and doing one load of washing then I can do the rest.'

I pick up my fork and begin to eat. I can't bear this and blink my eyes a lot because they keep getting stupid tears. It is my job to look after Dad and Charlie. Mine. Not some thieving, yelling person who never understood Charlie.

Dad insists on doing all the washing up and I don't argue. Charlie will need his bath soon so I run the water and make it nice in there. Just how he likes it with bubbles and the big, soft towel he prefers. I think about Tim. He tore part of his beach towel to bandage Charlie's bleeding toe. I'll ask Dad if he can replace it. Tim's parents might not be happy about him ruining his.

'Bubbles!' Charlie is on Dad's shoulders, hanging on as Dad ducks so both can safely get under the door frame. 'Thank you, sister of mine.'

It makes me giggle. He started saying things like that after being at his school for a week and I think it is cute.

'Glad you like it, little brother of the bubbles.'

He laughs and Dad swings him off his shoulders.

'We are going to play with the boats.' Charlie is standing, hanging on to the side of the bath and swaying a bit as he balances. 'Dad and I. Boys only. Okay?'

'Oh... I was going to... okay.'

Over Charlie's head, Dad winks at me. 'Wasn't there a book you were keen to read?'

I get the message. They are giving me some time to do what I want.

Dad is good with bathing Charlie and does it more and more. I guess little boys grow up and don't want their sisters around at certain times, just like I would never let Charlie see me unclothed. I shudder. Seeing myself without clothes is weird enough.

We joined the local library recently and Charlie and I have been there a few times. I wheel him down and then Dad picks us up later. Better than going to the beach all the time and I've got two books I want to read but sometimes I fall asleep before I begin. After grabbing the one I've started, I go into the living room and curl up on a chair with just a lamp on. The storm has gone but the rain keeps pattering away at the roof and there is a mournful wail of wind every so often.

I've got accustomed to the sounds here. Most of them. And it is strange not to hear the traffic on the street all the time or sirens as police cars and ambulances do their thing but also nice. As much as I don't like the dangerous ocean, the smell of salty air and the soothing whoosh of waves has become part of my new life. One day I'll go home and see Mum. But I think we are getting happy at last.

Now all I need is for Dad to forget about hiring someone and we will be fine.

The house is mostly dark and quiet.

Charlie went to bed a while ago after yawning so much that I told him his head would fall off. He kept checking his head was still there and Dad said he would be better off going to sleep to make sure it stayed attached.

Poor Charlie.

I shouldn't tease him.

Dad checks in on me when he gets himself a pot of tea and then he returns to his study and I keep reading. I read fast and get to the end before I expect. And then I yawn. It is after nine and I turn off the lamp then double-check the front and back doors are locked. There is lightning a long way away and I close the curtains so as not to see it anymore.

Book in hand, I go to say goodnight to Dad. His study door is only open a crack and before I can knock, he speaks. Not to me.

'I know. And that's my concern, believe me.'

I should walk away. But I want to say goodnight and now, I am curious about who he is talking to on the phone.

'She does too much. Way too much for a kid.'

Not a kid.

'If I can find someone local who she likes then—'

Then what? I inch closer.

'No, no, you don't need to do that. Apart from Becky working too hard, we are fine. We really are. Charlie's new teacher is doing amazing work with him. And I'm about to receive a decent lump sum payment for the work I just finished.'

So... money is okay. Charlie is okay.

Dad sighs, long and deep. 'I'll give it some thought, Ethel.'

Oh no! Not *her*.

'I guess it might be good for Becky to have a break. Just for a few weeks.'

Afraid Dad will hear me if I stay here, I cover my mouth with one hand and tiptoe to my bedroom. Once I have my door closed I throw myself face down on the bed and let out a whimper, hoping the pillow muffles it. I want to scream.

Aunt Ethel is horrible. She is Dad's older sister and thinks she's better than him. Every time she visits she goes on about her beautiful home in Perth which is all the way across the whole of Australia. It takes days to get there by train or car but she is rich and gets to fly across in a plane. The worst part is she is the principal of an exclusive all-girls school and last visit told Dad I should spend at least one term there. To improve my education. Pretty sure it annoyed Dad because he pointed out I've been ahead of my grade for several years, even in subjects I don't enjoy.

So why did he just say it might be good for me to have a break?

I don't want a break.

I don't want a housekeeper.

Everything I need is right here with Charlie and Dad.

SEVENTEEN

NOW

Dan had arrived right on eight and exchanged pleasantries with Pam, who was about to leave for the inn. She'd refused a lift from Sadie and then again from Dan. She wouldn't even take Sadie's car, saying it was too fancy and she wouldn't know how to start it. Once again it left Sadie wondering why her mother wasn't doing something about the van's tyres, if that was the issue. She needed to take a look at it herself.

She climbed into the four-wheel drive and they set off, waving at Pam as they left.

'Where are we going?'

Sadie had no idea why she'd agreed to go off with Dan yet again. It wasn't the same as last time, when they'd been worried about Rebecca and shared a common goal.

'There's a project I'm involved with. Sounds like something you might find interesting.'

'Why?'

He grinned. 'Is this you, or the journalist you?'

'Asking questions?'

'You do ask a lot of them.'

Sadie smiled in response, not that he saw because his eyes were on the road. He turned right at the end of her road.

'I've always been curious. Ask Mum. My favourite word growing up was "why" and it nearly drove her crazy. At school I probably made my teachers turn to alcohol. If I didn't understand the logic behind something then I would insist on more detail. And don't get me started on religious studies.'

He shot her a glance, eyebrows raised.

'Oh. I'm sorry. Are you religious?'

Dan chuckled, shaking his head. 'Not me. Not having grown up the way I did. But I'm a big believer in the shrine of a trillion stars in the midnight sky.'

Good grief, if you don't stop saying everything right and looking so darned gorgeous I am going to fall for you. Stop it.

Her eyes drifted out of the passenger window as they took another turn, this time into a narrower road. Shrine of a trillion stars. Sadie was caught between acknowledging the power of his simple statement and her default of keeping everyone, no matter how special, at arm's length. Building a barrier wasn't so hard. It just needed a few bricks to begin with... bricks formed by disappointment. Or sadness.

'You were saying?' he said. 'Religious studies.'

'Oh, them. A lot didn't make sense but what really got my interest was how people didn't like to answer direct questions. I was continually told not to pester everyone and go and read quietly.'

Especially by her own father.

'You are a child, Sadie, and have no understanding of what you are questioning.' Dad's face had been red with fury and she could see all the warning signs but hated the unfairness of his refusal to answer her questions.

'I'm fourteen, Dad. And how can I understand if you won't talk to me about it? Is it really your religion's belief that women shouldn't be well educated or just you being cruel?'

*He'd walked away from her. Got in the van and driven off,
leaving her heart racing and disappointment building early
bricks for her barriers.*

'And did you?'

Dan's voice cut through the memory.

'Did I... oh, read? You bet. If adults weren't willing or able
to help me understand something then books were my go-to.
And when the internet was available at school... game changer.'

'And this natural and keen curiosity led to journalism.'

'In a roundabout way,' Sadie said. 'I loved research and
began an arts degree with that in mind. The idea of being able
to immerse myself in questions and answers and actually find
resolution was mind blowing. But my first professor redirected
me to journalism. She said my mind and drive would waste
away in dusty old offices and I had a world to conquer.'

She rarely spoke about her past but between Rebecca and
Dan was spilling her guts. It didn't sit well with the caution
learned by too many life lessons. She'd said enough.

'And that progressed into your documentaries?'

Don't give up, do you?

The vehicle slowed as it reached a T-intersection which was
the road leading inland. They were two or three residential
blocks from the main shopping street of Rivers End. Sadie
checked her bearings. She knew there were only a couple of old
houses out here among acres of open land reaching to the
primary school but in front of her was a construction site. Dan
crossed the road and nosed into a makeshift driveway, passing
the framework of a large building before stopping in a dirt
carpark.

'Come and take a look.'

He was out of the four-wheel drive before she could ask
what they were looking at and by the time she'd climbed out,
had collected two hard hats from a pile hanging off temporary
fencing beside a closed mesh gate.

'You need this, and you need to sign in.' Dan checked the inside of the hard hat, adjusting a strap. 'See if this fits.'

Sadie had worn them in the past when shooting on building sites so knew what to expect. 'You got it right first time.' She took the clipboard and pen he held out and added her name and signature. These went onto another hook on the fence and then he pushed the gate open.

'This is my biggest job to date and one I'm thrilled to work on.' Dan led the way between two portable buildings. 'Have you heard what we're doing here?'

'Last time I looked, this was open paddocks, so no.'

Dan glanced back. 'No questions?'

'I'm saving them up.' Her need to ask a million things was buried beneath the unsettling memory of arguing with her father.

'Excellent.'

The site was busy and noisy as tradies got on with their respective jobs. Closest was the framework she'd seen as they drove in. At the far end of it a roof was taking shape. They stepped onto a concrete slab with internal frames for rooms and doorways waiting for plastering and plumbing pipes in place ready for bathroom and kitchen fittings.

'Over here is the main entry.' Dan strode through a couple of rooms to the front of the building which faced the main road but was set back about twenty metres. He turned around, his arms wide as if welcoming a guest to his home. 'Imagine if you will... a light-filled lobby with lots of plants and a water feature. Skylights and large windows to bring nature closer. An oval-shaped reception area – kind of like two semicircles with space between for staff to easily enter and exit. Plenty of places to sit, meet up with friends and family, or look out at what will be pretty gardens at the front.'

What was he building? Not a hospital... Green Bay's was only twenty minutes away.

'To the left,' he pointed, 'is the dining area. Perfect for couples wanting a romantic evening or a group of friends getting together. It also faces out to the gardens and the kitchen is situated between there and the café.'

Just like at a fancy boutique hotel.

A horrible sinking sensation pooled in her gut.

Dan headed to the imaginary kitchen and Sadie trudged behind, trying – and failing – to push away a rising tide of outrage. Was he actually building something in direct competition to her mother's inn?

'The kitchen is state of the art. Large enough to service both the dining room, the café – which is perfect for breakfasts and casual lunches – and in-room meals. Oh, and staff meals. See where the framework ends? On the other side is a gorgeous atrium which will have another water feature... a pond with fish, most likely, and with a clear roof for all-weather use.'

His face was alight when he smiled at her. He was so proud of himself and who wouldn't be? It sounded like a resort. Oh, what if it was one of those health retreats? That would be good for the town. Her heart lifted a fraction. She managed a semi-encouraging nod which must have satisfied him because his smile widened.

'So what else?'

'Finally, a question!' He was off again, striding through the imaginary atrium and zig-zagging around portable toilets.

This time they walked at least a hundred metres, out in the open, across ground which was churned up by trucks and work vehicles. She stayed behind him but the view of powerful legs and muscular shoulders striding away didn't help her state of mind. It was purely physical attraction and completely one-sided but because he was a decent man it was messing with her. Much better to consider he wasn't as nice as he first seemed. Not if he wasn't being honest with Pam.

He had his camera out and was scrolling when she reached him.

'Here is an artist's impression from this vantage.' He offered her his phone.

It was appealing, she had to give him that. Lots of guest rooms, all with doors leading onto what would be a parklike environment.

'The building to our right will house an indoor pool, spa, and sauna. Beyond it, a gymnasium set up for the guests. There really isn't much we haven't thought of.' He accepted the phone back. 'The owners are already sourcing staff from around the country. A few hotels in the cities might find themselves losing their best chefs and housekeepers.' He laughed.

It *had* to be a hotel. A health retreat would source nutrition-ists and natural therapists and the like. No, this was a boutique, high-end hotel.

'What do you think, Sadie?'

'I don't understand.'

'Oh. Do you mean the affordability? That is kind of the whole point of bringing you here.'

Dan gazed at her with such expectation that she almost second-guessed herself. *Almost.* A rogue thought fought for her attention, urging her to take a step back and listen before continuing down the risky path of half-formed conclusions. The thought got squashed. Pam was all that mattered and she'd had enough of seeing her taken advantage of.

'What's wrong? I can see in your eyes you want to say some-thing and I get the feeling it isn't complimentary,' he said.

'I... look, I'll walk home. Thanks for showing me this... whatever it is. And maybe let Mum know what you're building so she can factor in the conflict of interest.' Sadie stalked away before she could say more. Not that her throat would let her because it was tight, the same as her chest. And it *wasn't* because she was acting out of character. Was it?

'Where are you going?' Dan sounded amused as he caught up. 'You need to skirt around the building, yup, that way. Did you remember an appointment? I'll drive you back.'

'No. And no, you won't.'

Nothing more was said by either of them until they were clear of the building site. Dan hadn't got the message and still matched her stride for stride, checking his phone as he walked as if the pace she'd set was normal. Probably was to him with those long, muscular legs. But at the edge of the road, as they stopped for traffic, he put the phone away.

'Why does this construction upset you, Sadie?'

She shaded her eyes with a hand and looked up him. There were little lines around his eyes she'd never noticed and she wished she knew if he was genuinely puzzled. 'I just think it is a bit much to expect me to be enthusiastic about something which will affect Mum.'

'Even if she decides to live here, she won't want to move in for years yet.'

'Sorry... move in?'

Now, he frowned. 'What did you mean about a conflict of interest?'

Oh for goodness' sake, are you going to pretend?

'You want to rebuild Mum's inn. You are currently building an upmarket hotel. How on earth can there not be a conflict of interest?' Her tone was sharper than she intended and a glint came into his eyes. Probably not accustomed to being challenged if he was the boss. 'And I get it. I do, Dan. Rivers End is growing and that' – she gestured back at the site – 'modern establishment with world-class chefs and water features will attract guests from near and far, not that the average person will find it affordable, no doubt. But that leads to Rivers End Inn, which even when rebuilt will offer cheaper accommodation and basic facilities. Perfect for those with less money. Best of both worlds and you get the credit.'

The traffic cleared and she began crossing, hoping action would help her control the temper she'd thought she'd left in her teenage years.

Again, Dan kept pace.

On the other side she stopped again, turning to glare at him with her hands on her hips. 'Don't you need to work?'

She had no hope of reading his expression and it bothered her no end. Normally her people skills, including body language, were excellent but he had somehow turned his face to stone and his eyes to something dark and stormy.

'Let me get this straight. You think I'm building a hotel here *and* plan to rebuild a inn for Pam. Why would I do that?'

Before she could control herself, Sadie rolled her eyes. 'Money. What the hell else? Mum needs to know what she's up against and hopefully she'll accept a developer's offer before forking out money to someone who would take—'

'Take what, Sadie?' His voice was quiet and calm. Eerily calm.

'Advantage, Dan. Someone who would take advantage of a woman who just lost her husband and whose world is upside-down.'

Something changed in him. His head dropped and his hands, which were beside him, briefly tapped his legs. When he raised his eyes she could read them again. They were hurt. Dan went to speak then shook his head and turned. In a minute he was across the road and then, was out of sight.

And just like that, another layer of bricks in Sadie's mental barrier were laid.

EIGHTEEN

'Oh, Sadie. You didn't.'

Pam held one side of a sheet and Sadie the other. There was still nobody cleaning the inn other than the two of them and they had another room to do after this.

'Mum, he is only interested in money and his reputation as a builder.'

'Oh deary me, love.' Pam was doing a poor job of holding back a smile. 'Pass those pillows over.'

Sadie did so and then worked on the quilt. 'Why is this funny?'

'I doubt if poor Dan found it funny. If anything, it sounds as if you were quite rude and that really isn't a good start to a relationship, now is it?'

Stepping back from the bed, Sadie's mouth dropped open. How on earth was she meant to respond? She probably was rude to have spoken her mind but sometimes people only got the message when it was delivered clearly. And what relationship?

'I was direct. Not horrible or anything but I admit I probably offended him. And you need to stop imagining there is any kind of relationship because you know I'm heading home in a couple of weeks. Why would you want me to start something I can't finish?'

'Why *wouldn't* I want my daughter to find happiness?' Pam surveyed the room. 'One more to go.'

'We need to hire someone.'

'Feel free to find a suitable person. I've been looking.'

Sadie made a note on her phone to remind her to put an ad up on local social media pages.

They finished the other room and started yet another load of washing, not returning to the conversation. But Pam had obviously been mulling it over. While Sadie put the kettle on for a pot of tea, her mother perched on the arm of a chair.

'What makes you think Dan is building a hotel?'

'He showed me an artist's impression of the finished build... well, at least from the rear of the building where the rooms all go out onto a park of sorts. And he joked about city hotels being about to lose their top chefs and housekeepers. At first I'd thought it might be a health resort.'

'Did anything else occur to you?'

Sadie glanced at her mother.

'For that matter, did you ask Dan what he is building?'

'No. I... okay, so I made an educated guess based on the information at hand.'

'Is that what you do with your documentaries?'

Not even close. But... this is different.

Sadie carried two cups to the sofa, handing one to her mother who sank onto one of the seats. 'All I could see was the risk to you, Mummy. Imagine how much of your trade will disappear if there is some flashy new place a couple of blocks away. I did try to rationalise it though.'

'How?'

'Well, I imagine such a high-end place will attract a high-end rate and Dan didn't mention anything about families staying there, whereas you've always welcomed children and having a pool and play area will only serve to encourage that demographic.'

Perhaps she'd been a little hasty. The two properties might complement each other.

'Of course he wouldn't have mentioned families staying there. All the children will be middle-aged themselves.'

Sadie blinked. Was her mother losing it?

With a chuckle, Pam shuffled back a bit to make herself comfortable. 'Dan is building a retirement village. Assisted living, they call it. And very affordable.'

As her hands suddenly shook, tea spilled from the cup and Sadie gasped as hot liquid scorched her wrist. She got to her feet, put the cup down, and ran water over the pink mark.

'There's some aloe cream in the first-aid kit.'

What on earth had she done? Sadie prided herself on facts. Logic. Making decisions based upon the information at hand. But she'd completely misunderstood what Dan had shown her.

No, you deliberately put your own spin on it because you wanted to push him away.

She dried her skin and dug out the cream. The aloe was soothing and after putting it away, she picked up her cup.

'Careful. The tea is hot.'

'Geez, thanks, Mum.' Returning to her seat, she nursed the cup. 'You've known all along?'

'Everyone in town knows. The land was earmarked for the purpose years ago but the plan to build a multi-storey facility which was more prison than home for the elderly was continually rejected by council and then, out of the blue, someone bought the entire corner. Think it is around ten acres. New plans were approved in a matter of weeks and Dan's company won the tender to build it.'

Little things fell into place.

Plenty of places to sit, meet up with friends and family, or look out at what will be pretty gardens at the front.

Visitors and residents. Not guests.

He'd used the term dining room rather than restaurant.

Sadie groaned.

'You need to find him and apologise, love.'

Or leave town and never return.

Instead of doing what she knew she must – eventually – Sadie buried herself in work on her laptop at home. Lina had rung, saving her from continuing the conversation with her mother, and she'd excused herself. There was nothing more to do at the inn and Pam seemed content to stay there with more paperwork and wait for the afternoon's arrivals.

The call from Lina was brief, letting her know there'd be a proposal in her inbox later today. Although they were both free-lancers, they were part of a small group which regularly worked together on projects. These documentaries used a low-budget, fast-turnaround model which suited the streaming service who had so far taken four out of five of their finished shows, produced by a small studio.

Sadie attended to paying bills for her apartment and updating her professional profile on a few sites now that the last doco wasn't far off releasing its screening dates. After joining the couple of local social media pages she put up notices of the job at the inn.

She didn't bother with lunch. Every time she stopped, even for a glass of water, her mind returned to her embarrassing behaviour with Dan. It was best she kept busy. But it was no good ignoring her lapse of social skills and good manners. Sadie sighed deeply and pushed the chair away from the computer. Her wrist still stung where she'd burned it and she went in search of more aloe cream. Finding a tube in the main bathroom, she rubbed it on, then asked her reflection, 'What were you thinking?' She stared at her eyes in the hope of finding some response. Her skin was lightly tanned from the swimming and walking and it suited her better than constant make-up and too much time indoors. She released her hair from its ponytail and it cradled her shoulders. From a distance she didn't look her age, but if she peered too closely there were little lines which hadn't been there a few months ago. She didn't care, not really, but the world of television could be cruel to women in front of a camera... or at least, the decision-makers could be. There were so many projects she yearned to do and sometimes feared there wasn't enough time before she was no longer considered suitable to front them.

Being unkind to total strangers was not a good way to build a reputation.

'He's not really a stranger.'

Tired of talking to herself, Sadie returned to her room and reviewed the facts, turning the chair in slow circles.

Dan hadn't told her what he was building. He'd said a few throwaway lines and expected her to join the dots.

Which she had. And come up with the wrong answer. Understandable, but wrong.

Why had she overreacted? All she'd had to do was ask for clarification but instead she'd jumped to conclusions and then accused him of being out to take her mother for a ride.

His eyes had shown his pain.

She faced the laptop and typed in Dan's company name. When she found his contact number she dialled, heart racing a little. If he refused to speak to her she'd have to come up with another way of apologising.

'This is Dan Harrington. Please leave a detailed message and I'll return the call as soon as possible.'

Sadie put on her professional voice. 'Dan, this is Sadie

Forest. Would it be possible to meet with you... at your convenience of course. Please let me know.'

Argh. That was awful and he wouldn't ring back. He'd wash his hands of her and rightly so. At least he wouldn't ever think badly of her mother. Would he?

The laptop dinged as an email arrived, the proposal she'd been waiting for. These early concept emails were more to get expressions of interest from the usual team. This concept followed on from the doco about homeless teens. It was all about the struggles low-income people had with keeping a roof over their heads. Instead of the movie-length which Lina had expected, it had been adjusted to be in four parts. It delved into demographics which were all close to Sadie's heart. Teens. Families at risk. Disabled. And the elderly.

For the first time in hours she smiled as an idea formed. Maybe there was a way to show Dan she was a better person than he'd been exposed to, and do some good at the same time.

NINETEEN

Dan's house was nothing like she expected.

For some reason she'd expected a builder to have something super-modern, large, even gaudy. But as she sat in her car in his driveway, Sadie was impressed. The home looked as if it was newish but was old-fashioned in style. White weatherboards, a wide wrap-around verandah with railings and furniture and lots of hanging pots, reminding her a bit of Rebecca's cottage but on a much grander scale. The metal roof was dark grey and the colour extended to posts and accents, making for a welcoming and attractive frontage. If she had to describe the house it was as an Australian farmhouse and all of a sudden she wanted to go inside and see if he had laid timber floorboards and had a country kitchen.

An hour earlier, she'd received a text message from him with an address and a time. Nothing else. She'd rung Pam to let her know she'd be out briefly and her mother just laughed and told her she'd see her later. Much later. But all she was doing was offering a sincere apology and talking about her idea... assuming he didn't use his own choice words and send her packing.

Before leaving she'd changed from her shorts into an ankle-length skirt and white blouse and put her hair up into a tight bun. The type she wore when working. It gave her a sense of confidence. And she added mascara and lipstick.

In her rear-vision mirror she watched the four-wheel drive approach and all the calming breathing and positive thoughts of the last couple of hours swirled into a mess of anxiety.

He drove around her car and into a garage, whose door had opened as he approached. With a final glance in the mirror, Sadie climbed out and wandered across, stopping about halfway.

Dan was on the phone and as he exited the garage he made eye contact and held up a finger. The garage door slowly closed and he stood, legs slightly apart, finishing a conversation. Something about early morning deliveries and upping the security on the site. Then he hung up and pocketed the phone.

For a moment... a few heartbeats... he stared at Sadie. Then he headed for the front steps. 'Coffee?'

She glanced at her car. Sadie hated confrontations. Hated arguments. Hated being surrounded by anger and bitterness and snide comments and... but this wasn't her family. This wasn't her father pivoting from outright fury to cold control. Or her mother daring to find a few words of strength only to fade into the background. Sadie followed.

He waited at the door, holding it open. 'Sorry about the call. We found some evidence of theft and there is very little room in the budget for replacing stolen timber.'

'That's awful. Why would anyone do that?'

Sadie slipped past him.

The wide hallway was everything she had imagined. Floorboards, panelled walls, a gorgeous hall runner, and tasteful lighting with lamps along the walls and a few overhead lights.

Dan closed the door and pulled off his boots, dropping them onto a rack.

Sadie went to remove hers.

'You're fine. I've been ankle-deep in mud today.'

And it will take less time to throw me out if I don't have to stop to put shoes on.

She hoped she hadn't said that aloud because Dan gave her the strangest glance as he passed her, padding in his socks to the far end of the hallway. He turned to the right and she followed. If he was offering coffee he wasn't too mad. Surely.

His back was to her when she stopped just inside the doorway. What a stunning kitchen. Right out of a magazine with a large, ash timber island bench complete with sink on one side and stools on the other. White timber cupboards lined two walls and a door to one side gave a glimpse into a butler's pantry. In contrast the appliances were black, all in the vintage style so popular in modern homes. The white and black might have been too stark if not for the bowls with fruit and vegetables, herbs hanging to dry, as well as more plants and brightly coloured tea towels.

'Grab a seat, Sadie. How do you prefer your coffee?' Dan moved away from a coffee machine to collect mugs from a cupboard. 'I can make almost anything.'

'Actually, just black is fine.'

'Espresso or long black?'

'Long black. Had too many today to risk espresso.'

He turned back to the job of making coffee but Sadie was certain his lips had flicked up for an instant.

She perched on an end stool and watched him work. As attractive as she found him physically, something more intrigued her. Something apart from the need to put things right. Despite her sharp words earlier he hadn't responded in kind. He'd not arced up like someone might when under attack nor retaliated by using cutting language. Instead, he'd bowed out. Not because he was weak or afraid... she was sure it was because of an inner strength. Self-respect.

'Why are you so sad, Sadie Forest?'

Her eyes had drifted away from him and she'd not noticed the coffee machine had stopped. He carried two mugs around the counter and placed them down, then pulled up the stool closest to her.

'Do I look sad?'

'Yes.'

His phone beeped and he glanced at it then turned it face down on the counter. Picking up his mug, his eyes returned to her face but he said nothing.

'This morning... I was... wrong.'

An eyebrow lifted a fraction.

'And I apologise for what I said.'

'Which part in particular?'

She lifted her chin and forced her voice not to waver. 'I know you are not the kind of man to take advantage of anyone, let alone a grieving woman. That was unforgivable and I whole-heartedly apologise. And... for accusing you of trying to have the best of both worlds. I should have asked questions instead of jumping to conclusions.'

There. She'd said what she came to say. But she found herself holding her breath.

'I had expected questions. Just not ones about my integrity.' He lifted his mug and sipped.

'The way I spoke, what I said, it isn't me. I'm not about to excuse myself with reasons though and I am sorry. I really am, Dan.'

'Then we won't speak of it again.'

That's it?

When she finally tried her coffee she let out a small sound of pleasure. Was there anything this man didn't do well? Oh yes, he was terrible at explaining stuff.

'This is very good, thank you. Mum told me the assisted living home is going to be affordable. Do you happen to know anything about the pricing? Or can point me in the right direction of someone who does?'

'As I said this morning, Pam is a long way from moving in.'

About to assure him she wasn't planning on pushing her mother into care of any kind, she caught the glint of humour on his face.

'Oh I don't know. She's always wanted a nice water feature.'

'I'll add one to the inn plans.'

His smile warmed her heart and made it go a little faster. 'But no, not for Mum. I do have a reason for asking though.'

'I can put you in touch with one of the people behind it. The company is based in Melbourne but one of the owners has a holiday home in Rivers End Heights and comes down here most weekends.'

'Oh, yes please.'

'Care to share? Your reason?'

Sadie told Dan about the email she'd received and touched on the subject matter of her previous documentaries. 'So being able to take a deep dive into affordable housing for the various demographics who are most vulnerable is a logical step. Rivers End has an ageing population and I imagine some of the elderly manage at home with little local assistance. It is a lovely community but as it's growing so fast it's bound to take time for the infrastructures – both physical and in services – to catch up.'

'Exactly why this was the location chosen for the pilot facility. Rather than building in a population-dense area, they wanted to know what actually works and doesn't before expanding.'

'I could say something about test dummies.'

He shook his head. 'Far from it. This one will always get the first of everything. First to have above-standard-size accommodation in a single-storey building, with exceptionally easy access and beautiful grounds – plus there will be a small suburb, if you will, for those wishing to have small standalone cottages. First to experience in-house water therapies, massage, physio and more all on call. And first to try different menus developed with the approval of the residents.'

'Very lucky test dummies.' Sadie grinned. 'Should I be reserving my future space there?'

Dan's phone rang and he lifted it, standing when he saw the caller. 'Sorry, it's a supplier and I need to run out to the car to grab some info. Go for a wander out the back if you're interested in the garden.'

Sadie only waited until he was out of the kitchen and then was on her feet. The back door was directly off the kitchen and she unlocked it and stepped onto the verandah. Out here was as pleasant as the front including a long table with eight chairs and a covered barbecue against a wall. She went down the few steps onto a cobbled area which was partly covered by a large pergola and then followed a meandering path.

Unlike Rebecca's cottage in the valley, Dan had built into the side of a hill and Sadie couldn't resist seeing what was further up the path as it climbed, weaving past cleverly designed vegetable gardens, an abundance of flowers, and higher up, fruit trees. There was a small grove of cherries and oranges and beneath them, a stone bench.

She sat, her eyes drawn to the horizon.

The ocean stretched out forever from this vantage and it was one of the most beautiful vistas Sadie had ever seen. Here in the cool shadows, a sense of calm and belonging crept into her heart. The quiet was profound. Only birdsong filtered through the motionless air. There was no sign of the house or its tanks and outbuildings and she might well have been the only human on the planet

She never wanted to leave.

'This is one of my favourite places to unwind.'

Dan wandered up the path and when he reached the bench he joined her.

For a while they sat side by side. Dan was close enough to reach out and touch and Sadie almost gave in to a sudden urge to feel his skin against hers. It was nothing more than the moment. Relief that he'd accepted her apology. A physical response to being beside a man who was both physically and emotionally attractive.

'Sadie?'

She didn't want to look at him. What if he saw her messed-up thoughts?

'I have to go out again. There's a meeting to attend with the developer and yes, we work with one.'

At the smile in his tone she had to glance his way. And it was infectious, the way his eyes showed his amusement every bit as much as his lips even though she didn't understand what he was driving at.

'Otherwise I'd... well... would you have dinner with me another night?'

His smile was gone.

Was that apprehension on his face?

Are you nervous?

Goosebumps rose on Sadie's arms and she rubbed them, wincing when her hand accidentally touched the burn.

In an instant, warm fingers encircled her wrist. Electricity sparked through her body and it was all Sadie could do not to visibly react. What the heck was wrong with her? Dan gently extended her arm until he saw the red mark.

'What happened?'

'Um. Nothing. Spilled hot tea earlier.'

'Have you treated it? Does Pam have an aloe plant?'

'I held it under cold water and have twice used aloe cream. It will be fine.'

He wasn't releasing her. Could he feel the blood pounding through her veins?

'Yes.'

Dan's eyes moved to Sadie's. 'Yes?'

'Yes, I'll have dinner with you.'

As if he noticed he was holding on to her wrist, Dan let go. 'Okay. When?'

'I'm free anytime. Unless there's something Mum needs me for. But Dan... you do know I'm leaving Rivers End soon. A bit under three weeks and I'm heading home.'

'Home.'

'Sydney.'

'Of course.'

For a moment – an instant – he leaned a fraction closer.

'What about Rebecca?' Sadie had no idea why she blurted that out and from the confusion on Dan's face, neither did he. 'What I mean is, do you think Rebecca would move in to the assisted living complex in time?'

'Clearly you don't know her well. Do you mind if we walk and talk?'

He stood, offering a hand which she pretended not to see. Touching him again was a terrible idea. A wonderful idea. But not happening. There was just enough room on the path for them to stroll down side by side.

'Rebecca is fiercely independent. I think she'll live in her cottage until the day she... well, until then,' Dan said.

'I find her fascinating. She's highly intelligent. Talented. And has a kind heart although I get the feeling she keeps it well hidden.'

'She is an amazing person.' Dan glanced at Sadie. 'Why the interest? Is this the journalist in you?'

'Well, maybe. There's definitely a story there.'

'I don't understand.'

'People are interesting. Older people mostly because they've experienced life in all its facets but something about Rebecca and her cottage and cat go a step beyond idle interest. I'm going to ask her if I can interview her.'

Dan stopped dead.

'What?' Sadie asked.

'She won't agree. I'm sure she won't.'

'Then she will say so. But if she does then I might write an article about her, even if she chooses to be anonymous.'

'Some things are best left alone, Sadie.' Dan started down the hill again.

She knew he was right.

But she hadn't got so far in life by ignoring her gut.

TWENTY

62 YEARS AGO

Thank goodness Dad hasn't said another word about a housekeeper. For the past three weeks I've done extra stuff but been careful he didn't see. Like making a trip to the grocery store by myself when we were low on a few things. He'd gone to pick up Charlie and told me he would be an hour or so because there was a meeting with the teacher. So I ran down the hill and rushed around the store and even was polite to Mrs McKenzie. After leaving with two carry bags, I went past the gift shop. And stopped.

In the window was a lamp. But not just any old lamp. This one was in the shape of a lighthouse and I went inside and asked how much it cost. Far more than the little bit of pocket money I've saved. The lady behind the counter was nice and offered me a much less expensive lamp but it wasn't the same as the white lighthouse with red trimming and a lightbulb in the very top.

I was home before Dad and Charlie and proud of myself for taking the initiative and saving Dad from having to go out again.

But I thought about the lighthouse a bit and today, on the beach with Charlie, I really can't get it out of my mind.

'Can we go out there?' Charlie squints as he stares at the column of rocks in the little inlet. 'I can swim far enough.'

'Oh my goodness, no, Charlie. The water will be terribly deep and the currents might pull you into the far reaches of the sea.' And I can't swim to go with Charlie or save him if he gets into trouble. It occurs to me I need to learn more than the little bit which keeps my head above water in a pool. The bit Dad forced me to learn for emergencies.

'How did they get like that?'

'Like what?'

'Tall. All on top of each other without falling over.'

'Maybe Dad knows.'

'Or Tim. Here he is. Hi, Tim!'

Great.

He appears from around the base of the cliff wearing shorts and sandals with a bag slung over his shoulder. The tide is right out and flat rocks are exposed to the late afternoon sun which glints off the rockpools. Dad let me give Tim a new towel the last time I saw him and he even smiled. Better than staying cross at me for pushing him, I guess.

'Hey, little buddy,' Tim says. He drops his bag onto the sand near us. 'Hello, Becky.'

I make some grunting response. It isn't easy to be friendly when I hardly know him.

'Seeing as the tide is out, shall we look for shells?'

He isn't asking me and when Charlie raises his arms Tim lifts him onto his back as if he weighs nothing.

'Come on, Becky. We're shell hunters,' Charlie says.

Before I can even open my mouth they are crossing the golden sand and I scramble to my feet, knocking over the water bottle. I'd forgotten to tighten the lid and water bubbles out until I set it right. There's not a lot left which means another trip up to the house. Or we can go back early and play a board game. Without Tim.

The two of them are laughing as I catch up. Instead of going to the rockpools they've stopped on the sand. There's something out in the water and Charlie is beside himself. All I see is a shadow in the waves and then a fin.

'A shark!'

'Nah. Dolphins. Look, there's a pod out by the rocks.'

Tim points and I finally see the shapes are sleek and swift. They splash about, playing in the surf and seeming to race each other to the rocks and back toward the shore. Are they curious about us? One leaps almost fully out of the water and I gasp and then laugh as wonder rushes through my body. Charlie is high on Tim's shoulders and it is only when warm water covers my toes I notice how close we are to the danger of the depths.

'Come away. Both of you, please.'

I retreat out of reach of the waves but I might as well tell the dolphins to grow legs because Tim and Charlie stay in the sea. Admittedly, the waves near the beach lap rather than surge and even a dozen steps in, the water only comes up to Tim's knees. But my heart is thudding and my mouth is dry and I might be sick if they go any further.

Then I see it.

'Charlie, look!' I yell at him over the sound of the sea and cawing seagulls.

He and Tim stare at me. Did they even hear? I gesture at the rocks in the bay and then they both look in that direction.

The sun has dropped a little behind the column and there is a glow around the very top rock. Charlie's hands are trying to clap and he is so excited that he almost overbalances but Tim grips him around the waist to keep him steady.

'Lighthouse, Becky! Lighthouse!'

And there are silly tears blurring my eyes as I call back. 'It is Charlie's Lighthouse!'

.   .   .

Well, Dad is full of surprises. He arrives at the beach a little later with a picnic blanket and a basket of things to eat. And some more water as well as fizzy drinks, which we are rarely allowed to have. I don't even know when he got those but he must have been hiding them. We sit with our feet dangling in the lagoon, apart from Charlie who chose to lie on a towel on his stomach. He does that sometimes when he gets tired of sitting. Tim stays. I thought I'd mind but he isn't so bad after all. As long as he doesn't say too much.

'I watched you lot from the window having so much fun,' Dad says. He's in shorts and T-shirt and looks relaxed. 'And then I found all this extra food in the fridge.'

Whoops.

'Seems someone has been busy cooking.' He winks at me.

'I didn't want anything going to waste and besides, I wanted to try some new recipes. Like these little sausage rolls.' I put two on my plate. 'This one is the usual kind with meat and stuff but then I had a lot of leftover veggies and cheese. It is a bit different but I like the flavours. There's pumpkin and potato and some herbs and onion as well as cheese.'

Dad pulls a bottle of tomato sauce from the basket and shakes it until a blob drops over his. 'Well I like trying new food.'

Charlie is already stuffing his face. He eats pretty much anything, thank goodness. Fussy eaters make things too hard. I glance at Tim whose hand hovers over the rolls.

'Which is the veggie one?'

Fussy?

'That one, Tim.' Dad points.

Tim puts two of them on his plate then picks one up and bites into it. I can't help watching as he chews. Not that I care if he likes it. But most people would prefer a sausage roll made the way they are used to.

'Really tasty, Becky.'

He says that with a quick grin then picks up the second one.

I'm a bit shocked and not at all sure why Dad is smiling. I mean, they are nice little rolls. Everyone should try them. Then I realise this is the first time anyone outside the family has tried my cooking. And liked it!

We all eat for a while. Charlie asks for a hand to help him sit again and both Dad and Tim do it before I can. So I have a choice. I can feel mad about Tim helping or I can deal with it. Charlie obviously sees him as a friend and he's never had one before. The kids his age back home only ever made fun of him. And Tim is older but I guess he is kind.

'My lighthouse lit up,' Charlie says.

Dad immediately looks out to the rocks. The sun is closer to the horizon and the glow is long gone.

'Do you know how the rocks got to be a lighthouse shape?'

Tim and Dad have an animated conversation about their theories and I tune out and begin to pack up the picnic. It was thoughtful for Dad to do this and now I don't have to worry about cooking dinner although I have some little puddings which can heat up in the oven to serve with ice cream later on.

'We should go, Becky.'

'Almost ready.'

'No, silly, we should go to apple-ostles.'

I stop what I'm doing. 'To what?'

Charlie screws up his face. 'Twenty-two appointments.'

Tim covers his mouth but his eyes give away how amused he is. He'd better not be laughing at my brother.

'Twelve Apostles, Charlie,' Dad says and he is smiling as well. 'They are limestone formations close to the coastline and not very far away from here. We were talking about how Charlie's lighthouse might well be a mini limestone stack. Weren't you listening?'

I feel heat rise up over my face and return to putting everything into the picnic basket. 'Oh, them.' I have no idea about limestone rocks with biblical names but I'm going to go to the library and find out. 'It sounds fun to visit.' Actually, not even one little bit but the others go back to talking about rocks and geology and I can do what I do best. Make sure everything is done properly.

We skip the puddings because Charlie is super tired after being at the beach for so long, so he has a bath and goes to bed. Dad reads to him for a while. I've already emptied the picnic basket and cleaned everything we used so look for something to do. Night time is harder because Dad is around more and if I do any of the noisy cleaning it will stop Charlie settling down. But there is a basket of washing I need to fold so I tip everything onto the sofa and start.

'You should be reading. Or drawing. Never see you with your sketch pad out these days.' Dad joins me and begins to roll socks. 'I can finish this.'

'Almost done though.'

'Did you enjoy the picnic?'

Apart from putting up with Tim?

'It was fun. And it stopped Charlie going on about wanting to swim out to the rocks.'

'Swim?' Dad shook his head. 'Possible but not recommended.'

'I said that.'

'A boat though... something small. That would be the safest way to go out there as long as the conditions were right.'

The shorts I'm folding slip out of my fingers and I stare at Dad. 'Don't tell Charlie that. All he wants is to go out there and it's a terrible idea!'

'Hey, okay, don't get upset, sweetie. I'm only telling you.'

I grab at the shorts and fold them badly. Then refold properly.

'But there is something important I'd like to discuss. I'm sure you think I don't notice how much you do around here. And lately you're doing even more.' He tosses the last of the rolled up socks back into the basket. 'And we'd talked about you having more time for yourself.'

Oh no. Oh, please don't say we're getting help.

'Whatever are you doing to those shorts?'

They are unfolded again and I've managed to turn them inside-out.

'Daddy... I love helping out.'

'I think I've been unfair though. From today I'm doubling your pocket money and I'm insisting we set up a roster of jobs so that I help out more and even Charlie can do some little chores.'

The shorts end up on the floor as I throw myself at Dad. He laughs and hugs me. 'I guess that's a yes.'

He gives me a whole pound note and says it is for all the extra stuff I've been doing. From now on I will get two shillings pocket money each week. Later, I tuck them into an old sock with the other money I've saved and roll it up and push it to the back of the drawer.

I'll be able to get Charlie the lighthouse lamp.

And then he won't need to worry about visiting the real one.

TWENTY-ONE

NOW

Sadie reread her handwritten notes for the third time and still couldn't work out what she had missed. The feeling that she'd forgotten an important piece of the picture nagged at her.

This was how she always started an investigation. Handwritten notes. Images if available. Sometimes she'd sketch something she'd remembered. The first thing she'd done this morning was copy the thoughts she'd added to her phone the other day.

- *What is the history of the cottage by the lake?*
  (Whisper Lake)
- *Who is Rebecca?*
- *Why has she wandered from home at least twice?*
- *Who does she want me to help her find?*

She only knew a little about the cottage. Rebecca purchased it without an inspection about three years prior. Dan had replaced the roof and, from the sound of it, Rebecca had done additional work herself to make it into the inviting home it was now. Sadie made a note to find out which realtor had sold it and look into its history.

The second question was the most relevant. Who was Rebecca Meyers... Becky? On the surface she was a retired teacher. A cooking teacher who'd lived in Mildura. But for how long? Was that where she'd always lived?

She tapped a query into her laptop.

Rebecca Meyers.

A few results popped up but none matched the woman in question.

Sadie tried a dozen different ways, using cook, chef, teacher, combinations of the same, Mildura, artist, Rivers End. When she failed to find anything, Sadie sent an email to Lina with what she knew – name, description, age, current location, past location, possible career. And finished it with a polite 'no hurry!'.

Whatever had drawn the woman to that part of the coast on two occasions – and about a year apart – was powerful enough to have made her leave home without her handbag. No phone or keys. No water. Probably not even any money. Perhaps the bus driver had taken pity on her and given her a lift to Driftwood Cove. Every interaction with Rebecca revealed an intelligent mind and normal grasp of reality apart from those few minutes on the bench when she'd called herself Becky and been in an almost dreamlike state.

- *Depending on what Lina finds – birth, education, work*
- *Focus on any connection to the region*

The cat was her only companion. Percy. Did Rebecca not become lonely so far from neighbours and with no apparent family or friends close by? Even if she considered Dan to be a friend, he wouldn't be there daily. Some people dreamed of solitude but few enjoyed the reality of it. Rebecca did. Certainly from the outside. She'd created not only a comfortable home but also a vegetable garden and small orchard and must spend a lot of time in the kitchen if her pantry full of bottled produce was an indicator.

- *No car. Has a bicycle for transport.*
- *Has a rowboat but Dan says she never uses it*
- *Does she have a family?*

The little pier was old. Perhaps the rowboat was already there when Rebecca moved in and she had no interest in using it. Attaching it to the post was a very long rope and now that she thought about how she'd pulled the boat in to tie up closer, Sadie was sure the rope wasn't old. Nor the rowboat. But there was something else about it she couldn't remember so she went downstairs and made coffee rather than keep going around in circles.

Her mother had been full of questions last night when she arrived back from Dan's. What was Daniel's home like? Was he willing to start over? Why hadn't Sadie stayed for dinner?

Sadie grinned as she poured coffee.

It was abundantly obvious Pam wanted Sadie to stay in Rivers End and she was going to throw an eligible man her way to seal the deal. As if a man was enough to make her change the life she'd fought so darned hard for. Fifteen years of working and studying and putting herself into dangerous situations at times in order to interview people who were otherwise overlooked. Having to deal with unpleasant editors and demanding producers and compete against her peers in order to get the jobs she wanted. Everything else in her life was a sacrifice she'd been willing to make. And it wasn't as though she'd never had male company. Just nobody serious or willing to deal with her lifestyle.

Was that what happened to Rebecca? Never found a person she cared enough for to change her life? Had she fought for what she had? Sadie thought so. It was the journey to where Rebecca was now which intrigued her. But if it was anywhere near Sadie's experiences, did that mean she'd end up living in seclusion with a bossy cat?

It was a sobering idea and rather than dwell on it, Sadie returned to her notes. This time she wrote about the lake from the moment she'd noticed it in her phone camera. The walk through that magical forest. A black cat with green eyes and an insistence she follow. Starting a new page she sketched Whisper Lake, complete with pier and rowboat, and that was when she remembered the oil painting.

Sadie closed her eyes and cast her mind back.

The painting in the hallway of Rebecca's cottage was extraordinary even though the techniques used were not conventional. It was definitely an amateur work but the passion poured into its creation elevated it beyond the normal. Against a blue-black background, upon a partly submerged flat rock in an angry sea, a white lighthouse with red trim shone a soft light... a halo of sorts. And far beneath the glowing top of the lighthouse, a tiny wooden rowboat was at the mercy of the waves.

Sadie opened her eyes and wrote down everything she remembered. It wasn't nearly enough. There'd been details she'd not noticed but how could she have known it might be important? At the time her focus was on finding a person she'd never met and it was only the dark splendour of the painting which stopped her for long enough to recall so much.

And the signature... Becky M.

Not Rebecca. Not Meyers in full. The woman didn't seem to use Becky as a shortening of her name now, apart from the one time when Sadie found her on the bench and asked if she was Rebecca.

Today, I am Becky.

Becky was probably her childhood nickname, even young adult. So being there at the little seaside town was part of something to do with her youth. Maybe. There'd been the comment about the old homes being pulled down.

Families lived there once. Children. All gone.

'Why does this even matter?' Sadie muttered as she stood and began to toss things into her handbag. Notebook, phone, house keys.

'I need to find them. Will you help me?'

What was it about the elderly woman which tugged so hard at Sadie's heart?

There was only one way to find out.

The drive to Driftwood Cove was a bit unsettling. Last time Sadie had been a passenger with a man she'd literally just met behind the wheel. As she passed the turn-off to Willow Bay it was as if he was catching her eye again, silently telling her not to bother rising to the bait Mick Hammond was dangling. That was another mystery – how someone with so few people-skills and a nasty streak became a police officer. She wasn't inclined to find out. Staying away from that man was the best advice she had for herself. For anyone.

But the other man, the one with a gentle soul and a smile which made her heart skip a beat? He was worth thinking about. If he lived in Sydney she would pursue him. Or let him pursue her. Perhaps he had a brother living there. She was smiling when she parked in the shade of the pines lining the street between the beach and the shops.

In her haste to get here she'd ignored the rumbling of her stomach after skipping breakfast and now was so hungry that she went into the café on the corner. As the young woman behind the counter toasted a sandwich for her, Sadie considered asking a few questions. Had she ever heard of Becky Meyers? Did she know who used to own the old places up the hill?

But more than fifty years might have passed since Rebecca

lived here. How would a young person have that kind of local knowledge? And a quick search on her phone showed no real estate agents in town.

Sadie headed to the park and sat at the same table she'd shared with her mother only a few days ago. How cross had they both been that day! Dad had a lot to answer for and Sadie still hadn't opened the brief about the trust. She'd do it once she was back in Sydney rather than spoil her time in Rivers End.

A lone seagull landed and circled her and she tossed it a tiny piece of tomato. Whatever signal that sent to the masses resulted in the descent of a flock of bickering birds including two who were audacious enough to land on the table.

'Go on with you. Don't you prefer fish?'

There was a clear view up the path she'd taken the other day when she was looking for Rebecca. The cliff face jutted out a bit and there might well be a way around it to the next bay. At least when the tide was low, which it wasn't at present. Lunch finished and stomach happy, Sadie left the seagulls to their endless cawing and complaints and went for a walk.

The weather was nicer than the last time she climbed this hill. At the bench she sat and gazed out to sea as Rebecca had – so focused on something only she could see. Trancelike. But there was nothing out there today apart from some sailing boats and a hazy, distant horizon. This was the last part of the path which had a view before skirting around the old cottages toward the road. Sadie followed the path. The cottages – of which there were three – were boarded up and quite hidden behind over-grown bushes. Beyond them was a narrow block of land and then the first of the big new homes.

Rebecca had been cutting about them.

They were similar to some of the homes around Sydney Harbour. Oversized with multiple levels which each had a massive balcony to take full advantage of the views. What was it Rebecca had said?

Views aren't everything.

Doubling back to the narrow block, Sadie crossed its length to the edge of a rather steep descent. It wasn't a complete drop to the sea but dangerous for anyone not accustomed to the difficult ground. There was construction fencing along it and she was able to walk between it and the back fences of two cottages whose gardens didn't go all the way to the edge. They were typical weatherboard homes of the first half of the last century, not large and boxy in shape. She came to a stop when the fence of the third cottage blocked her path.

This one was a lot larger than the first two and was raised on pylons thanks to the drop from the street. There were lots of missing palings in the fence and she slipped between a gap into the garden.

This was private property and yet again she was casually exploring without permission. But unlike the little valley where Rebecca lived, this was abandoned. Bushes along the fences were woody and overgrown. There was a small lawn, if one could be so kind, of straw-coloured grass which was knee high and scratchy on her bare legs as she stepped carefully through it to reach a concrete path around a broken clothes line. From there the path led to the cottage. There was no grass here, just more concrete taking up the majority of the yard. A long ramp doubled back on itself leading up to a small deck at the back of the house, and a set of stairs did the same.

Further from the house in the direction of the sea was a shed whose door hung from the top hinges. Inside was empty apart from a wooden sled with a rope attached to one end and a very old style of surfboard, paint peeling away. There was a basketball hoop set against the better end of the shed but not at the usual height, being only a little bit above her head. Must have been done for kids.

Beyond the shed the ground dipped away, the concrete swapped for a mix of dirt and sand and tufts of grass as a rough track meandered all the way down to a tiny beach. Phone out, Sadie took photographs of everything. The perfect private beach, the odd limestone stack of rocks in the inlet which from the look of them were suffering the same erosion as the Twelve Apostles further down the coast, and then along the edge of the rugged cliff. It was easy to see why the old cottages were being demolished to make way for luxury homes with the incredible view from here. She photographed the shed and the garden and the back of the home then slipped her phone away.

It was sad. Once there would have been laughter and playing kids and people running down to the beach. Families living normal lives in their sweet little town.

And what of the residents of this home? If she took a look... peered through the windows for a moment... it could do no harm. And then she'd leave.

'What are you doing here?'

With a gasp, Sadie spun around from the bottom of the ramp.

An old man stood near the shed, glaring at her from under a floppy fishing hat.

Hand over her heart, she took a couple of steps in his direction. Surely he didn't live here? She stopped at the outrage on his deeply lined face.

He was at least seventy-five, maybe more, but stood straight and tall with white hair touching his shoulders. There was a bag over one shoulder with a beach towel peeking out and he wore shorts and T-shirt and sandals.

'I'm so sorry... is this your home?'

'Who's asking?'

'My name is Sadie Forest. And you are?'

'None of your business. This isn't your property and I'd like you to leave.'

'I mean no harm. I was walking past and felt drawn to the

place. If this isn't your home then do you know the owners? Or anyone who once lived here?'

'You a developer? Another one? All we see is this town being overrun with your kind, tearing down one house to make way for another. Like I said, this isn't your property and you can either leave or I can call the police.'

Sadie nodded and headed back to the gap in the fence. 'Not a developer. Just curious.' She ducked through to the other side and peered over the fence to gaze at him. 'You've lived in the town for a long time, I take it? Would you let me ask you a few questions about the region and the people?'

He lifted and then dropped a hand in an arc as if to push her away across the distance and turned, disappearing down the track before she could say anything more.

With her heart still thudding, Sadie leaned against the fence.

She couldn't do this... snoop around. It wasn't as if she knew for sure that Rebecca once lived here. Gut feelings only counted if there were facts behind them but this was a waste of time. Before too long these cottages would be demolished and replaced. If the old man had a connection with this home then he wasn't open to a discussion. And in a couple of weeks she'd be on the way back to her life in Sydney. There was a ton of work to do to help Mum before then and this urge to uncover the history of a woman she barely knew was little more than a distraction.

Time to stop interfering.

It was better this way. She wouldn't upset Rebecca more by asking questions because the woman had changed her mind about needing help finding the mystery people. She could keep herself busy until she left Rivers End, which was a blessing in disguise because getting too close to the older woman, or her neighbour – especially him – wasn't going to lead to anything other than disappointment.

TWENTY-TWO

'Alright. I'll do it.'

Pam had just arrived home and came straight to the kitchen to make her announcement.

'Great. Sounds good. What exactly are you doing?' Sadie's eyes scanned the shelves of the fridge. Nothing jumped out at her to cook tonight. At home she ate out or ordered in at least three or four times a week and she was running out of ideas. If Dan had called and asked her out she probably would have accepted even with her new resolve to keep her distance.

'Let's go out. For dinner.'

Sadie closed the fridge and turned. 'I'm sorry. I thought my mother just said she'd like to go out for dinner.'

'Nothing wrong with your hearing, young lady. Just your attitude.'

Trying not to laugh, Sadie put her hands on the table. 'Tonight?'

'Tonight. Before I change my mind.'

'Suits me, Mum. Anywhere in mind?'

'You choose. I need a quick shower first.'

With that, Pam was on her way upstairs, humming to herself.

This was refreshing. Another step forward. If she enjoyed herself tonight Pam might be willing to expand her friendships and have some fun. Sadie pulled out her phone and made a note. *Find friends for Mum.*

Rather than taking a stab at booking somewhere, Sadie decided Rivers End was small enough for them to take a leisurely stroll and check out menus. She needed to freshen up if they were going out. After applying a light amount of make-up, she brushed her hair and put on a wide, white hairband. With a grin she added a touch of perfume, not for any reason other than to enjoy the scent.

Pam insisted they walk to town and that suited Sadie. On the way down Ryan Road she quizzed her mother about the residents.

'I really don't know them well, love. Although Joan has those lovely fresh eggs you've been eating. That's her little place over there.' Pam gestured at a pretty property with a cottage garden and white fences. 'She's a widow. Used to live in Green Bay but had always wanted to raise chooks and sell flowers and came here about two years ago. Her garden is quite inspiring. Do you see how she has the little stand out the front?' There was a multi-tiered timber construction with a metal roof on the road side of the fence. 'Every morning she fills it with tubs of flowers and cartons of eggs and by nightfall she's sold out. Getting quite the reputation for quality.'

'She sounds nice. Do you visit each other?'

Her mother frowned. 'Now that you mention it, not really. I do go and buy eggs from her and we always have a chat. And since your father passed away she's been dropping eggs to me. Leaving them at the front door with a note. Always a kind note.'

Perfect.

'Tell me more about Daniel's house. Is it big? A family home?'

'Mum.'

'He seems like the type of man to like children. And you always wanted a dog and I'd imagine there'd be room there.'

This was getting too much. Enough of the matchmaking.

Before she could snap out the words in her mind, Sadie pulled herself up. Things had changed.

In the past, Sadie's response to her mother's persistence would have been to shut down. Make a lame excuse and avoid the questions. Pam always got the message, sooner or later. It had driven a wedge between them as much as the other troubles around Dad and when Sadie moved out of home there'd been few questions, not even about her new life. Pam hadn't even known much about Sadie's career. And when she did show interest in it and Sadie's world in Sydney, she'd been hesitant, careful with how she asked.

It was my fault. I pushed her away.

Sadie stopped dead on the path.

Pam was a few steps ahead before she noticed and turned back. 'Your face is bright red, Sadie. Are you unwell?'

With a small cry, Sadie threw her arms around Pam. 'I'm so sorry, Mummy.'

'My darling girl, what on earth?' Pam cuddled her tightly. 'Who has hurt my princess?'

The use of the nickname from her childhood pushed Sadie over the edge and she burst into tears. 'I never knew... understood... how could I be so mean...?' She pulled away a bit to find a tissue in her handbag. 'It took me until just now to realise.'

There was no finding anything as her hands fumbled around inside the bag but Pam had a packet in hers and held them out. 'Dry those tears, Sadie. Take a few slow breaths. Or do you want to sit on the ground for a bit?'

Her mother spoke in a soft, soothing tone which almost

resurrected the tears. Sadie gulped them down and blew her nose. The rush of emotion simmered beneath the surface as she finally got some semblance of control back.

'I'm okay. My face is a mess though.'

Taking a tissue, Pam held Sadie's chin and gently dabbed around her eyes. 'Wearing waterproof mascara I guess. Apart from a little bit of redness you'd never know you've just been bawling your eyes out.' She smiled but there was worry in her eyes. 'There is nothing to be sorry for. Not to me.'

There was a soft nicker from the other side of the fence and then the muzzle of a pony popped over the top.

'Hello there, Dusty.' Pam reached across to scratch behind the pony's ears. 'This is my daughter, Sadie.'

'You know the pony by name. But not all your neighbours?'

'Well, animals aren't too nosy... having said that, leave my pockets alone because I've got nothing for you.' With a final pat, Pam stepped out of the reach of Dusty's lips which were flapping around in an attempt to grab the bottom of her blouse. 'What if we go out another night?'

'Not a chance, Mum.' Sadie slipped her arm through Pam's. 'I've waited fifteen years to take my mother out for dinner, so let's go.'

The main street of the town was a delight to wander along. Other people were out and about enjoying the warm evening air and while most of the shops were closed, there was plenty of window shopping to be done. Sadie and Pam stopped at shop after shop, making up verbal lists of what they'd buy. Clothes, shoes, books – these were all discussed at length and with humour. Whenever they came across a place to eat they'd read the menu, ask each other if they wanted to eat there, then unanimously decide to keep looking and maybe come back.

Sadie's heart rate had settled down after the surge of ridiculous emotion. Even though the crying had helped, it was showing weakness and she hadn't wanted anyone – particularly her own mother – to witness such a loss of control. They'd not spoken of the reason but once Sadie had sorted a few things in her head then she'd explain herself.

'Oh, this is the place I mentioned. The beauty salon.'

They stopped outside the large window. It was dark inside although at the far end of the shop, big glass doors led to a court-yard where there was a raised spa. And two people were in the spa – too far to identify, apart from being a man and woman.

'Well, I have heard that the service and quality is exemplary. Not that I've ever done such a thing.'

'Mum, never? But didn't you used to have your hair done here when it was a hairdresser's?'

'For a while. But your father thought it an unnecessary expense so I learned to cut my own hair.' Pam flicked the end of her bob. 'It does the job.'

They settled on the bistro in the pub for dinner, the one at the far end of the town. The music was to Pam's liking and not too loud and the menu had plenty of options. Seated at a table beside the window, they clinked their glasses of wine together.

'I haven't been in here for years. Decades. There used to be big booths everywhere but these tables are nicer.' Pam's eyes roamed the bistro. 'For a pub it looks family friendly.' She smiled at Sadie. 'This was a good choice.'

A big difference from the woman who only recently was distraught at the concept of eating out. How far her mother had come so quickly.

'Mum? With that... moment, back there, I'd had an epiphany.'

'Sounds painful.' The smile widened as if encouraging Sadie to continue.

'Kind of. I remembered how I was as a teenager whenever you asked a question I was a bit uncomfortable with. Or would have meant I'd have had to share my feelings.' She looked down. 'Never been good with showing them.'

Pam reached for her hand. 'Go on.'

'I realised I must have done it so often, closing up, shutting you out, that you gave up asking.'

Feeling a tightening of her mother's fingers around hers, Sadie raised her eyes. 'I don't know why but I stopped sharing how I feel so long ago. Not even certain how much I feel compared to other people because I'd rather be logical than emotional, even though that seems to have gone out the window recently, but the point is that I'm sorry, Mum. And I'm going to be more open with anything you want to ask.'

Even just saying the words released a tight band inside her she'd not noticed until tonight. She had to be careful in case the safety net fell and instead intended to unwind it bit by bit. When her eyes misted up she blinked but didn't make an effort to fight the feeling.

'Now, which of you lovelies is having the eggplant parmigiana?'

Sadie and Pam sat back as the server, a forty-something, cheery woman with 'Tessa' on the front of her shirt, held two plates aloft.

'Mine, thank you,' Sadie said.

'Then yours is the veggie burger.' Tessa lowered each plate. 'Nice to see our new plant-based meals getting so much love. I'll fetch some tomato sauce for the chips... or aioli?'

'Any chance of both?' Pam asked with a grin. 'My daughter and I have never been out to dinner together as adults and we want to try it all.'

'On their way.'

'You do know I am trusting you with the suggestion of this burger.' Pam used a fork to poke at the patty. 'Never had a fancy plant meal.'

'Sure you have. Every time you eat a meal without meat,

Mum. We don't need to be vegetarian to enjoy these and I kind of like the look of yours. Didn't the menu say it was made from mushrooms and red beans and onion... Actually, would you like to swap?'

Pure reverse psychology at play.

'Absolutely not, young lady. Mind you...' Pam took a good look at the golden-crumbed eggplant smothered in cheese and surrounded by fat chips and salad. 'What if we share?'

As if on cue, Tessa arrived back with two small plates and a trio of condiments. 'Most folk like to try each other's food since the menu upgrade. And here is some sauce, aioli, and a little relish I was given by a local retired chef. Enjoy.'

'Thank you so much,' Sadie said. What a lovely woman.

'Are you thinking what I am, love?' Pam put some of the relish on her plate. 'Rebecca's doing?'

Sadie helped herself to a spoonful of each condiment and then carefully sliced some of her parmigiana and transferred it to a small plate. Pam did the same with her burger, which was a bit trickier but she managed to keep it intact after a couple of close calls.

'Would you know by the taste?' Sadie put a bit of relish on her tongue and her tastebuds lit up. Sweet and savoury and fruity and tart. 'Whoever made it, I want to find them and buy a whole box of this!' She added some to a chip and bit in. So good.

For a while they ate, only the occasional sigh of enjoyment breaking the silence between them. Pam devoured the burger and her share of the parma followed.

Sadie was used to quality dining with all the options in Sydney but here, in her hometown, she was falling in love with the simple and beautiful food on her plate. 'I would move back to Rivers End just to be able to eat here whenever I want.' Sadie put the small plate on top of the dinner plate. 'Since when was it this darned good?'

'No idea. Dad and I stopped eating out a long time ago.

Another waste of his precious money.' Pam rolled her eyes. 'I loved him. But he made it challenging at times.'

Most of the time.

'I wonder what he'd think about the plans to upgrade the inn?' Pam nestled the almost-empty wine glass between her fingers. 'Back when he designed it there were fewer options and we had so little money that it was amazing we built what we did. Sometimes he'd say how much he wanted to redo the rooms, like, properly. New carpet, curtains, fittings. More than just the beds. And even get a new computer in the office.'

'But it never happened.'

'There was never enough extra money.'

'Well, at least we know why. He was too busy putting money into what he thought was important rather than taking care of what was needed now.'

Pam bit her bottom lip and Sadie patted her arm. 'Sorry, forget I said that. I guess he did what he believed was right and if he hadn't put money away, you wouldn't be contemplating the upgrade now.'

There was only a small nod in return.

'If we have another glass of wine are you going to be okay to walk home?'

Now, a smile. 'Stagger. But why not.'

The idea of stumbling home along Ryan Road in the dark, singing loudly and disturbing the neighbours was too much for Sadie and she snickered.

'Are you laughing at your old mother?'

'Not even close. Let's get some more wine and dessert. I'm sure I saw something chocolaty and decadent on the menu. And Mum? Do you know any sea shanties?'

'She has black glossy fur which is so soft and big green eyes and she sits on my lap and...' Charlie screws up his face, searching for a word. 'Pur-ring. Yes, she purrs.'

'So you get to ride the pony, pet the cat, and do art as much as you want?'

'All day if I decide to.'

I give Dad a long look and he shrugs. 'Sorry, Becky. I know your school isn't nearly as interesting.'

'You can say that again.'

'Dad said your school isn't nearly—'

'Okay, okay. Thanks, Charlie.'

'Are you cross, my best sister?'

Only at the annoying kids at school.

'I'm your only sister.'

'Still the best.'

I give him a hug and he squirms. 'No hugs. Dad needs to say yes. So, can we?' Once I release him, Charlie slides off the armchair.

We're in the lounge room about to play a board game which Dad is setting up on the big coffee table in the middle. I've been putting cushions on the carpet for us to sit and had just placed Charlie's small chair near Dad. It is really just a regular chair from the dining room but the legs are cut down so that he can sit on it without having to climb up. And the height suits him for playing games. He's been watching all of this from an armchair while he tells us about his day at school. And a lot about the cat.

Charlie takes a moment to balance himself. And then he walks straight to Dad on the other side of the coffee table.

'Whoa! Charlie, that is fantastic work!' Dad's hands grab Charlie at the last moment, when his legs begin to bow. 'Not even wearing callipers. I'm really proud of you, son.'

Charlie beams. 'Me too. Proud.'

I want to hug him some more but instead I run to the kitchen. 'This calls for a celebration of ice-cold milk and chocolate cake.'

Better to be in the kitchen so I can wipe my eyes. All I seem to do is cry since we got here. I did cry back at home but only when my bedroom door was shut and I could be in private to think about Mum and stuff. These are happiness tears though. Much better than the other kind. Charlie just walked the furthest I've ever seen! I won't tease him about his school anymore because whatever is happening there is helping him get more independent. Back home there was a special place we went a few times which gave us the exercises and stuff but they were always so busy and didn't have a lot of money for more staff and facilities. One day I want to help out there. Or anywhere to help people who need a hand.

Once I've put three slices of cake on plates and poured two glasses of milk – and one of water because Dad doesn't drink milk – I carefully carry them in on a tray.

Charlie is in his own chair now looking at the game and Dad gets up and takes the tray. 'Sure this won't spoil dinner?'

'Probably, but how often do we get to celebrate?'

Charlie glances at me with a big smile. 'I'll eat cake *and* eat every bite of dinner.'

I sit close to Charlie and help him with the cake. If the plate was flat on a surface he could manage, but it is too hard to hold and eat. He still manages to get chocolate all over his mouth and Dad goes to find a face washer.

'You have to help, Becky.'

'Ah... I am?'

'Nah, not this. The kitten.' He whispered the last bit. 'We'll tell Dad.'

I have my doubts. We've never had a pet, not even a goldfish. And I understood why Dad always said no when I asked for a puppy or a kitten. We lived in an apartment on a busy street. It wasn't practical. Or fair on the pet. Or me.

'Let's get that face cleaned up and start the game. If anyone hadn't noticed, I'm cooking tonight and I need a bit more time than our super-chef.' Dad cleaned up Charlie's face. 'Better.'

We start the game and there's a lot of laughter and accusations of cheating. Same as always. I feel Charlie looking at me a couple of times but I've asked far too often and if he really wants a kitten then he has to start the conversation. Not that I like his chances. To everyone's surprise I win. Of all the games we play this one is usually split between Dad and Charlie to win, so that's nice.

'Shall I pack up or do you have time after dinner for more rounds, Dad?' I ask.

'Are you kidding? After you just smashed us it is game on. An evening of beating you two at this and other games awaits.'

Dad gets to his feet.

'When can we get our kitten, Daddy?'

Charlie rarely says Daddy. Always Dad or if he feels more grown up, Father.

From the expression of surprise on Dad's face, he is a bit

shocked but whether it is from Charlie saying Daddy or asking for a kitten, who knows?

'Ah... I have to cook now.'

Dad goes to the kitchen.

'We won't give up, *Daddy*,' I add.

Charlie giggles.

After a minute, Dad walks back in and stands in the doorway, arms crossed. 'Are you both serious about this?'

'Yes.'

'Very serious.'

The seconds tick past. I can feel them. Dad doesn't move and his face doesn't change. I can't tell what he's thinking. Charlie reaches out for me and I take his hand.

'Who is going to care for a kitten?'

'Me.'

'Me.'

Another long silence. Charlie's fingers dig into the palm of my hand.

'Do you have a name for this potential new family member?'

Charlie gasps. I blink. Is Dad for real?

'Percy,' Charlie says.

'Percy? Where did that name come from?'

'Because Miss Carlisle's cat purrs a lot, Dad. I'd like a kitten just like hers.'

Dad's arms drop and he comes over to us, leaning down to look at me, then Charlie. I think I'm holding my breath and am pretty sure Charlie is as well.

'Percy, hmm. Sounds like a nice name. Let's have a chat to Miss Carlisle and see if she knows anyone with kittens.'

TWENTY-FOUR

NOW

The house was quiet. Everything was quiet – apart from Sadie's mind which refused to settle for the night. Although the walk home was a lot less rowdy than she'd joked about earlier, it had exhausted her mother and they'd stopped a couple of times to let her catch her breath. Sadie had offered to call an Uber... not that Pam knew what they were, but they'd finally made it back almost at midnight. She'd taken Pam's arm and helped her up the stairs to her bedroom and kissed her goodnight.

That was an hour ago.

Sadie stared out of her open bedroom window, enjoying the cooler night air. An owl hooted. So peaceful. No traffic or sirens or pedestrians outside. Nor was there a party on the same floor with booming music or one of the endless arguments from the couple upstairs.

I could live here again.

It was a ridiculous idea.

Every part of her life was integrated with Sydney. Almost every part. She'd missed her mother far more than she'd realised. It was easier to put up a wall and use her father as the reason why she'd moved a thousand kilometres away and only returned once in fifteen years. But every day since she'd arrived was a revelation as she got to know her mother all over again, and this time as an adult. She liked Pam as well as loved her and although she still didn't understand why her mother hadn't abandoned her marriage, there were moments when she glimpsed the love her parents once shared.

Some things didn't need to make sense to be true.

She flopped onto the seat at the desk and opened the laptop to see if the email had arrived with a projected start date for this new documentary. But there was no update. Her idea of inter-viewing the owners of the new assisted living centre still excited Sadie. Being able to bring something different to the forefront might change lives.

Dan hadn't given her any contact details yet. For that matter, he hadn't suggested a day for their dinner.

'Why do I even care?' Saying it aloud didn't help. Her voice was plaintive and it made her chuckle. A relationship wasn't on her to-do list, let alone a long-distance one. What she needed to focus on was helping Pam navigate the next couple of weeks with finalising paperwork and things to address such as the van and other odds and ends. Dan would have to become a pleasant memory... an occasional fantasy of what another lifetime might have been.

Maybe if she kept telling herself that she'd really believe it.

An email came in from Lina.

Okay, so who is this Rebecca Meyers? As in, why is she impor-tant? Here's what I found. Nothing. I mean, there's plenty of people around the world with that name but nobody of the approximate age and locations you provided. I tried different ways to spell the name, heck, I wrote a tiny program to find this person but she must be in witness protection or completely off the grid. Come on, girl, give me something else to go on!

With no idea what to reply, she closed the laptop, turned off the lamp and climbed into bed. Her mind was firing all over the place. People left a footprint. Rebecca must have changed her name, and recently, because if there'd been no result from Mildura, where she'd said she used to live and work, then there had to be another explanation.

Was Meyers her maiden name? If she'd been married and then either divorced or widowed, she might have reverted to it. But surely a birth notice would have resulted from what Lina called her 'tiny program'. Lina was brilliant at coding and would have worked with broad parameters. Or had Rebecca's birth name been changed for some reason? Sadie was tired. Bone tired. Her brain needed to stop and let her rest.

She'd already decided not to delve into Rebecca's story, given her mistake of trespassing at the seaside cottage and upsetting an elderly gentleman, and her tendency to follow a lead without much thought. It was still a bad idea.

Hugging the pillow in her arms, she squeezed her eyes shut.

A really bad idea.

* * *

Sadie parked her car and had scarcely had the chance to climb out and stretch before Percy appeared with her tail high and a loud meow.

'Well hello there.' Sadie squatted to pet the cat, who rubbed her face against her fingers. 'Where's your human?'

'I'm around here.'

'Here' was the front verandah of the cottage where Rebecca sat on her rocking chair. She closed a book as Sadie stepped onto the timber decking and placed it on a low table beside a small pitcher and half-full glass.

'Would you care for some iced tea, Sadie?' She shuffled forward as if to stand.

'Love some, but I can get a glass if you prefer to stay seated.'
Rebecca stilled.

'Cupboard to the left of the fridge?'

With a small smile, Rebecca nodded. 'You're either observant from having tea with me or rifled through my kitchen the first time you were here.'

'Definitely rifled... I mean, observant.'

Sadie wasn't waiting around for Rebecca to change her mind and after removing her shoes, went in through the open door. She hurried to the kitchen and collected a glass and then slowed on her way back to absorb as much as possible. It wasn't the rooms off the hallway which interested her, but the painting, and she took a moment to pause in front of it.

It was richer in detail than she remembered and there was so much raw talent that it was hard to move on, but she did so before Rebecca noticed how long she'd been inside.

'Shall I pour you another?'

Sadie lifted the jug when Rebecca nodded. She'd sat back in the chair and was letting it rock ever so gently. Once she'd filled two glasses, Sadie sank onto a wicker bench. 'This is a lovely spot.'

'Very peaceful. Until the cockatoos come to call and then it's a riot of squawking and bickering.'

Percy stalked along the railing.

'Is Percy afraid of the cockatoos?'

Rebecca snorted. 'That cat is unafraid of the world. She's made friends with one of them and I've caught them at the end of the pier more than once, staring over the side, probably hoping some poor fish will spontaneously leap out into their respective mouths. Mind you, cockatoos aren't known for their love of fish so my furry friend has most likely corrupted the bird.'

'Well, she's a wonderful cat. Any reason for the name? Percy seems a bit more... masculine.'

Profound sorrow creased the other woman's face and she drew in a long, shuddering breath and looked away. Percy was close enough to jump straight down from the railing onto her lap and then stood on her hind legs to tap ever so gently at her owner's face. Whatever nerve Sadie had touched ran deep and she couldn't stop herself from leaning over for Rebecca's hand. The wrinkled skin was surprising in its softness and when Rebecca turned it over to hold Sadie's, her grasp was strong.

Percy lowered herself onto her haunches and glared at Sadie but Rebecca's spare hand found her fur and stroked it.

'I am so sorry... I hadn't intended to cause distress.'

Rebecca's fingers squeezed a bit more and then released Sadie's hand and, with a sad smile, she met her eyes. She picked up her glass and drank and Sadie did the same. The iced tea was sweet and lemony and minty all at once.

'Only the tea came from off the property,' Rebecca said. 'And if I could work out how to grow it, I would.'

The cat curled on her lap now but her eyes were open, staring at Sadie.

'Percy is a special name from a special person. I've named all of my cats Percy to remember... to remember them.'

'What a beautiful thing to do.' She chose her words carefully. 'I feel I have put myself on Percy's hitlist though.'

Rebecca laughed.

'Cats have long memories. If they take a dislike to a person then it won't end well,' Sadie said.

'I believe you are still a friend of the feline. She might be sending you death-stares right now but you were kind to her and she won't hold a grudge.'

A breeze drifted across from the lake, casting ripples across the water. The rowboat was far from the pier, bobbing as the wind caught it. Rebecca must have set it loose again. There was a connection between that little boat and the painting and Rebecca was the only one who knew it. But was it worth risking more upset by asking? From the expression on the cat's face it wasn't.

'Mum wanted me to thank you for the pickles. Especially the chillies, some of which made their way into a delicious curry the other night.'

'She is most welcome. If she needs some more fruit to preserve then I have an abundance of plums and peaches. In fact, why don't I fill that container of yours with some to take home?' Rebecca gently lifted Percy onto the floor, ignoring the growl of annoyance, and pushed herself to her feet. 'I'll go and do that.'

Sadie collected the glasses and pitcher. 'I'll wash these up in that case.' She wasn't about to wait out here and miss the chance to take another look at the painting, and followed Rebecca in. The other woman set a fair pace and although Sadie dawdled she couldn't exactly stop dead without it being obvious. Along the walls were more paintings, much smaller and less dramatic than the lighthouse. And so many books in the shelves lining the lower part of the walls.

'What an impressive collection of books.' Sadie went to the sink. 'Mum reads a lot... well, she does lately. Visits the book-shop in town any chance she can get.'

'Books, bottling, our love of our gardens. Your mother is a woman of good taste. Does she own a cat?' Rebecca half-smiled at Sadie as she collected the container from a cupboard. 'Or enjoy a dry sherry?'

'No cats, I'm afraid, although I expect that might change now that my fa— um, now that circumstances are different, but she does love sherry. First alcoholic drink she ever tried and even though I'm slowly expanding her taste into wine, I think she'll always enjoy sherry.'

Rebecca disappeared through the door toward the back of the cottage, her voice carrying. 'First drink? Surely not as a young woman, because sherry is definitely for oldies like me.'

Am I saying too much?

There was a trust growing here and it mattered a lot that Rebecca got something back for every little snippet she gave. She returned, carrying a bucket which she deposited on the table with a grunt. It overflowed with stone fruit. Sadie dried her hands and joined Rebecca, her mouth beginning to water at the rich, fresh ripe-fruit smell.

'From what she's told me – which isn't much – Mum never drank before my father died and I certainly don't remember her ever doing so. He was against alcohol unless used in cooking, although I suspect he enjoyed a beer or two away from home at times. But it was different for her. She'd never do anything to go against his wishes.'

Rebecca began to put the fruit on the table, sorting as she went, and Sadie joined in. 'He didn't strike me as a controlling husband. I imagine your mother got a little lost though beside his strong personality and while he was the one with bluff and bravado, she had the grace. And a quick mind.'

Peach in one hand and plum in the other, Sadie stopped sorting and stared at Rebecca. This wasn't the first time someone had spoken about her father as if he was a different man from the one she remembered, and the way Rebecca described her parents was... compelling.

'Peaches on this pile. Your father and mother came to the cottage about a week after I moved in and they brought with them a basket of fresh produce from their garden as well as seedlings for half a dozen plants Pam had raised from seed. As well, there was a sturdy young peach tree and an apple tree which your father planted for me on the spot. I'd barely unpacked, let alone considered the garden, but he dug up the ground where you now see my garden beds.'

Sadie sank onto a nearby chair.

'Your father was generous with his time and efforts and

from the few hours they were here, seemed to dote on your mother. A little possessive perhaps, but the love was evident.'

'No... but...'

'Perhaps put the fruit down, darling.' Rebecca leaned over, hands out. 'Here, I'll have them. It upsets you, talking about your father. I understand.'

Her fingers had squeezed the fruit hard enough to break the skin and crimson juice flowed onto the table. Rebecca dropped them into a small compost bin on the counter then wet a dish cloth and gave it to Sadie for her fingers. After cleaning them and the table, Sadie got up and rinsed the cloth. She'd still not said a word and didn't know where to begin.

'We are a pair.' Rebecca was sorting again.

'I don't understand.' Sadie watched, not trusting her hands at the moment.

'We've managed to touch deep-seated pain in each other. I imagine not a soul lives who doesn't endure heartache or tragedy and while some folk are able to put it behind them, others – perhaps those with the gift and curse of empathy – are never the same. To the onlooker we are strong and industrious, living our lives with few outward signs of the struggle which is what really drives us in every single thing we do.'

The words were profound. Meaningful. And delivered in the softest tone. But Rebecca might have been talking about the weather, her hands moving back and forward to pick up, identify, and then place fruit in the appropriate pile. And when she glanced at Sadie, her eyes showed not one sign of the gravity of their conversation.

She was a poster girl for concealing the struggle.

'Can I trust you to pack as many of these that fit into the container while I duck outside to pick some fresh herbs for Pam?' Rebecca smiled. 'Gentle hands, Sadie. To go with your gentle heart.'

Left alone, Sadie took a few calming breaths. She'd visited

to find out more about Rebecca and discovered something about herself. There was unfinished business with her father and new information which she didn't know how to process. In the time she'd been back in Rivers End she'd never felt so alone or so uncertain than here in the kitchen of a kind stranger.

TWENTY-FIVE

Hours later, unsettling emotions still haunted Sadie – enough for her to have rashly agreed to have dinner that night with Dan. The minute she'd said yes, she'd wished the word back but he'd mentioned something about texting her details and said goodbye. She'd only agreed because Pam would be home in an hour or so and Sadie wasn't ready to talk to her. Not about Dad.

When the text came through she was on her laptop replying to Lina's email from last night. She gave Lina a few more snippets of information plus a photograph she'd sneakily taken of the painting while Rebecca was outside picking herbs. Sadie had battled with herself over the ethics of taking the photo, let alone sharing it, but Lina was trustworthy and it was only for research purposes. When a second message dinged, Sadie read them both.

> Six pm. Do you know the mooring point along the river closest to your house? I'll be there.

Well, sure she did. But what an odd place to meet.

> Hope a picnic appeals. Swimming optional.
> Dan.

A picnic. Perfect. She sent a smiley face in return and finished her email by adding she'd just been asked out on a picnic. Lina hated the great outdoors and would probably warn her about the risks of being outside in what she'd call 'the wilds'.

Halfway through applying some light make-up, Lina rang.

'I've put you on speaker, hon. Can't hold the phone and do mascara.'

'Mascara implies this isn't an entirely wilderness-based excursion,' Lina said. 'I hope it is more glampic than picnic.'

'Glampic? Is that like glamping for camping? Cute. And I only know I'm meeting him at the river.'

'River! What if you drown?'

'Same river I used to paddle a board down as a kid.' Sadie moved on to her hair. 'Everyone knows how to swim these days. Don't you?'

'Yes but that's beside the point. And the point is why haven't you told me about this man? Who is he? An old flame? Oh, I like that idea... someone you snuck out of the house at night to see and then you cast him asunder in your quest to fulfil your destiny.'

'"Cast him asunder"? I'm not planning on ripping him into pieces. Are you quite alright?'

Sadie braided her hair at the back of her head.

'Details please,' Lina said.

'There's not much to tell. Dan is a local builder who my mother knows. And he happens to be Rebecca's closest neighbour. He was the person I went looking for her with that time. When she disappeared from her cottage.'

Hair and make-up done, Sadie took the phone into the bedroom. 'I'm dropping you onto the bed so I can get ready.'

'Put me on video so I can see what you choose to wear.'

'Never happening.' Sadie undressed and slipped into the black one-piece swimsuit she favoured. 'This is just a friendly dinner. Nothing more.'

'Is he handsome?'

'I guess.'

Lina made some muffled sound. 'You guess?'

'We've only met a couple of times.'

'You said he's a builder which means he must be built.' Lina laughed loudly at her poor attempt of a joke. 'And you never go out on dates... oh. You like him.'

Lina knew her too well. And now she'd never hear the end of it.

'How is my apartment?'

'Changing the subject. You *really* like him.'

Sadie was happy with her choice of a deep blue maxi dress and sat to strap on a pair of sandals. 'Okay, yes. I do. But it will be one date because long distance is impossible.'

Lina didn't answer and Sadie checked the phone to make sure the connection was still live.

'I might be off base, Sades, but from a few things you've said recently I get the feeling you like being back home. Close to your mother and the place you grew up. People move all the time. If Dan is potentially *the one*, why not move home to Rivers End?'

Sadie closed her eyes. If only life was so simple. She opened them and picked up the phone, turning the speaker off to hold it against her ear. 'My whole life is in Sydney. My career. And friends.'

Lina's voice was gentle. 'I'm your only close friend and I'd miss you but as for your career, well you can be anything you want, particularly now with the experience and exposure you've got. Heck, you could live in Rivers End and fly up to Sydney for a few weeks at a time to film if it came to that. The rest can be done remotely.'

'I'm home, Sadie.' Pam's voice echoed up the stairs.

'That's Mum.'

'Off you go. Just think about what I said, okay?'

'Okay. Love you, Lina.'

'Back at you.'

Sadie tossed her phone into a small backpack which already had her hat, purse, sunscreen, and towel. She had to let Pam know about the date and then cut across country and if she didn't go now, she'd be late.

At the back of the property, beyond the vegetable garden and small orchard, a gate led to an empty paddock and then a small forest – bushland which had avoided any clearing years ago and quietly thrived. The dead leaves, bark, and twigs from towering gum trees and blackwoods crunched under Sadie's sandals as she hurried between tree trunks. There wasn't a path as such but the years away didn't stop her remembering the easiest route to cover the distance and in minutes she was in the late afternoon sunshine again. From here it was only fifty or so metres to the river.

She reached the mooring point with time to spare and glanced back the way she'd come. The house was invisible beyond the bushes and trees. So many times she'd run or walked through the bushland, sometimes to meet friends or enjoy the solitude, other times to hide from the anger of her father. There was always a sense of peace and safety there.

A soft swoosh, swoosh, swoosh on the water drew her attention and she gasped. A tandem canoe was approaching and Dan was paddling, his muscular arms making it look easy.

Sadie met him at the mooring point, a slightly indented spot with a tie-up post and tiny platform. A ridiculous bubble of joy had her wanting to jump up and down and clap her hands. She'd never been on a date where the man paddled to a picnic. And when his eyes met and then held hers, sparks tore through her body. Little jolts of electricity.

He expertly slid the canoe alongside the platform. The

canoe was old, timber, but beautiful. In between the two seats was a picnic basket. 'Your chariot awaits.'

'Oh, we're going somewhere?'

'Happy to paddle a bit?' He held his hand out. 'Okay to climb in?'

'Yes and yes.' Sadie shrugged off the backpack and lowered it in front of the seat she was taking, then she accepted his hand long enough to step in and sit. 'Thanks, been ages since I was on the river.' She turned enough to look at him, which was a mistake as he was far too close and way too good-looking. And that smile. He wore three-quarter-length pants and a white T-shirt under an unbuttoned shirt the colour of tangerines. If a man could look this fine in casual clothes, what would a suit do to him?

'You don't need to actually help,' he said. 'You can just enjoy the ride.'

Sadie picked up the paddle. 'I will but I also enjoy this part.'

He pushed the canoe away from the platform.

They fell into an easy pattern and the river's current helped them along with its primeval need to reach the sea. This was bliss. No talking. Nobody else out on the water. Just two people in harmony, nestled within a small boat, the only sound the slicing of timber through water on repeat.

There were few homes close to the banks, mostly paddocks, and then the bridge was ahead. Sadie had sometimes stopped her paddleboard beneath its span, listening to cars travelling above. But the canoe was under and beyond it in seconds and then Sadie lifted her paddle. From here there was little effort to make, other than navigating a couple of turns and best done by one person.

'Have you been along here before, Dan?'

'Several times a week. Best way to get to the beach in my opinion.'

She agreed.

The break in the cliff approached. Rivers End was built behind the limestone cliffs sheltering the town from the winds of winter buffeting off the Southern Ocean. Most towns were built with sea views but not so much here, unless you owned one of the handful of homes lucky enough to be built up high. There were several ways to the beach. Stone steps from near the cemetery; a couple of paths across a lower section which dropped onto sand dunes; rugged tracks from the far cliff, and this channel.

About twenty metres in width, and fifty in length, a natural tunnel had formed millennia ago. The river took up much of the width but there was a path beside it which was the most commonly used way onto the sand.

As the canoe entered the channel, the temperature plummeted. Sadie dipped her fingers into the water which was already much cooler beneath the weight and shelter of the limestone. On a really hot day it was an oasis and Sadie and her friends had often sat for hours in its shade, bobbing in the water on paddleboards.

'Always feel I should sing as I traverse this part,' Dan said. 'Echoes bring out the child in me.'

'I may have done that once or twice.'

'Shall we sing now?'

Sadie glanced back at Dan to see if he was joking but his face was serious as he gazed up at the rocky roof.

'Go right ahead,' she said.

He grinned and looked at her. 'Too late. We're almost through.'

Even as he spoke they were on the beach side of the cliff. A warm breeze lifted tendrils of Sadie's hair which had come free of her braid and in seconds her lips tasted deliciously salty. The river merged into a shallow lagoon with just a narrow stream of water snaking through the sand to the tideline.

'I think this is final stop for the afternoon rail service. All passengers please alight.'

Sadie removed her sandals, hitched up her skirt, and carefully stepped out into knee-high water. 'Hang on, wasn't this a chariot earlier? When did it become a train?' She collected her backpack and shrugged it on.

'When we went through the magic portal.' Dan gestured back at the channel. 'All who enter as one entity, leave as another.' He climbed out and then pulled the canoe onto the sand beside the lagoon. 'I was a stressed-out small-business owner but now I'm a carefree beach bum. How about you?'

'Hmm. I was an emotional timebomb waiting to go off.'

Dan held his hand out. 'Sounds... dangerous. What are you now?'

'Sure you want me to take your hand?'

'I don't mind a bit of excitement and risk.'

She took it but didn't move. 'I'm... actually, I'm hungry.'

His hand was warm and enveloped hers and the skin-to-skin contact was messing with her but there wasn't a chance in the world she was letting go.

'Good thing I have the means to satisfy your hunger.' The corners of his lips rose and he gently pulled her up onto the sand, not breaking eye contact. He still held her fingers and Sadie fought a sudden longing to lean closer and touch his chest. She was certain his body was as toned as it looked under that T-shirt but it couldn't hurt to confirm these things.

'Where would you like to eat?'

She blinked.

Dan released her hand to lift the picnic basket out of the canoe. 'We can sit here or at the base of the dunes, or on the jetty, or—'

'Jetty sounds wonderful.'

'Jetty it is. I've never had a picnic there.'

Along the beach people swam, surfed, sunned, and strolled.

Several dogs ran back and forward in the surf. Nobody was on the jetty and Sadie stopped long enough to put her sandals on before following Dan. The timber boards creaked and the sea sploshed against the pylons. Her spirits rose, senses heightened by the environment and the man a couple of metres ahead.

He stopped as if realising she wasn't right next to him and when she caught up, they continued to the end without a word.

Companionable silence.

Sadie had heard the term but for the first time in her life she understood it. She and Dan had paddled for almost half an hour without speaking. There'd been no need. They'd been in synch with each other, adjusting the speed and motion of the canoe, slowing to admire a sweet foal with its mother on the banks and increasing again where the scenery was less interesting. It was a kind of decompression and being here above the ocean with the breeze in her face was sublime.

'How hungry are you, Sadie Forest?' Dan lowered the picnic basket. 'Would you like a swim first?'

'What would you prefer?'

'I'd prefer to know what you want. What would you do if you were here alone?'

The water was clear and calm and inviting. Her stomach could wait. She dropped her backpack onto the boards, pulled her dress off in one motion and slid it under the backpack in case the wind stole it away. Then without hesitation, she dived cleanly into the sea. The water parted, welcoming her to its realm and she kicked to reach the bottom, skimming along it between dancing seaweed until her lungs forced her up.

Head above the surface, she paddled on the spot, a little distance from the end of the jetty.

Where was Dan?

Had he dived in she'd surely have seen him.

She rotated three-sixty-degrees. He wasn't here. He wasn't on the jetty. Had he hurt himself?

Heart racing, she took a breath and submerged. And there he was, sitting cross-legged on the floor of the sea, tiny bubbles ascending as he flapped his arms up and down to hold his position. Of all the cocky...

Sadie settled opposite him, also cross-legged but instead of waving her arms around, she gripped the base of two hefty sea plants to keep herself still. Pity she couldn't say a word but she was pretty sure he got the message that this was a game he wouldn't win.

His eyes narrowed and then he kicked himself upwards.

She held on for as long as she could, lungs on fire, then, with a push of her feet against the seabed, Sadie shot upward. Dan was close when she surfaced, doing everything in her power not to gasp for air. He watched her. So he should. She was a waterbaby. And competitive. He might set a challenge but she would finish it.

'Hungry yet?' Dan didn't even sound out of breath.

'Would you like me to fetch some seaweed to add to dinner? I'll only be a few minutes down there.'

'Perhaps next time.'

There was an odd glint in his eyes. Maybe it was from the setting sun. Then he smiled and in a quick motion began swimming back to the jetty in slow, effortless strokes. Sadie decided against making a race of it. Instead, she turned onto her back and took her time following, letting her feet propel her with gentle kicks rather than put much effort in. For a while she floated, drifting with the current.

'Planning on joining me? I have an important question.'

Dan gazed down from the top of the jetty. She was close enough to the steps on one side to climb up and at the top, she perched on the timber boards, legs dangling as she wrung sea water from her braid.

He'd laid out a picnic blanket and was unpacking the basket.

'What is the question?'

'Oh... you've emerged from the depths, mermaid. Red or white wine?'

This was difficult. Not choosing wine, but knowing she'd found someone she could fall for so far from her home and career. Sadie glanced upward. If this was her father's afterlife way of making her life even more complicated, then he was doing a great job.

TWENTY-SIX

62 YEARS AGO

I am so happy today.

Last day of school term *and* I'm on my way to buy the lighthouse lamp.

The lady at the gift shop is so kind and has let me pay her a little bit every week after I gave her a down payment with the pound note from Dad. It's been a few weeks but Mum used to say that little steps still get you where you want to go. And I have wanted this so much.

Next week is Charlie's birthday. All attempts to find a black kitten with green eyes have failed so far, but Miss Carlisle says her friend's cat is having babies in a few weeks and that's where her kitty came from. He kind of understands he needs to be patient but I know he's hoping a kitten will magically appear on his special day. At least the lamp might cheer him up if he's disappointed.

'There you are, my dear. One lighthouse lamp plus two lightbulbs. Best to keep the light shining, isn't it?' Mrs Murphy smiles as she gently slides the lighthouse, and then a small box, into a large paper carry bag. 'And this should hide it from young Charlie if he happens to see you carry it in.'

Mrs Murphy might be a bit nosy but unlike Mrs McKenzie at the grocery store, she doesn't ask personal questions or jump to conclusions. She met Charlie once when we were all out shopping for a new tablecloth and had a long and cheerful conversation with him.

'Thank you for the bag. And for letting me take a while to pay it off.'

'It's my pleasure. Did you say it was for his birthday?'

'Yes, in a few days.'

'Let me just add something then... ah, perfect.' Mrs Murphy slips folded wrapping paper into the bag. 'That is a nice bright birthday paper.'

'Oh. I'm sorry, I didn't bring any more money to pay for that.'

'Go on with you. There's no charge.'

I can't let a stranger give me something of value. But she has another customer so I take the carry bag and remind myself to bring Mrs Murphy a bunch of the flowers growing wild in our front garden.

After crossing the road I take off my shoes and dangle them from my fingers as I walk barefoot in the grass. If the tide is all the way out I might walk the long way, around the cliff on the flat rocks and then go up to our house from our beach. But I shade my eyes with my hand and it looks as if there's still too much surf and although I can see that some of the rocks are right out of the water, it's too risky.

The worst part of walking up the main hill is going past the swings at the end of the grass. There's always a group of boys there, older than me. They wear the uniform of the high school which is in another town because Driftwood Cove is too small for more than a primary school. I guess the bus drops them off and they hang around for a while. I get all the way past without any childish comments but then my fingers are being tugged at. One of the boys has grabbed my shoes.

'Let go.' I stop walking and turn around, making myself as tall as possible and giving him a stern look.

'Want me to let go of your shoes?' He sneers at me. 'Then give me the bag.'

I release the shoes and hold the paper bag against my chest with both arms. Nobody is getting the lamp from me. Once I get home I'll tell Dad what happened and he might be able to find these mean boys and get my shoes back.

'You're Charlie Chuckles' sister. He chuckles instead of talking. And waddles instead of walking.'

I spin around to run away but the boys surround me and I can't see any escape route. Someone reaches for the carry bag and I take a few steps back and trip over something, landing on my behind. My shoes have been tossed onto the ground. I still have hold of the carry bag but they circle me and start chanting.

We want the bag. We want the bag.

Why isn't anyone coming to help? I open my mouth to scream but nothing comes out. Like in a nightmare. But I scramble to my feet so at least my legs work. Dropping my head and one shoulder I charge between two of the boys and almost get through, but one gets hold of one of my arms and drags me to a standstill. He laughs. They all do and between two of them they pry the carry bag from me.

'No, no, no.' I have words again but not loud ones.

'What's this in here?'

They are peering into the bag. They are going to steal the lighthouse lamp and I just want to die.

'Oi, leave her alone!'

Another boy runs at us all and he pushes a couple of the others aside. The one holding the carry bag stumbles and drops it and as I throw myself onto the ground to protect it, another boy kicks it.

But then they run and scatter.

Apart from the boy who came to help.

Tim squats beside me. 'Did they hurt you, Becky?'

I can't answer. Tears are streaming down my face and when I look inside the bag, I feel sick to my stomach. They broke the lamp.

'Becky?'

'Get away from me.'

I drag myself to my feet and force the shoes onto my feet and then start running.

He runs with me.

'Wait. Please, what did they do? What is in the bag?'

'Leave me alone!' I scream at him and next time I look, he's gone.

Dad and Charlie are already home from school. I sneak inside the house and go to Mum's room.

I can't stop shaking.

After putting the carry bag on the dressing table, I sink onto the carpet and wrap my arms around myself. It was all for nothing. Almost every penny I saved went to buy the lighthouse lamp and now it is useless. It was the perfect gift for Charlie. How could I have been so stupid as to let those boys do this?

'Becky?'

I jump. I hadn't heard Dad open the door and when he looks at me his eyes widen and he steps in.

'Don't let Charlie come here.' I sound so angry.

Dad closes the door. 'He's reading in the loungeroom. What on earth is wrong, sweetie?'

'Nothing is wrong!'

'You know we don't tell lies in this family.' Dad squats beside me. 'You've been crying and your face is red. Rebecca?'

My lips are twitching and my throat has such a big lump that I can't get any words out again and all I can do is stare at him. He sits on the floor and lifts me onto his lap. He hasn't done that in ages and I have to help a bit as I'm heavier now than he probably realised. For a couple of minutes I lean against his chest and he holds me tightly.

'What's in the carry bag?'

'It doesn't matter anymore.' My voice is muffled against his shirt.

'Clearly it does matter. A great deal.'

He adjusts us both so I am upright and he can see my face. I don't want him fussing about this. Any of this.

'I bought a present for Charlie. For his birthday.'

'And it is in there?'

I nod. I don't want to answer anything. There's a horrible feeling in my chest.

'May I see it?'

The pressure behind my eyes hurts and I blink but tears make it hard to see.

'Oh... Becky?'

'The boys at the swings... they took my shoes... pushed me... I tried to save the bag but... all around me calling Charlie dreadful names... couldn't stop them... Daddy, they broke the lamp.'

Dad wraps his arms around me and makes soothing noises. I cry, again, but after a while I feel a bit better and take a big breath. Dad gives me one of his hankies and I wipe my eyes and blow my nose. He gets to his feet and opens the bag.

'Once you feel up to it we'll have a proper talk about what happened. Sounds to me like a bunch of nasty bullies who need adult intervention. For now I am more concerned about your distress. And looking at this.' He is gentle about lifting the lamp out. 'A lighthouse in a lamp? What a clever idea for Charlie.' Dad turns it this way and that then checks the bag. 'I think the lightbulbs are broken, but there's only a couple of chips out of this and if you don't mind helping, we can fix it up.'

I jump up. 'Really? But I heard it smash and there's glass everywhere and some of the paint.'

He shows me the damage. It is much less than I thought.

'How will we fix it?'

'My father and I used to make model airplanes and I think I remember how to touch up little flaws. We might need a trip to a shop that sells what I have in mind but I'm confident this will be like new by Charlie's birthday.'

And those silly tears start all over but now I am smiling and hopeful as well as angry at those awful boys. Something else nags at the back of my mind. Tim helped me and I was mean to him. So now I need to fix more than just the lighthouse lamp.

TWENTY-SEVEN

NOW

Resplendent shafts of light coloured the ocean gold and pink and orange as the sun touched the horizon. The wind dropped and the air cooled a little. Most of the sunseekers had packed up and left but other people wandered the length of the beach. At the end of the jetty the splashing of water beneath the timber boards was a quiet serenade.

Sadie sighed deeply and dragged her eyes from the view.

Dan was watching her with the half-smile she was beginning to recognise. She didn't know him well enough to be certain but if part of it wasn't amusement and another part attraction, then she was in the wrong business. People-watching and working with folk from a large cross-section of experiences came with insight into body language. And he was trying to work her out. Had been since he'd collected her on the side of the river. And she was happy to let him puzzle away.

They'd both dressed once their swimwear was dry and Sadie had let her hair free from its braid. Now it was wavy and soft from the sea water.

'Have you had enough to eat?' Dan asked.

'Did we leave much?'

He'd progressively packed away anything cold as they served themselves out of containers.

'A couple of bread rolls, some potato salad, and a chicken drumstick. Enough for my lunch tomorrow.' Dan reached for the bottle of white wine. 'Refill?'

'Not driving, so yes please.'

He held it aloft as if reconsidering and Sadie stretched her arm with the glass.

'We *do* have to paddle upstream,' he said.

She grinned. 'We?'

'Oh. So that's how it is. Happy to help when it is all downstream and easy but then you'll leave me to do the grunt work when it gets more difficult.'

'Yes. May I have more wine, please?'

'Unsure. Shall we barter?'

'For wine. Absolutely.' Sadie shuffled closer to Dan until they were merely centimetres apart. All she'd need to do to touch him was lean his way. Her skin was alive with anticipation. She lowered her glass onto the board. 'I'm listening.'

Dan placed the bottle between them. 'Ask me anything. But for every answer I want one from you.'

'That's all? Okay... where did you move from to come to Rivers End, as in, where did you grow up?'

'I grew up in a caravan. My parents moved every few months and I don't remember having an actual house until I began to study and lived in a shared flat.'

'Was that hard? Being uprooted all the time?'

'That is two questions,' he said. 'But I hadn't fully answered the first one so will let that pass, for now.'

'Generous.'

'Hugely.'

He moved the wine bottle a fraction away from her and she giggled. He waggled his eyebrows up and down and that made it worse but she managed to control herself and gestured for him to continue.

'You asked where did I move from to come here. It was Tasmania. Once I left home – for want of a better word – I studied in Melbourne at RMIT which is excellent for learning a trade. Then I went to Tasmania and did a business degree while working as an apprentice for a builder in Hobart. I rented a house. A whole house just for me, and learned more in those few years than anything before. Or since.'

Something stirred deep in Sadie. Displacement was something she understood from personal experience and from the documentaries but many people who grew up drifting never made it out. Not the way this man had.

He drew in a breath. 'Your turn. Why did you leave Rivers End? You have your family here. A lifetime of memories. Security. Was it to pursue your career?'

Oh boy. This was getting deep.

'Starting from the end... no, it wasn't to pursue my career, not exactly. I left home the day after I graduated high school. Going to Sydney offered the best opportunities with distance between me and home. I had no money and nothing to fall back on.' Sadie glanced at the bottle.

Dan noticed. He lifted it and dribbled a couple of mouthfuls into each of their glasses. Sadie quickly drank hers while he didn't touch his. The silence dragged. Not companionable now. It was expectant.

'Why? Well, I don't know where to begin. A need to find out exactly who Sadie was or could be and I couldn't do that here. Mum and Dad were impossible to live with. Dad in particular.' Frustration coloured her tone. 'He held the view that I should not pursue higher education and was expected to work at the inn until I married. I refused to accept such nonsense and Mum rarely spoke up in my defence.'

'Families can be hard. My parents never argued. Just one

long cold silence which stretched across the years.' Dan opened the wine and filled both their glasses. 'Enough bartering for one evening.'

'It is a wonder anyone stays married.'

'There are happy marriages.'

Sadie scoffed. 'Show me one.'

Dan handed Sadie her glass then gestured at the beach. 'They look happy.'

A couple strolled hand in hand along the sand, deep in conversation. They were in no hurry, allowing the waves to roll over their feet, more intent on each other than their surroundings. Both were in their seventies and behind them, occasionally dashing into the shallows, was a sleek kelpie with a shiny black coat. Near the beach end of the jetty they stopped to wait for the dog.

'Catch up, Jag,' the woman called with a lilting Irish accent.

The man said something and she laughed and then he took her into his arms and kissed her as if they were newlyweds.

'We shouldn't be caught watching.' Dan's whisper was near her ear and his warm breath sent chills down her spine. She turned her face slightly and their lips were almost touching. If she just lifted her chin a little...

'They won't see us here.' She couldn't move. He hadn't either and they were oh-so-close. Teasing her with the smallest of smiles. Her eyes moved to his. 'I feel...'

'What do you feel?'

'As though you're trying to work me out.'

'Oh, mermaid. If we shared a thousand lifetimes I'd never know enough about you to be satisfied.'

Her heart stopped and her eyes fluttered shut and then open and just before his mouth reached hers, she turned her head and leaned back. Self-preservation. Fear, if she was honest with herself. Sadie drew her legs up in front of her body and held them with an arm, taking a sip from her glass in the hope

Dan might see her indifference. Her lack of interest in kissing him. Most men who tried to get close emotionally got the message quickly and those who didn't never saw her again. But the concept of never seeing *this* man again burned a hole in her soul.

'We should swim again,' she said, gazing at the ocean.

'We should?'

Why didn't he sound the least bit put out?

He'd probably never intended to kiss her anyway.

'Just before complete darkness is the best time. There's a subtle shift in the water, almost like the fish and other marine life who live around the jetty and close to the beach go somewhere to sleep and are replaced with creatures of the night.'

'Such as sharks.'

She shrugged. 'True. But every time you enter the sea you risk encountering one.'

The urge to swim was overwhelming and she finished the wine, her eyes on the beach. The older couple were climbing the stone steps near the cemetery. There was something familiar about the man but almost everyone she'd ever met here was familiar to a degree. They did give the impression of sharing a deep and abiding love.

Wine glass empty and returned to the picnic basket, Sadie slipped out of her sundress again, acutely aware of Dan's eyes following her movements. Then she began climbing down the steps.

'No diving?'

'Not when it's dark.'

He wandered over and sat on the end of the boards, legs hanging over the edge. 'You'd rather not headbutt a shark?'

That made her laugh as she eased into the water. She swam a few strokes freestyle then dogpaddled closer again. 'Are you coming in?'

'I think one of us needs to keep watch for fins slicing

through the surface. Besides, drinking and swimming and darkness are a potent mix.'

'But if there is a shark... you'll rescue me?' She didn't wait for an answer, lifting clasped hands high above her head and spinning like a ballerina as she sank. It was much gloomier here so close to the thick pylons than she expected and she kicked upwards. Dan hadn't moved which was oddly disappointing. Sadie had expected him to follow her in.

Did he think she was being foolish?

Years of barrier building had kept her safe from the impact of other people's opinions. Journalism was a tough gig. It didn't matter what Dan – who she'd only known for a few days – thought about her actions or life choices.

'Have I mentioned I have dessert up here?'

On the other hand...

'Gently down the stream, happily, rapidly, paddling along, night-time is for dreams.'

'Nor are those the right words, not all of them,' Sadie said.

'I haven't heard your version yet.'

'And you won't. Are you certain you didn't drink the bottle of red wine while I was swimming?' She half-turned to look at Dan, determined to keep her face as serious as her voice but it was impossible when he smiled. For the past ten minutes of the paddle back he'd regaled her with songs about the water. He had a good voice but an aversion to the correct lyrics which kind of made it more endearing.

'Did you enjoy dessert?'

'Strawberries, blackberries, cherries served with crème fraîche and a drizzle of balsamic. It was delicious.' Everything had been delicious. 'Thank you, Dan. I mean it, tonight was wonderful.'

He nodded, the smile still on his lips when she faced

forward again and got back to paddling. A few minutes later the canoe slid against the platform and Sadie dropped the paddle into position. 'Are we a chariot again?'

'Nope. I thought it was obvious we were in Venice on the canals in a gondola.'

'Ah. That's why the singing.'

The canoe rocked as Dan climbed onto the platform. When Sadie stepped up, he reached down to collect the backpack and put it over one shoulder then tossed the rope from the canoe around the post. And then he held out a hand for her. 'I'll leave you at your back gate.'

'Oh, no. I mean, there's no need to walk me home.'

'Pretty sure Pam will take me to task if I don't.'

His hand was waiting and his eyes were warm and sparkling... if that was really a thing. It was an irresistible combination and she curled her fingers around his. It felt nice. 'Come on, then. But no singing.'

Dan's chuckle was soft and his fingers tightened around hers as they crossed the open grass. They paused closer to the small forest and Sadie turned on the light on her phone. It cast shadows of low-hanging branches and bushes onto the wide trunks of the old gums and there was almost no natural light under the heavy canopy. Some people might find the experience disturbing but Sadie loved it and felt safe. Even if Dan wasn't with her, she'd have enjoyed the walk but his presence brought a new element. She just hadn't identified it yet.

'I feel I should whisper,' Dan said.

A jolt surged through Sadie as if his warm breath was on her skin again. Just from the word, whisper. She didn't answer, afraid her voice would give away the unsettling feelings. Somehow she had to control these responses – change the subject before things got out of hand.

'How well do you know Rebecca?'

'How have we gone from tiptoeing through a forest to talking about my neighbour?'

'I meant to ask earlier. She clearly likes you a lot.'

'Goes both ways. Rebecca keeps to herself. She's rarely spoken of her life before moving to Rivers End apart from having lived in Mildura for many years. I know she is an accomplished chef and taught cooking and that she has always owned a black cat with green eyes called Percy.'

'Yes, she told me as much. The cat thing is to remind her of someone special.'

'I didn't know that.'

'What about her paintings? Particularly the lighthouse?'

Dan didn't answer and when Sadie looked at him, his forehead was wrinkled in thought.

'It's just that she's so talented and it is... haunting,' Sadie said.

'Haunting is the right word.' He sighed. 'I don't know anything more. But the lighthouse painting is important to her. I've seen her gaze at it more than once as if remembering something.'

They emerged from the trees and crossed the last paddock. Sadie released Dan's hand and turned off the torch, putting the phone into her pocket. She didn't reach back out to hold it again and he didn't offer. Had she pushed too hard? Dan was a private person, same as Rebecca, and she'd put him on the spot.

'Sadie?'

'Hmm.'

'Wait a sec. Look up.'

In the still of the night they stopped and gazed up. Without meaning to, she nestled against Dan, her back to his chest. His arms encircled her and it was the most natural feeling in the world. Above, the sky was incredible.

'A shrine of a trillion stars,' Sadie murmured.

'You remembered.'

She turned herself inside his arms until they were face to face, her arms sliding around his neck. 'Some things are unforgettable.'

Dan brushed her hair back. 'So soft.' Then his fingers trailed down her cheek and brushed her lips. 'Some... people, are unforgettable.' He pulled her even closer and captured her lips with his mouth.

TWENTY-EIGHT

Sadie hadn't slept so well in... well, forever. Even as a child she'd struggled to settle at night and nothing really changed as an adult apart from being able to stay up as late as she needed to be tired. But last night she'd slipped into bed after changing into PJs and brushing her teeth and hair – which was silky soft after being wet in the braid – then watched the sky through her window for a few minutes.

A text message had arrived.

> Made it through the enchanted forest and my pirate ship is ready to embark on the final leg home. Sleep well.

Dan had added an emoji of a mermaid.

She found one of a parrot and sent that with a smiley face and 'Goodnight'. And then she'd turned the phone off and wrapped her arms around herself and slept.

As the sun rose she was drawn outside and spent an hour working in the vegetable garden, singing softly to herself. She cleared one vegetable bed of weeds and found several withered potato vines. After some gentle digging it was obvious there were potatoes in there. She had few happier childhood memories than filling a bucket with potatoes with Pam. Just when you thought you'd got the last one, another peeked through the soil. Well she wasn't going to waste the chance to relive the experience. Sadie went in search of her mother.

By now, Pam would normally be bustling around the kitchen but the lights were still off and more importantly, the kettle was cold. No note left that she'd already gone to the inn. Sadie hadn't seen her last night but had sent her a text once she and Dan arrived at the beach.

She stopped and checked her phone. She hadn't dreamed the reply.

> You and Daniel enjoy every second and don't worry about rushing home.

Had Pam even been home last night? She wandered around the house and even tapped on Pam's bedroom door, which was slightly open and allowed her to check the bed was made. Most peculiar.

Sadie retraced her steps from the moment she'd left Dan at the gate... after a few more kisses. Through the veggie garden to the back yard then letting herself in by the back door. The house had been in darkness – apart from the light over the stairs and Sadie hadn't put that on before she left.

'Okay, mother of mine, where are you?'

Although not ready to panic yet, Sadie was puzzled. Most likely she'd left for the inn early for some reason and had forgotten the usual note. Returning to the kitchen she filled the kettle and turned it on, then phoned Pam's mobile.

'You've reached Pam Carson and Rivers End Inn. Please leave your name, phone number, and a short message and I'll be in touch very soon. Have a nice day.'

Such a polite message.

'Just Sadie. Found some potatoes in the garden but can't find you.'

The kettle was close to boiling when Pam called back.

'Hi Mum.'

Heavy breathing.

'Are you okay?'

Puffing.

'Mummy? Where are you?'

'Sadie?'

'Yes. Where are you?'

'Oh goodness. I just heard your voice in my pocket.'

Pam sounded out of breath. The other night she'd had to stop to rest on the way home. What if she was having health issues? Sadie hurtled from the kitchen, grabbing her car and house keys from the table near the front door.

'Mum, tell me where you are and I'll come get you.'

She swung the door open.

And her jaw dropped.

Dressed in shorts, an oversized T-shirt, and runners, Pam was halfway up the driveway. Power walking. An empty water bottle was in one hand and the phone in the other and she had one of those caps on her head which only had a peak, but no top.

'I'm almost home... oh. Hello.' Pam hung up when she saw Sadie. 'Where are you off to?' Giving Sadie a peck on the cheek as she passed, Pam went inside and pulled off her runners. 'Need a shower!'

'Hang on a sec... you've been walking?' Sadie closed the door. 'When did you leave?'

Pam checked her watch and, for the first time, Sadie realised it was one which kept track of the wearer's vitals.

'Just over half an hour. Got to the end of Ryan Road and back, then to Joan's and back. Not bad going but I think tomorrow I'll aim for two lengths of the road. Why are you looking concerned, love?'

'I didn't know you had one of those... or that you were into fitness.'

'This arrived in the post yesterday. Ever shop online? Best invention. And really, after the other night when I got tired walking home after our dinner, I decided it was time to begin taking a good look at my fitness.' Pam grinned. 'So where were you going? Meeting Daniel for breakfast?'

'No. I was coming to find you.'

'Me? I'm right here. And starving.'

With a small shake of her head, Sadie headed back to the kitchen, calling over her shoulder. 'Have a shower. I'll make us both breakfast.'

'Lovely. And then we can have a nice chat about your date with Daniel.'

For once Pam was in no hurry to go to the inn. There'd been no guests last night and none expected until later afternoon, so after breakfast, she happily joined Sadie in the vegetable garden.

'I don't remember how long ago I planted potatoes and I'm not expecting them to be edible. Not this old.'

But when Sadie climbed into the bed with a garden fork, Pam's eyes widened and she clapped her hands as huge, healthy potatoes emerged from the soil. She collected while Sadie dug until the bucket was full.

'We might need a wheelbarrow.'

'Do you still have one?' Sadie climbed down. 'Didn't see one in the garden shed.'

'Are you certain?' Pam creased her forehead. 'I'll take a quick look in case there was stuff on top of it.'

'Okay. Well I'll grab your old laundry basket just in case.'

They went in different directions.

The basket was falling apart so Sadie let herself into the garage through the side door. There'd always been big plastic containers and the like on the shelves and who knew what else. Sadie expected it to be full to the brim after Pam had said on the first day she arrived there was no room in there for another car.

Or had she imagined that?

The van her parents had owned for at least twenty years was parked in its usual spot but the rest of the garage was empty. Almost empty. There was a wheelbarrow at the back and a pair of Dad's boots just inside the door. Sadie stared at them. They were almost new. The same brand of work boots he'd always worn. Why were they here? Forgotten, or maybe Pam hadn't had the heart to move them yet.

But the garage itself... the walls of shelves remained but nothing on them. No tools of any kind. The ride-on mower was gone. Dad's huge collection of nails and screws and bolts which last seen were separated by type and size into glass jars. The woodworking bench. Everything.

She squatted and touched the boots. As a kid she'd got pocket money for shining his two pairs of formal shoes and his work boots each week. Sadie could almost smell the polish. He'd always given her a two-dollar coin for her efforts and she'd saved them in a glass jar of her own. She must have been eleven or twelve when out of the blue he'd told her not to polish them anymore and cut off the pocket money. Pam always gave her a little but Sadie had missed her job.

I missed helping Dad.

It had all changed at once. Her father changed. She straightened and was drawn to the van where she ran a hand over its side then leaned her forehead on it. Pam had spoken of a visit by three men who'd come for dinner and pulled her father back into his childhood religion. Why hadn't she tried to learn more about him and why he'd become so distant? It was time to start facing the past. A tear dripped from her eye and she wiped it.

'Oh no. Oh no, Sadie, come out of there please.'

Pam stood outside the door, both hands on her heart, her face white.

'Mum?'

'You can't be in here.'

Sadie collected the wheelbarrow on her way. 'I was after one of those big containers you used to have out here. To put the potatoes in. But I found the wheelbarrow.' She pushed it outside and Pam stepped back.

'Close it.'

Sadie pulled the door shut. 'Why are you upset I was in there?'

'I have to go to work.'

'Is someone checking in early?'

Pam might have just seen a ghost from her eyes, expression, the way her body slumped. Sadie put her arms around her mother and for a moment, Pam was tense and rigid against her, then with a sob, she kind of crumpled and her weight sagged.

'Hey, hey, let's sit for a minute.' Sadie managed to move them both to a bench and they sat, Pam still leaning against her. 'I thought the garage was too full for my car... but it was that you didn't want me looking in there. Mum, I don't understand.'

Pam didn't answer but she straightened, shaking from head to toe, clasping her hands tightly together and staring straight ahead. Even her lips trembled and it was all Sadie could do not to wrap her back up in a hug. What on earth was this about?

'I saw Dad's boots are inside the door. Do you remember how I used to polish his shoes and boots each week? I loved making them all clean and shiny and then getting that coin to add to my collection. Would you like me to move them? Is that what's upsetting you?'

There was no sign that Pam even heard her.

'The van looks okay. I know you worried it might need new tyres so how about I help you source them and then you'll have transport again?'

Pushing herself to her feet, Pam shook her head. 'I have to go to work.'

Sadie stood. 'You said that already. But we're digging up potatoes and there's nobody coming to the inn for hours. What if we have another cup of coffee? Or I can make some tea if you prefer?'

'Stop mothering me.'

'Then talk to me! All I know is you were happy until you found me in the garage so how about you tell me what the problem is? Please, Mum.' Sadie took Pam's hand. It was icy despite being in the morning sun. She held it between her own, trying to warm Pam's fingers. 'You feel so cold.'

Pam lifted her chin. 'You always thought I should leave your father but I loved him deeply, Sadie. Somehow I always saw him without the flaws. There are things you don't know about his health and his change of heart but if you'd been here more or kept in touch then I'd have told you. Not one visit after you walked out for the second time eight years ago.'

'But I had to go. Dad didn't want me here and there are things he said that you don't know about.'

'*I* wanted you here. All I knew was you stormed in after a conversation with your father and packed and were gone before I could turn around. You never said a word to me about why.'

'Because you wouldn't have done anything. You always sided with him.'

We can't do this.

Sadie stopped herself from pointing out that she had sent email after email over the years and got no response because there was truth in Pam's words. She could have tried harder. Visited. Phoned. But how would that have changed anything?

'I think it best if you head home soon.'

Her mother might as well have thrown a bucket of ice water over her. Sadie dropped Pam's hand and stepped back. 'Are you telling me to leave?'

'You have a life in Sydney. A beautiful apartment and a successful career. I've enjoyed seeing you again but there's no need for you to stay any longer. Please excuse me. I have to go to work.'

Face set like stone, Pam crossed her arms.

Sadie turned and ran.

Pam called out something but the words were lost as she rounded the side of the house and sprinted toward the back gate. Not bothering to open it, she climbed the fence and kept running until she reached the sanctuary of the tall trees, then she slowed, gazing around until she found it.

The hollowed tree of her childhood.

And there she made herself as small as she could and gave in to the grief of a lifetime.

TWENTY-NINE

62 YEARS AGO

'I'm sorry I yelled at you.'

No, that won't do.

'My sincere apologies for being so rude.'

I roll my eyes at my feeble attempts to find the right words. I'm almost at Tim's house and all the way I have struggled to come up with the perfect apology. I'd hoped he might be at the beach yesterday but there was no sign of him and even Charlie got impatient to go home when it got close to nightfall and I still waited. There'd been no other way to do this but visit him at home and hope he didn't slam the door in my face.

'Who are you talking to?'

Tim rides past me on a bicycle then turns in a big, slow curve to come back.

'Nobody.'

I'm impressed by how he can make his bike go so slow without it falling over.

'Going on a picnic?'

'Oh. This?' I lift the little basket a bit. 'I made some jam biscuits. And veggie sausage rolls.'

He circles me again then hops off the bike. 'Someone is lucky. Anyway, this is my house.'

'I know.'

If I don't hurry up and say something he'll go inside. He is being way too nice and my guilty feelings about the other day just get worse.

I take a deep breath and hold out the basket. 'These are for you, Tim. Because I was horrible to you when you chased off those nasty boys and I am really, really sorry.'

'For me? Thank you, Becky, but you didn't have to. Those kids need their behinds kicked for what they did and said and when I told Mum and Dad, they called the school about it so I think they'll leave you alone now.'

Unsure if I'm happy they'll be in trouble, or worried they'll come looking for me, I have to admire Tim's honesty and courage.

'Um, thanks. Do you accept my apology?'

I'm still holding the basket outstretched and he finally takes it with a big smile.

'I do. You were upset and I wished I'd arrived a bit sooner. Did they break what was in your carry bag?'

'A bit. But I thought it was destroyed which made me so angry. Dad fixed it up.'

We stand looking at each other and the silence is awkward.

'How do you get your bike to go so slow?' I blurt it out without a thought.

'Balance. Practice. You got a bike?'

'I wish.'

'Know how to ride?'

I shake my head. I can barely swim. Too scared to ride a pony. And never tried a bike before. Pretty dismal record.

'There's nothing better, apart from the sea of course. They can go where cars don't and keep you fit. Mum doesn't use hers anymore. I could ask if you could borrow it to learn. If you like.'

Nobody does nice stuff for me. It makes me feel... scared. A bit. Maybe I'm just so used to looking after Charlie and Dad that I forget I need to have fun as well. Different fun than at home.

'If she wouldn't mind...'

'I'll ask her tonight.'

I'm smiling.

We say goodbye and I take my time going home. No need to rush during the school holidays. Tim's house is a couple of streets inland from ours and although I can smell the ocean from here, there's no view. I wonder if he is sad not to be closer to the beach because he loves it enough to swim almost every day. I'd prefer to live further away. Maybe then Dad and Charlie wouldn't take such big risks all the time.

I feel myself getting worried and at the end of the street I stop walking and count to ten, breathing in and out until I'm calm again. Dad taught me to do that ages ago and I forgot how helpful it is. The other thing he taught me is to count my blessings when I'm unhappy.

Starting off home again, I count mine.

'I have the best brother in the whole world. Charlie is funny and loves me and is smart. Now that is a blessing.'

Good thing the streets are quiet if I'm going to talk aloud as I walk.

'The sun is shining and the town is much nicer than expected. Tim is friendly now that I know him better. And he cares a lot about Charlie. Another blessing.'

When I get home I might bake an apple pie.

'Dad is strong and kind and loving. He fixes things and says sensible things and funny things and plays games really well. And he will never let me or Charlie down. I love him a lot and will never, ever leave.'

Well, maybe one day, when Charlie is grown and has his own life and Dad doesn't need the extra help. I might have my own family and a job I love. An artist or a dancer. But I'll get a house right next door. Nothing will ever stop that happening.

I can't remember being as happy as this moment.

* * *

The apple pie turned out perfectly and I couldn't wait to eat it after dinner. But then for the next couple of days, no more treats because I have big plans for Charlie's birthday.

Dad and I had a special meeting last night after Charlie was asleep. We made a list of what we need to buy for his birthday dinner including the ingredients for the best chocolate cake ever. And we wrapped his gifts, including the lighthouse lamp which looks as good as new. There is a new board game, a Lincoln Logs set, some toy cars, and a sketchbook with coloured pencils. Miss Carlisle suggested the sketchbook and Lincoln Logs to help Charlie's fine motor skills and he's going to love them.

Just before dinner, Dad gets a phone call and is in his office for a while with the door closed. It has to be for his work as he rarely closes the door and I turn the stove down really low so the potatoes don't overcook. I'll mash them once he's finished. Everything else is ready and Charlie is reading in the lounge room so Dad will need to take him to wash his hands as well.

'Rightio. Sorry if I held things up, Becky. Can I pour the water out of the potatoes?'

'I can do that if you sort Charlie out.'

'Will do.' Dad hesitates and I look up at him, ready to pick up the pot and take it to the sink. 'We'll have a visitor for Charlie's birthday.'

Why is Dad looking grim?

My heart sinks.

'Yes. I just had a call from Aunt Ethel. She's in Melbourne and wants to surprise Charlie. So keep it between us.'

There's nothing to say. Nothing which won't upset Dad who doesn't like me speaking my mind about his sister. I think he expects me to answer though. 'I'll mash these, Dad.' I have a tea towel in each hand and take a hold of the handles, still looking at him. 'Dinner in five minutes.'

But I'd forgotten the coil is still on and the end of one tea towel must have touched it because all of a sudden something appears in the corner of my eyes and before I can move, a flame streaks up the tea towel to my hand and I scream.

'Poor Becky. Poor special sister.' Charlie has tears on his face and is rocking back and forward.

He does that only when he is really upset.

I've done that to him.

'Becky is okay, son. Just let's keep ice on this for a bit.' Even Dad has tears but his are deep inside his eyes, glistening but not falling.

The only person not crying is me.

'Dad, I can hold this if you can mash the potatoes. And the rest of dinner will be ruined if it doesn't come out of the oven.'

I'm sitting at the table holding ice, wrapped in a tea towel – but not one on fire – against my arm where the flames got me. The minute the pain began and I screamed, I dropped the tea towel and kind of fell back and Dad caught me. I didn't know he could move so fast. Then my arm was over the sink and cold water was pouring over it from the tap and Charlie was yelling.

'Dinner will wait, Rebecca.'

He's angry. I understand. I've messed everything up and now there's noise and chaos and upset instead of a nice dinner. It is all Aunt Ethel's fault. She shouldn't be coming here. I know in my bones something awful is happening.

Dad checks the burn. There's a big red mark on my arm, a bit up from my wrist. Dad peers at it. 'I'll get some aloe vera.

Hold the ice on.' Then he's gone again. We always keep an aloe vera plant. Dad knows botany and how some plants can heal and has different ones growing out the back.

'Charlie, please stop rocking. I'm really okay and I'm sorry I startled you.'

'Burned.'

'Yes. But it will heal.'

'Fire. A flame, Becky.'

'But Dad put it out. It was just a mistake. I lost my concentration for a second and will never do that again. Now I have a reminder on my arm and I'll show you soon. You can tell me what it reminds you of.'

He stops rocking. 'Like a picture?'

'Exactly. Do you know, some people get tattoos on their body to remind them of something important?'

He is puzzled.

'There's a special ink that changes the skin. I guess like drawing on your hand but it stays forever.'

'Even with washing?'

'Even with.'

This has him thinking and the tears are gone, thank goodness.

Dad returns with a chunk of aloe. The juice oozes from the part Dad broke and I move the tea towel so he can rub it on. The relief is instant. Cool and calming. He stares at me with the oddest expression.

'I'm alright, Dad. Just a silly accident.'

He doesn't say anything and that sick feeling is back in my stomach. Whatever is coming, I won't like it.

'Lighthouse, Becky.'

Dad and I both look at Charlie.

'I'll get a lighthouse tatty-too. Then I'll always remember being here with you and Dad.'

Thunder rumbles in the distance.

THIRTY

NOW

The tears had stopped falling a long time ago and the grief had dulled to an endless ache.

It wasn't about her mother telling her to leave even though the shock sent her reeling. There was something else so deep and important – a turning point in her life with the details just out of reach. The strongest sense of needing to make life-changing decisions but her brain couldn't process it yet. Maybe it never would.

What had Pam said?

You always thought I should leave your father but I loved him with all my heart, Sadie. Somehow I always saw him without the flaws. There are things you don't know about his health and his change of heart.

How had her mother still loved – unconditionally, it seemed – a man who treated her with dismissal and disrespect? And what about his health? Why hadn't Pam made it a priority to talk to her about Ron's health? Round and round it went, intensifying her own heartbreak with her father.

He'd been her cheerleader for so long. Encouraged her to try new things. Swim faster and further and dive deeper. Be in charge of her own choices. Was it wise to paddle downstream alone? What were the risks? And what was she going to do with her life as an adult? Hidden away were memories of conversations about Sadie being anything she chose. About her taking chances and believing in herself. She'd thought the whole world revolved around her dad.

Tears welled up again, stinging her eyes, and she blinked them away.

Virtually overnight he'd stopped talking to her like a young adult and relegated her to being a child, and much younger than she was. He no longer answered her questions or tolerated her following him everywhere. One time, after she'd raised her voice in protest because he wouldn't answer a question, he'd struck her so hard she'd fallen. This wasn't something she'd told her mother. But she'd learned. Keep out of his way. Give him no reason to lash out. There'd been no more lessons at the beach. No help with homework. No coming to her important school and sports days. Somehow, Dad had stopped loving her.

Sadie climbed out of the hollow tree, stretching muscles made sore by confinement and tension. She lowered herself onto the ground and lay on her back on a bed of dried leaves to stare at the sky. How often had she done this in the past? When she hit puberty this had become her go-to place to escape. And all through high school, between the normal stresses of study and dealing with her difficulties with her father, she'd been here more than in the house. Well, it felt that way.

The last time she'd seen her father was here, in this clearing. The memory hit her hard enough to make her body shake and she released a low moan. Eight years ago she'd arrived unannounced and stayed all of two days. He'd barely spoken to her in that time and the hope she'd brought with her had withered to almost nothing. She'd come out here to think and had started at the crunch of a foot on a twig.

'Are you ever going to grow up and stop running from anything you don't like?'

He'd stood, arms crossed, head shaking in disappointment or disapproval.

'I'm not running, Dad. I came home to try and put the past in the past but every time I start a conversation, you just stare at me or walk away.'

'Such as launching an attack on me about how I treat your mother? She's a grown woman who can make up her own mind about me without you interfering all the time. This is why I didn't want you doing more studies. Look at yourself. Making judgements about your own parents instead of pitching in when we needed you to help run the business.'

'And what about my life? I do good things with my work but you don't even acknowledge what I achieve. So much for telling me I could be anything I wanted.'

He turned his back and then stopped long enough to give her a look she'd never forget. 'I didn't expect you to turn into a selfish woman who'd forget her only family.'

Sadie's heart still hurt from those words between them. The canopy above was denser than she remembered but not so much as to completely hide the sky or the clouds as they slowly drifted across. Her breathing slowed and her heart settled into its normal beat.

Pam had said Sadie hadn't kept in touch and while there was truth in it with her lack of visits and rare phone calls, she *had* emailed regularly. This was something she had to get to the bottom of – not to prove a point but to clear up the misunderstanding.

At least one misunderstanding.

'I don't want to leave. Not yet.'

Saying it aloud made it real, and Sadie sat up, startling a rabbit which was hopping by. It tore away then stopped on its haunches at a distance, ears flattened and nose twitching.

Scared, it had run. Now it stopped to look at what scared it.

'And I'm not so bad. Sorry, bunny.'

She took her time to stand rather than frighten the poor creature again but when she looked, it had disappeared. And if she didn't stand her own ground she'd do the same. She'd already run. Not just today but from her entire history all those years ago.

Sadie left the trees behind and stopped at the spot she'd been with Dan last night. Those beautiful, tender moments were burned into her mind. It was hardly the first time she'd kissed a man. But it was the first time she'd kissed a man who was genuinely his own person and one who was invested in who she was. He'd seen through the games – outdoing him on the sea floor, taking risks swimming at night to get a reaction – and nothing so far had scared him off. And he'd accepted her apology for misjudging him at face value which spoke volumes about his personality.

She touched her lips. There was more going on than physical attraction but no denying the desire between them. And it would amount to nothing if she ran again. Here she was. Halfway between the sanctuary of the trees and the anguish of the house. A middle ground, born from history and hope. And she had no idea what it meant.

Her phone beeped. It had a few times while she was sobbing in the hollowed tree but she'd ignored the messages, expecting Pam was reminding her to leave. But there wasn't even one message from her mother. The first three were from Lina and she scrolled past without opening because the one just received came from Dan.

> Would you and Pam join me for dinner tonight at my house? I'd love to cook for you.

Oh lord. What timing.

Before she could respond, another message.

Or I could meet you at midnight with
champagne and strawberries in the place
between your childhood and your future.

Sadie gazed at the sky. The sun was out, not the stars, but all she could see was a shrine.

Pam stood in the bed of potatoes, digging and tossing the poor things into the wheelbarrow. Sweat poured down her face as she used more force than required to turn the soil. She threw one potato so hard that it bounced right out of the wheelbarrow and rolled to a stop at Sadie's feet. Without a word, Sadie picked it up and placed it with the others.

Her mother leaned on the garden fork and wiped her brow.

'Not bad for a forgotten crop,' Sadie said.

Although Pam's face was stern, she didn't seem angry anymore. All that hard work must have let her get some of the emotions out of her system. But when her mother began to climb out, Sadie resisted the urge to offer an arm. Twice she'd been told not to mother and she wasn't letting it happen a third time.

'I think that's about it. I'll leave the bed for a week then turn it again.'

'In that case, where would you like this?' Sadie lifted the handles of the wheelbarrow. 'My gosh there must be fifty kilos in here.'

'Close to the back door. I want to get them packed away before the sun ruins them.'

Leaving her mother to bring the garden fork, Sadie wheeled the barrow, bumping over the long grass, to the back of the house, then turned it around and pulled it up onto the verandah. It was only one step high and there was space against the wall away from the sun.

She didn't go inside, waiting for Pam to put the fork away in the garden shed. There was a lot to be said but the outcome depended upon how well she managed her own emotions as well as Pam's willingness to meet her partway. Otherwise, she'd be packing her things and leaving.

Pam stepped onto the verandah, glancing at the wheelbarrow. 'Good thinking. After a cup of tea I'll get onto doing them.'

'Not going to the inn?'

'Later. Once I know you're okay.' On that strange note, Pam went inside. 'Coming?'

After pulling off her shoes, Sadie followed. Pam had disappeared, probably to freshen up, so she filled the kettle and began making a pot of tea. By 'okay', did her mother mean 'okay to pack and go' or 'okay about the past' or something altogether different?

'There's some gingerbread cookies in the pantry. Inside an airtight container.'

'When did you make those?' Sadie collected the container and opened it. 'Oh my goodness, these smell incredible.'

'Sit. I'll finish the tea.'

Pam had changed her top and washed her face. Once Sadie was at the table, Pam bustled around collecting cups and plates for the cookies.

Sadie's phone beeped again and she turned it face down. She'd reply to Dan once she knew what was going on and she still had to read the messages from Lina. A cup of tea appeared in front of her and the container of cookies moved closer.

'Try one. I did some baking last night. And I bottled the peaches and plums Rebecca sent.'

'Oh, Mum. That's wonderful. Did you enjoy doing that again?'

Finally, a smile, albeit fleeting. 'Hadn't realised how much I missed it. And although I'm certain Rebecca has plenty of her own, I'd like to give her one of each.'

This was real progress. Next thing would be getting the two ladies together to talk about books and gardens.

They drank tea and ate a cookie each.

The phone beeped.

'Answer it.'

Sadie turned it over. Another one from Dan.

Does Pam enjoy fish? I caught some whiting.

'It's from Dan, asking if you enjoy whiting.'

'Me?' Her mother nodded. 'Anything from the sea is lovely. Why?'

'When I was almost home he messaged to ask us both to his house tonight for dinner.'

Pam's eyes lit up. 'You said yes?'

'I haven't replied yet.'

'Then tell him we'd love to.'

'And then what, Mum? We have a nice dinner, small talk, then I have to pack and leave? What did you mean about knowing I was okay?'

Helping herself to another cookie, Pam tilted her head. 'In all the years of you disappearing when things got tough I've never left the property. Why would I start now?' She bit into the gingerbread.

'Never? But Mummy, half the time I'm sure you didn't even know where I was. Sometimes I even said I was going to visit a friend but ended up in the forest instead.'

'In or near the hollowed-out tree. The first few times I followed you but once I knew you were safe, I let you be. Everyone needs their own private place so I figured you'd head there today. And I expected you'd do some thinking and want to talk once we'd both settled down again.'

Sadie didn't know what to say. She'd never known her

mother followed her or knew where she was and it gave her a sudden sense of... comfort.

Pam put her hand on Sadie's arm and their eyes met. 'I was wrong to tell you to leave. This is your home as much as mine and you are welcome to stay here as long as you want. I see you struggling with memories. About your father, I expect. And if you want, really want, I'll try to answer your questions. But first, you let Daniel know we'll be round tonight and ask what we can bring.'

They'd moved to the garden and sat on the bench surrounded by roses.

'So much neglect,' Pam said. 'But Ron refused to let anyone help, even those men from his church. Not that they offered after he stopped taking an active role there but I'd have reached out to them had he agreed. So he'd try his best and do a bit here and there and meanwhile the place fell down around us.'

The bitterness in her tone was alien.

'After you left to go to Sydney, days after you finished your schooling, Ron spent a few months sulking. He wanted to come and find you and reconcile but was too proud and too inarticulate to do so. His beliefs encouraged him to turn his back on the past and I imagine it was a whole lot easier than putting things right with you. Sadie, the religion he followed was there at a moment when he doubted himself as a person and they took full advantage of his fears. I blame them.'

'Why would he doubt himself? He was always so strong and in control of everything.'

Pam shuffled on the bench, her lips tightening for a minute. She reached up to pull an open rose closer and smell its fragrance. 'So perfect. Layers which unfold over time, each creating its own beautiful image.'

'That's lovely, Mum.'

'Thanks. It is how humans are, or should be. Changing all the time and hopefully becoming what we are meant to be.'

Releasing the rose, Pam sighed and then took one of Sadie's hands.

'Do you remember your grandparents?'

'A bit.'

Sadie had never met Pam's parents, who'd died a long time ago. Dad's parents were distant, unfriendly, and intolerant of a small child. His father died when she was about seven and she'd only seen his mother a few times after that.

'When you were about eleven or twelve, his mother demanded he visit. You probably don't remember but he was away for a week and he came back a real mess. I'm not one to speak badly of the deceased but she wasn't a pleasant person and your father had a horrible childhood.'

'Oh... oh, I never knew.'

'Whatever she said to him, he lost all his belief in himself as a father and husband. I found him outside wandering the garden, night after night, sometimes in tears, but he refused to see someone to help him and wasn't about to let me to. About that time he fell in with that stupid group of men again and at first it was good. He was more focused. Less distraught. I thought he was on his way back.'

'Except he wasn't.'

Pam nodded. 'The thing is, Sadie, like so many men of his age he'd been taught to be strong no matter what, and whatever happened during the week with his mother made that impossible. I think she forced him back to that church and in doing so, he lost a big part of himself. He never meant to hurt you. Setting up the trust was a way of showing you he loved you, I'm sure of it.'

'But he didn't love me.' Sadie took her hand away. 'He stopped and it... broke me. Inside.' She whispered the last word as tears forced their way into her eyes. 'How could he do that?'

'I'm not excusing him. Not for one minute, but you know that not every rose blooms. Many of them stay tightly closed and disease kills them.'

'But Daddy wasn't a rose.'

Pam put her around Sadie's shoulders. 'No. He was a person and one with baggage we'll never know about. Then, three or four years ago his heart began to play up and it was like he could see his own mortality. He all but left the church, love. And while he was never the man I married, he stopped being so bossy and tried to make it up by helping others.'

'Like I said, Mum. He didn't love me because he had time to put things right and didn't even bother to try. I honestly don't know what to think.'

'Think about the good memories. I know you have them. And think about your own happiness because only one person is responsible for that, and it's you.'

When did Pam get so wise? Probably always was. And she'd made peace with Dad but Sadie wasn't so sure she had the same courage or compassion. Some things were unforgiveable.

THIRTY-ONE

Sadie dropped Pam at the inn to wait for the guests, leaving her car there to walk to the supermarket. It wasn't as though they were urgent for shopping but she was restless, even after helping her mother sort and store the potatoes. She was sure she smelled like a potato and the thought made her smile.

A woman heading toward her smiled in return, obviously assuming it was meant for her, and why not? Smiles were free.

Instead of shopping she wandered for a while and ended up at the café on the corner. After ordering a coffee, Sadie chose a seat outside beneath a colourful umbrella. She enjoyed people-watching and from here had a good view of the intersection.

On one corner was the same real estate agent she remembered always being there. She had a vague memory of a cheerful, bustling woman working there, always with a friendly word. Colourful flowerpots sat beneath the two big display windows. After coffee she'd drop in and see if they'd been the sellers of Rebecca's cottage. There were still so many unanswered questions.

'If it isn't our town's claim to fame, the little TV star herself.'

Sadie frowned as Mick Hammond dropped his bulk into a

chair opposite. He was in uniform but carried an unlit cigarette. 'Please don't light that near me.'

He sneered and tucked it into his top pocket. 'Afraid it might give you more wrinkles?'

Had she not just sat down she'd have left without a word but her coffee was too nice to abandon.

'Heard you found the old bat.'

'Did you blackmail someone to become a cop? I can't imagine you passing an IQ test, let alone a physical.'

'Ouch.' He patted his gut. 'Used to be lean and mean.'

'You forget we went to the same school, Mick. The mean part is true.'

'And haven't you turned into a nasty little bi—'

'Careful, Constable. I don't put up with bullies anymore and it won't take much for me to make a complaint about you. Is there a reason you have intruded?' Sadie finally added an edge to her tone. He made her skin crawl but she'd dealt with worse types. 'No?'

He grunted as he stood. 'Being friendly. Stardom's gone to your head.'

'Goodbye, Mick.'

Sadie stared at him until he finally got the message and lumbered away. He was bad for the town. Even if he did nothing wrong, it was the lack of care for the residents of Rivers End and his unkind view of the world which had her shaking her head over his choice of career. And to not even have bothered following up on Rebecca... how could he wear his uniform with any pride?

Lina messaged her.

Have you read anything I've sent? 😊

Whoops. Nope. Sadie scrolled back through the ones she'd missed.

> You should have the same email from the
> studio I just received. Let me know once you
> read it.

Darn. She'd not got near her laptop today but another hour wouldn't matter. If it was urgent someone would have phoned.

> I've had some thoughts about your mystery
> woman. Happy to talk when you're not too
> busy.

Rebecca still played on her mind and if she was to get any closer to understanding why she was a bit obsessed with the older woman then she needed all the help on offer.

> Which brings me to my next point. How was
> the dreamy date? Hmm?

Dreamy. Magical. Life-changing.
Sadie tapped a message back.

> Away from home so will check emails later,
> thanks for the heads up. If you're up later
> tonight I'll call about Rebecca but I'll message
> first. And it was a nice dinner.

She turned the phone off. Lina would want more details and she had no inclination to answer questions, let alone ones she hadn't even answered for herself. Her gaze moved to the other corner. As much a part of the town as the beach and the river, the jewellery shop was an institution. It was one thing she did remember clearly, generation after generation of master jewellers from one family creating exquisite pieces for the local community. Pam's wedding ring was made there. And a necklace her father gave her when she turned ten.

The memory jolted her. A starfish on a fine chain. Where was it now?

'Excuse me... you *are* Sadie Forest, aren't you?'

The speaker was one of three women, all in their seventies or older, who stood a few feet away from her table. One had a walking stick and another had a sweet Cavalier King Charles spaniel on a lead.

'Hello, cutie. May I say hello?' Sadie waited for a nod from the owner and approached slowly, squatting to let the dog come to her. 'Who is this gorgeous little person?'

'James Regal is a dog, not a human.'

Sadie gazed up at the owner with a smile. The woman wore large sunglasses and was stern-faced, so clearly not a fan. 'You are right, of course. So it's James Regal.'

'Really, Marge? That was uncalled for.' The original speaker glared at Marge and loudly whispered, 'Miss Forest is a star.'

James Regal didn't care. He wanted his tummy rubbed and flopped onto his back on the pavement and Sadie happily obliged.

'She isn't stuck-up like most stars,' the woman with the walking stick also whispered. 'I quite like her.'

Instead of mentioning that she could hear them, Sadie gave the dog one more scratch and straightened. 'He's a great dog. I always wanted a dog growing up but it never happened, and these days I live in an apartment.'

Marge's face softened. 'Cavaliers are happy to live wherever their owner does, but it makes sense not to bring one into your life if you're very busy. I'd imagine you are with your wonderful documentaries.'

I take it back. You are a fan.

'Would you all like to join me? I can order some more coffee. Or whatever you'd like?'

The ladies didn't wait for a second invitation, pulling out chairs and sitting at her table in a matter of seconds. James

Regal settled underneath it, shuffling a bit to rest his chin on her foot. It felt nice.

'We don't need coffee, dear, but we do have some questions. And how rude of us not to introduce ourselves. I am Bess, this is Annette, and you've heard me use Marge's name.' Bess was the first of the women to have spoken to her. She had a quick smile and very short hair dyed bright red. Annette had the walking stick and a silver bun on top of her head, and Marge, who was looking a little less stern now, wore her salt-and-pepper hair in a bob.

'If we're intruding, please tell us,' Annette said. 'We just couldn't believe our eyes when we saw you sitting here.'

'We don't often get television stars in our town,' Bess added.

Sadie could barely keep herself from grinning at their sweetness.

'I'm truly not a star.'

All three faces were aghast and now she did smile.

'But I really appreciate you being so kind. My focus is always on telling a story and if I've reached nice people like you, then it makes it worthwhile.'

Marge removed her sunglasses and leaned forward a little. 'What you do is change lives. My cousin twice removed lives in Sydney and told me you personally helped a resident in the apartment building he was living in. They were being evicted. Do you remember?' Her gaze was intense and expectant.

'I do. They'd had their rent hiked months earlier but hadn't been advised so were suddenly presented with a big bill. The property manager there had to face a tribunal over their dodgy actions and the resident was excused from the debt and awarded some compensation for the suffering. He was eighty years old.'

How could she ever forget the pain that poor man endured?

'Well, you might say you are not a star, but what you did for him was like a whole sky full of stars.'

There was that shrine again. Sadie drew in a long breath. Was the universe trying to tell her something? James Regal was having a dream, his little body quivering against her foot as he chased some imaginary rabbit. Another sign.

'We all know your mum. She's such a brave woman, isn't she?' That was Annette. 'Fancy having to find your own husband dec—'

'Won't you look at the time!' Bess cut Annette off. 'Before we go, I want you to know that all your documentaries matter. Well, they do to us. All three of us have put our names down on the list to be considered for the new assisted living complex young Daniel is building, and that's because we saw you talking about the importance of protecting our own futures. None of that nonsense of us of being found dead in our homes, half-eaten by our cats.'

'Oh my goodness! You've been reading too many of those mystery books from the bookshop.' Annette pushed herself to her feet with her cane and gave Sadie a wide smile. 'Can't take her anywhere.'

All three began an animated conversation as they waved and wandered off, with James Regal yawning as he padded behind.

'What about my mother? And father...' It was pointless. None of them heard her over their own chatter and short of chasing them down the street Sadie could only finish Annette's sentence herself. 'Fancy having to find your own husband dec... deceased. Oh, Mum.'

* * *

'Why do you keep looking at me so oddly, love?' Pam put a hand on Sadie's arm the minute the car stopped in Dan's driveway. 'Is something wrong with my make-up?'

'Your make-up is perfect. And your hair, before you ask. Shall we go in?'

Pam wasn't convinced and Sadie couldn't blame her. She had no idea how to broach the subject of the details of her father's death and certainly wasn't about to spoil dinner tonight by doing it in a clumsy way. But she must be showing signs of something bothering her if Pam noticed.

'Come on, you've been so keen to get here, Mum, and Dan might be wondering why we're sitting here.' Not willing to wait, Sadie climbed out and went around to let her mother out. 'You'd be easy to steal. Get you into a car with anything but a manual handle and you'll be in a mini prison.'

'Don't make fun of your elders. Here, take my handbag.'

Once out of the car, Pam gazed around. 'What a pretty garden. From the road you'd never know this is here.'

'Wait until you see up behind the house, though. Best view of the ocean.'

'This far back from the coast? Well, I shall have to see for myself.'

Pam slid her arm through Sadie's and they wandered to the front steps. Since their talk earlier in the day there was a new closeness between them. There was still air to be cleared, but spending this time with her mother was precious.

The front door was wide open and when Sadie tapped, Dan's voice boomed from somewhere inside. 'Come in, come in.'

Both left their shoes at the front and waited in the hallway. Butterflies flapped around in Sadie's stomach. Last night may have been a dream or if it was real, Dan might regret it. But the minute he appeared from the end of the hallway, wearing a bright purple apron with *Go ahead, bake my day* blazoned across its front, her fears dissolved.

'Pam and Sadie, welcome. Shoes are fine as long as you've not just arrived from a muddy building site.'

Dan kissed Pam's cheek.

'In that case I might pop my sandals back on.'

While Pam did so, he turned to Sadie with a soft, 'Hey you.' His eyes were warm and his smile caught at her heart.

'Hi,' she said. It seemed inadequate but throwing herself into his arms and kissing him with her mother there wasn't happening. 'I know you said not to bring anything, but Mum was on a bottling and baking spree.'

'I was. Plums and peaches plus some gingerbread cookies. And I left the bag with them in the car. May I have the keys, love?'

'Shall I run out and get them?'

'No shoes.'

Sadie handed over the keys. 'This button for the boot.'

The minute Pam was out of sight, Dan pulled Sadie into his arms and gazed down at her. 'Do you think she did that on purpose?'

'We shouldn't disappoint her.'

Sadie lifted herself on her toes and Dan met her halfway. As short as the kiss was it left her buzzing with happiness, grinning like a child with a secret. When Pam returned, they were apart again, chatting about the weather.

'Here's your keys. And Daniel, here's your goodies. But why on earth are you discussing the weather? Couldn't you find anything else to... discuss?'

Dan smirked as he took the bag. 'Nothing wrong with comparing our perfect climate to Sydney's humidity. And thank you for these. Anything with ginger is a favourite and I hope your enjoyment of it extends to savoury dishes. Care to join me?'

Dinner was a delicious meal of whiting baked with ginger, chilli, and garlic, plus asparagus, green beans, and baby carrots cooked in a buttery sauce. Dan had asked who was the designated driver and then poured Pam a glass of sparkling wine and Sadie one of non-alcoholic apple cider. Sadie didn't need wine to feel intoxicated. It was enough listening in as Dan and Pam discussed the fine points of his building proposal. He encouraged her mother to consider more than the external look of the inn. At one point he wrote down a couple of websites for her to explore, places specialising in the fit-outs of boutique hotels and resorts so she could get some ideas of what was possible.

'The owners of the assisted living complex are working with the first company.'

'I met some future clients today,' Sadie said. 'Bess, Annette, and Marge. Oh, and James Regal.'

'Who is James Regal?' Pam asked.

'Marge's little dog.' Dan grinned. 'Don't tell her I said this, but JR is easier to get along with than she is.'

Pam looked horrified. 'Daniel Harrington! I have never heard you speak badly of anyone.' Then she laughed and Sadie and Dan joined in. 'But it is true. She says things as she sees them. When did you meet them?'

'I was at the corner café enjoying a coffee and people-watching but they were watching me and decided to introduce themselves. They sat with me for a while and we had a very nice conversation. Actually, they were very kind about my documentaries.'

And very informative.

'My company is renovating Marge's home in Driftwood Cove. She got divorced about ten years ago but neither she nor her ex moved out. This way it'll sell for enough for the both of them,' Dan said. 'She's not so bad.'

He started clearing the table and Sadie joined him. Pam was content to sit with her glass and watch, a half-smile on her face when Sadie glanced at her. Whatever was going on in her mother's head, whatever she thought was happening with Sadie and Dan... well, it was probably true.

'I'm going to put dessert in the oven which will take half an hour. Sadie, would you like to show Pam the lookout and I'll join you both in a minute?'

He was true to his word. They'd barely sat when he caught up and Pam made space between herself and Sadie. But first, he gestured to the darkening sky and sea. 'I love watching the sun set. From here I've seen so many and each one is a glorious nod to Mother Nature.'

'Have you considered poetry, novels, or painting instead of construction?' Sadie asked.

'All three.' Dan sat between them, his thigh touching Sadie's and sending delicious tingles of anticipation through her. 'But you are the one with that kind of talent.'

'She certainly is. Now, I am going to go and use your ladies' room, if I may. And I'll keep an eye on dessert.' Pam got to her feet with an overly obvious expression. 'Do you object to me pouring another glass of wine?'

'Pour away. We'll be down in a few minutes.'

Sadie wanted to laugh at her mother's behaviour but it didn't bother Dan and, for once, she was happy Pam was taking the initiative.

'Your mother keeps disappearing and leaving us alone.' Dan lifted one of Sadie's hands and began stroking her palm. 'I wonder why.'

'No idea.' She sounded breathless as she inched closer. Dan's touch was playing havoc with her senses.

'I wanted to ask you something about the documentaries,' he said.

'O-kay.'

'Your name. Sadie Forest, not Carson.'

'Ah. Forest is Mum's maiden name. I wanted something not associated with my life here.'

'Your life? Anything in particular?'

'An "anyone",' she said. 'My father didn't approve of what I was doing so changing my name seemed appropriate.'

And it probably contributed to their estrangement. He'd been a proud man and although nothing was said to Sadie, she could imagine him taking her decision as a personal affront. It explained why he insisted the inheritance recognised his name. Always exerting his control.

Or showing me I'd hurt him.

Before the thoughts could spiral much more, she put a hand onto Dan's leg.

'How long did I say we'd be?' he asked.

'A few minutes.'

Dan's arm had somehow gone around her shoulders and he effortlessly drew her against his chest. His eyes burned into hers.

'A few millennia wouldn't be enough, Sadie Carson Forest. I am terrified I'll wake up and have been in the most wonderful dream. And as much as I would enjoy the dream, I don't want the reality to end.'

And then he kissed her.

Aunt Ethel arrives just after lunch with a big suitcase and loud voice. I hear her from Mum's room, where I am playing with the jewellery box and softly talking to her about Charlie. How proud Mum would be to see him now. Eight years old. Walking on his own more and more. Doing well at school. And being the best brother ever. It was sad she'd never see him grow up. I promised her, like I often do, to look out for him and Dad. Be the best sister and daughter I can. And always keep her in my heart.

'Where are my niece and nephew?'

Oh goodness.

I rush out of Mum's room and close the door then hurry to the living room.

Her suitcase is in the middle of the floor and she has Charlie in her arms, kissing his face while he tries to avoid her lips.

'Such a big boy now!'

Dad closes the front door and moves the suitcase against the wall, giving me a look. The one reminding me to behave. But then he rolls his eyes and it is all I can do not to giggle.

'No kisses, Auntie!' Charlie wriggles hard enough that Aunt Ethel almost drops him and Dad is there in an instant to scoop him up.

'Too big for kisses? Never. Oh now, here's my darling girl.'

As soon as her arms are free, she holds them wide open and as much as I long to run the other way, I do what Dad would want and give her a hug. She smells awful, like always, saturated in the perfume she always wears. After a crushing hug she grabs my face and kisses me on the lips and I want to throw up. Ew.

'A cup of tea, Ethel?' Dad suggests.

'I'll make it.'

Anything to escape.

'Please, and I'm starving if you have any afternoon treats?'

Dad sits Charlie in his wheelchair, which is decorated with red ribbons for the birthday celebrations. 'You good here?'

'Very good. Birthday boy is always best.'

The second Aunt Ethel and Dad – carrying the suitcase – disappear up the hallway, I whisper to Charlie, 'That was disgusting.'

He looks very serious. 'Awful. Awful aunt. Awful aunt... what's an "a" word for hugs and stuff?'

Charlie recently began learning alliteration and assonance.

'Affection. But say it quietly.'

He nods. 'Awful aunt affection.' Then bursts into giggles.

At least he thinks she's funny. He doesn't know her like I do, with her constant carrying on at Dad to let me live with her for a while. I'm not some pet to share between houses.

'I'm sorry Dad hasn't found a kitten yet, Charlie.'

'At least he promised we will get Percy one day. And I love my lighthouse, Becky.'

I grin. I've smiled a lot today, from our breakfast of pancakes to opening of presents and then a lunch picnic on the beach with Charlie and Dad.

Hearing voices approach, I fill the kettle and get busy on making a pot of tea. In the cupboard is an airtight container with caramel cookies so I put some onto a plate. I pour milk into our one and only fancy milk jug and sugar cubes into a matching bowl. I expect Aunt Ethel prefers the nice china and sure enough, she smiles when she sees what I've prepared.

'I always did like the pattern on these. Thank you, Becca.'

Becky.

Dad carries the tray into the lounge room and sets it on the table where we play our board games. Aunt Ethel has taken off her big coat. She wears a smart skirt and matching blouse in pale yellow and has changed into slip-on shoes which look out of place, being bright orange.

She sits on an armchair and makes a big sigh. 'Such a long trip. Did your father tell you I'm travelling home by ocean liner?'

Who would ever do anything so dangerous?

Charlie's eyes are wide. 'A big boat?'

'Very big. It is called the *Marconi* and originally came from Italy. Most of the time it travels from Sydney to Perth and sometimes stops in Melbourne, so when I found out it was stopping there this time, I arranged to fly into the city. But then tomorrow night I'll leave very late to get to Melbourne in time to board during the next day.'

'How late?'

'So many questions, Charlie!' Aunt Ethel stirs two sugar cubes into the tea I poured and then lots of milk. 'Close to midnight, when you are fast asleep. I need to take my time driving back because the road is winding and narrow in places and it isn't my car, just one I rented.'

At least she's only here for one night. I can cope. 'Would you like one of these? I baked them yesterday and they are caramel with some crushed peanuts.' I hold out the plate and she takes one and tries it, nodding as she chews.

'Will you come to the beach, Auntie?' Charlie hasn't taken his eyes off her. 'We can swim.'

I glance out of the window at the grey sky. 'Charlie, looks like a storm is coming.'

'I'm not one for beaches, dear. Sand is so messy.'

At least we have one thing in common.

Dad and Aunt Ethel spend a lot of time talking in the lounge room after I take Charlie to play for a while with the Lincoln Logs in his room. But when I go to the kitchen to fetch glasses of water for us, they've gone outside and stand on the back deck. The door is closed so I can't hear a word but I see Dad shake his head a lot. Is she still going on about me?

My hands curl into tight fists. I'm not angry. This is more. I'm afraid.

I take the water back to Charlie's room and stand in his doorway for a minute. He is on his stomach, propped up with a pillow beneath his chest so his hands are free. Concentration furrows his brow as he lowers a cross-beam onto some uprights. He misses and the pieces fall but all he does is set them up again. And again. Third time he gets the distance right and has created one piece of a fence.

'Ooh... got it.' His voice is so low and his smile so wide. He notices me. 'Look, Becky.'

'Very good, Charlie. One fence at a time, huh?'

'I might be a builder when I grow up.'

After putting the glasses down I help Charlie sit and hand him one. 'You can be whatever you choose.'

'Anything? Lighthouse keeper.'

'Even that.'

He tilts his head. 'And you will be a famous chef.'

'Me? Nah. But I'd like to be an artist.'

'You draw nice pictures.'

'Thank you. I might need to start making your birthday dinner.'

'Okay, can Dad come get me soon?'

'I'll go ask him now.'

I plant a kiss on his forehead and he screws his face up.

'Not you too.'

'Except I'm allowed to. I'm your big sister.'

'I cannot believe how much I enjoyed such a strange dinner.' Aunt Ethel pushes her plate away after neatly placing her knife and fork together in its middle. 'Tomato soup with a crusty roll. Spaghetti on toast. And a bowl of mashed potato and gravy.'

'All my favourite things,' Charlie said. 'Birthday boy gets the choice. It was Dad's birthday a few weeks ago and we had steak. And Becky is next.'

'Well I enjoyed this very much.'

I begin clearing the plates. Charlie wants us all to play the new board game and then have his birthday cake. Dad gets up to help me. Aunt Ethel doesn't move from her chair.

Once we're in the kitchen, Dad fills the sink. 'This was a fun dinner, sweetie. Charlie has had a terrific day, despite the rain stopping him having a second trip to the beach. And wasn't it nice of Tim to bring him a present?'

He'd only stayed a few minutes to watch Charlie unwrap the little sailboat, which he said would be fun to play with in the lagoon. When I let him out of the front door he told me his mother was fine with me borrowing her bicycle for as long as I want and promised to bring it around soon. And then he ran off down the street with his raincoat flapping as the sky opened.

'Dad, is it okay if Tim teaches me to ride a bicycle?'

After turning off the tap, Dad gives me the biggest smile. 'Of course it is. I'm just not sure if the budget will stretch to a new one, but we can ask around for a second-hand bike.'

'Tim's mother said I can borrow hers. She doesn't ride anymore and I'd take really good care of it.' Suddenly it matters a lot for Dad to approve. 'I really want to learn to ride and can save up my pocket money to buy my own eventually.'

He dries his hands and hugs me. 'I'll talk to Tim's mum and see if she would like to sell it, once you've tried it out for size. And I'm paying, because you deserve a chance to get out and about and do things with new friends.'

I'm still smiling when I go into the lounge room where Aunt Ethel is trying to work out how to set up the new board game. Her back is to me and she is talking to Charlie and my heart leaps into my mouth.

'Just like you have a special school, I'm principal of a different type of special school.'

'What's special about it?'

'I have a girls-only boarding school and we only take very smart young ladies who want to excel.'

'Becky is very smart.'

'Oh my boy, I know. But living here in this little town she won't have the kind of opportunities she deserves.'

I've heard enough.

'Would you like me to finish setting this up, Auntie?'

She jumps and that tells me more than anything. She's trying to get Charlie on her side. Well I have my own plans about that. I kneel at the table and begin sorting cards, winking at Charlie. 'Did Dad tell you how well I've done at school this last term? My teacher says that considering I only arrived at the school partway through the year, she is impressed with my results.'

'You got all A's, didn't you?' Charlie says.

I shake my head and see a little triumphant smile on Aunt Ethel's face.

'No. Not all A's. All A plus.'

The smile drops. In fact, she purses her lips.

'And the high school I'll be attending has accelerated learning for advanced students and my teacher said I will be considered to go into it.'

'Imagine what you could achieve in a school which only focuses on excellence. And it is more than the usual subjects we teach, but also music and art at a high level.'

'Becky wants to be an artist.'

Thank goodness Dad comes in and before there's any further discussion about schools, we start playing.

When I get ready for bed much later, I am so full after eating too much of Charlie's birthday cake. I think he enjoyed every second of his special day. The storm is gone but the night is pretty cloudy when I go to close my curtains. There is some light though. Strange little lights moving around near the limestone column. But then they are gone and I think I must be so tired I'm seeing things. I climb into bed and ask Mum to help me get through the next twenty-four hours until Aunt Ethel leaves. Until she's gone, I'm not going to breathe easy.

THIRTY-THREE

NOW

Two days after the dinner at Dan's house, Sadie still hadn't found the right way to ask Pam about the comment from Annette, but she had found the starfish necklace in a tiny box in her dressing table.

It was even prettier than she remembered. A gold starfish with a blue gemstone in the centre. It hung from a delicate gold chain. She rarely wore jewellery but something about this piece was different, even though it was only made of gold plating and perhaps a type of quartz stone. The chain was too short for her adult neck, which gave her an excuse to visit the jeweller's.

She didn't recall ever being inside the old shop but many times had gazed in awe as a youngster at the windows crammed full of the most beautiful objects she'd ever seen. Dazzling rings, pendants, earrings, pearl strings, men's tie clips and cufflinks. And clocks. So many interesting clocks and watches. But it was the sculptures she'd loved the most. Porcelain statues and glass blown into horses, and dolphins, and dogs. When Dad gave her the necklace on her tenth birthday and said where it had come from, Sadie had almost cried with delight.

A bell jangled above when she pushed the door open and stepped inside.

It was darker in here, lit more by scattered wall lamps than anything overhead and several glass cabinets were softly illuminated from inside. A sense of history settled on Sadie. The building was one of the first built when Rivers End was established. The only sound was the steady ticking of clocks, some on the wall behind the long counter, and then a cluster of grandfather clocks set apart from the cabinets. There was a gap, roughly the size of a large grandfather clock, in the corner. Some lucky person would be enjoying their acquisition.

'Good afternoon.'

Had he been there the whole time, sitting behind the counter? Sadie hadn't heard footsteps.

'Oh, good afternoon. What a beautiful shop you have. As a child I used to stop outside on my way home from school to admire the window displays.'

'And you didn't come in?'

The gentleman was closer to ninety than eighty, with snow-white hair and kind eyes behind old-fashioned spectacles.

'My father would not have approved of me wasting the time of a fellow trader.' She removed the box from her handbag. 'This was my father's gift to me on my tenth birthday. I only just found it again and would like to wear it but the chain is too short.'

After opening the box, the gentleman stared at her for a moment then nodded. 'Sadie Carson. My condolences about the loss of your father.'

'Thank you. I'm shocked you would know who I am from an old necklace.'

A smile accentuated the lines on his face. 'I'm last in a long line of jewellers but my one real talent is recalling every piece of jewellery I've made and who owns it.' He gently extracted the necklace and held it aloft to bring to his eyeline. 'Your father wanted something to remind you of the sea, made in gold like the sand at sunset and with a sapphire to match your eyes, which this does.'

'That's a sapphire?'

'Well of course. And nine carat gold. Not many people buy something precious for a young child but clearly you've taken care of it.'

In the bottom of a drawer. Forgotten for more than two decades.

'The chain is not one which I can simply extend so if you approve I shall replace both pieces with longer ones.'

'Yes please. I'd like the starfish to sit here.' Sadie touched a spot a few inches beneath the 'V' on her neck. 'Do you need to measure?'

He climbed off a tall stool with a shake of his head. 'Not necessary.' He shuffled to the far end of the counter to collect a heavy book. Inside, written in beautiful cursive script, was a record of transactions. 'If I may take some details? And I should have introduced myself. George Campbell.'

Sadie answered his questions and George promised to phone her when it was ready to collect. She'd have loved to stay a while and browse but that would lead to buying and if it was clocks or the glass sculptures then she'd have to transport them all the way to Sydney.

Nevertheless, she lingered outside for a few minutes, transfixed by a dozen or so sea creatures along the bottom shelf. At the end, sitting upon a rock, was a mermaid. Smiling, Sadie bobbed down to see it better. Such a gorgeous design with an iridescent tail and long, flowing hair down her back and discreetly covering her breasts. Mermaids were her spirit creature and Dan calling her mermaid only served to strengthen their connection.

If she was going to buy a piece it would be this.

She straightened. The piece would be beautiful on the sideboard in her apartment. But every time she'd look at it, she'd think of Dan and that was the problem.

Thinking about Dan Harrington was a poor substitute for being with him.

With a heavy sigh, Sadie headed to her car.

Intending to go home to attend to the long-overdue checking of emails and finally talk to Lina – who'd been busy every time they'd tried to catch up – Sadie instead drove to Rebecca's cottage, stopping long enough to collect the goodies Pam had made.

Rebecca wasn't home but nor was the bicycle so she waited. When Percy made an appearance they went for a walk, ending up at the end of the pier. Sadie sat and removed her shoes so she could cool her feet in the lake the way she'd planned the first time she'd seen it. Percy spent some time peering into the water watching huge carp. The weather was beautiful as summer tapered into autumn and soon the deciduous trees would be a riot of colour before dropping their leaves.

She'd missed the changing of the seasons. Sydney was different. Long, humid summers. Wet winters. Not a lot in between. When she drove out of the city to the north or the south coast, or inland past the majestic Blue Mountains to Tablelands towns such as Orange, then she experienced spring and autumn. Even snow in Orange one day.

Rivers End was different again. A bit of humidity on summer days when storms were hovering around but otherwise warm enough to live outdoors with the odd really hot one. Winters which weren't as cold as the mountains only half an hour away but with lovely crisp evenings. And proper changing of the leaves.

But missing the changing of the seasons wasn't enough to make her move back.

Nor was her renewed passion for Rivers End beach and the ocean.

Pam came close... that is if her mother really wanted her here all the time. They'd clashed over Sadie's need to help and fix things and probably always would, but their newfound relationship meant the world.

And there was Dan. A few weeks ago she'd not known he existed yet now he filled her thoughts and – if she was honest with herself – her heart. No man had ever made her laugh and feel so alive, nor given her a sense of belonging. He was her match, neither more nor less than her own intellect and sense of humour and compassion.

Percy rubbed her head against Sadie's arm.

'What would you do, kitty cat? Should I go through the reasons why I shouldn't move back here?'

With a sudden meow, Percy trotted away. Rebecca was cycling toward the cottage and stepped off while the bicycle still moved with a nimbleness belying her age. She raised a hand in greeting when she spotted Sadie.

By the time Sadie reached the cottage, barefoot as she allowed the warm grass to dry her feet, the bicycle was in its usual place on the verandah and Rebecca was lifting two cloth bags of shopping from the steps. She waited for Sadie to join her then offered a small smile. 'Isn't the kettle on yet? The door is always unlocked.'

'Oh, I'd never just let myself in and... you're teasing me.' Sadie took the bags from Rebecca. 'But tea sounds nice.'

Rebecca opened the door and waved Sadie in first. Percy streaked past and was in the kitchen before Sadie was halfway along the hall. She tried not to but couldn't help gazing at the paintings along the walls and Rebecca noticed.

'Mostly ones I've done over my lifetime.'

'You are so talented.'

Rebecca made a scoffing sound as she passed Sadie. 'Persistent. I only had a few lessons and quickly realised I'd never conform to the rules, so they are certainly not worthy of hanging anywhere but in this cottage. Besides, I'm the only one who cares about my memories.'

That was not even close to being true.

Sadie followed her into the kitchen and deposited the bags on the table. 'I hope you don't mind me asking... one of the paintings draws me into it. I think about it a lot.'

Hands on the kettle ready to fill, Rebecca paused, her eyes bright. 'The lighthouse.' She blinked rapidly and then moved to the sink. 'Not today, Sadie. Ask me again after tomorrow.'

Goosebumps rose on Sadie's arms. What was significant about tomorrow? Was it the anniversary of the day it was painted... no, that made no sense. But the anniversary of whatever had inspired the painting did. The possibility of having a conversation about the lighthouse painting had to be enough for now, as Rebecca had seemed ready to cry.

'Oh, I almost forgot! Mum has been bottling again.'

Kettle on, Rebecca moved to the bags to unpack. 'I'm very happy to hear that.'

'She sent you bottles of peaches and plums from the lovely fruit you gave her. They're in the car so I must remember to give them to you before I go.'

'Well fancy that. I'll have to phone Pam and thank her.'

'I'll get you her number.'

'Already have it.'

Oh.

The kettle began to boil so Sadie took over tea-making duties while Rebecca finished unpacking. Sadie felt as at home here as she did at Dan's and whether that was the style of kitchen she enjoyed or the company... or a mix, most likely. Tea made and shopping put away, they sat at the table while Percy took her position on a spare chair again.

'It looked as though you and my cat were deep in conversation when I arrived home.'

'Percy is an excellent listener.'

'Indeed. But not so good with feedback, other than complaints about the standard of care she receives.' Rebecca gazed at Percy who immediately jumped the small distance onto her lap. 'But she more than makes up for that with her perception.'

Even if she believed she could create an engaging environment, Sadie couldn't have a cat or a dog in her apartment thanks to body corporate rules. No pets other than a small fish tank and even those needed approval on a case-by-case basis. She'd have to move if she introduced a furry creature into her life.

'What's troubling you, child?'

Mentally adding Rebecca to her earlier list of who and what she'd miss by going back to Sydney, Sadie knew she needed a sounding-board, and one more responsive than Percy.

'I've lived in Sydney for fifteen years which is pretty much my entire adult life, but being here again in Rivers End where the pace is slower and the scenery is breathtaking and the people...'

'You are torn in two directions.'

'I am. It isn't Sydney as such, although I love my apartment and the city but my career is based there and until recently I was certain it was everything to me. Yet here, I feel happy.'

'Our lives aren't always our own. We fit into what society expects. Sometimes – often – what our families expect. For what it is worth from an old woman who followed a difficult path, find a way to cut through the noise. Decide what really matters to you and you alone. And when you have to choose, you *must* go with your heart.'

'Even when you have to sacrifice something you've worked so very hard to achieve?'

'We all pick our own version of what is hard. Is it harder to leave? Or stay? Only you can make that decision,' Rebecca said.

Sipping her tea gave Sadie time to consider Rebecca's words. Was it as simple as following her heart? The concept was uncomfortable. Too many years expecting the worst to happen and building barriers to keep anything and everyone which might shatter her safe world at bay.

'My job matters to me. I believe it makes a difference to people who might not otherwise be seen.'

'Your documentaries. Yes, they bring important attention to social needs. You give a voice to those who have given up or never had a choice to make and that is a worthy job, Sadie. But tell me, would living here in your hometown exclude you from making those shows?'

'I'd need to be in Sydney for the filming as well as a couple of weeks prior, so around eight weeks at a time.'

'And Sydney is the only place you can make them?'

'Actually... no. But for the last few years I've worked with one studio.'

'We need cupcakes,' Rebecca announced as she stood. 'I made far too many earlier.'

'Good thing I like walking and swimming. Mum filled me up with gingerbread cookies yesterday and last night Dan made the most sumptuous apple crumble with homemade ice cream. Even Mum couldn't finish hers, it was so rich and she's the sweet tooth.'

Returning with a plate of delicately iced chocolate cupcakes, Rebecca nodded. 'He'd phoned me to ask if I'd also come along for your dinner last night but I was... occupied.'

'Making these? They look so pretty.'

'Charlie always nibbled the icing off first and would tell me I'd forgotten to do it and would I bring the bowl to add some more.' A dreamy smile lit Rebecca's face. '*More cupcakes, Becky!* Always more cupcakes.'

'Charlie is your son?' Sadie bit into decadent deliciousness. 'Oh, but he called you Becky, not Mum. So someone else special.'

The smile dropped. 'No children. He was my baby brother. Sadie, would you mind if we cut this visit short?' Once again Rebecca was on her feet. 'Please take your time finishing your tea and take some cupcakes home. Take the whole plate because I have another.'

'I'm happy to sit with you. In silence if you wish.'

Rebecca squeezed Sadie's shoulder. 'Please excuse me.' And then she was gone, Percy on her heels as she left the kitchen. A moment later the front door opened and closed.

Sadie covered her mouth with her hand as her heart thudded. Although Rebecca was expert at hiding her feelings, the pain which had flashed in her eyes was profound. Charlie... her baby brother who loved cupcakes with icing. A conversation about the painting she was willing to have, but not until after tomorrow. Sadie emptied the teapot and washed up.

Was Charlie one of the people Rebecca had asked Sadie to help her find?

How on earth could she take the cupcakes which meant so much? They went back into the fridge. And on the next shelf was a peculiar tray of items.

A small, unopened tin of spaghetti with two slices of white bread on a plate. A small crusty roll. A bowl of mashed potato and another of homemade tomato soup. And in an empty bowl was a note saying 'ice cream'. It was as if a small child was coming over for their favourite meal.

'Oh my gosh.' Sadie closed the fridge, chilled to the bone, not from having stood in front of it but by the heartbreaking conclusion which hit hard.

Charlie had died, probably in childhood. The contents of the tray were from his last day or possibly a birthday. Something which meant a great deal to Rebecca. And the cupcakes were from a memory she wanted to keep alive. And the painting?

Sadie grabbed her phone and keys and hurried to the hallway.

For the first time she was able to stand in front of the light-house painting without expecting to be caught doing something she shouldn't. Rebecca had indicated she would answer questions soon. So why not answer them today? She peered more closely at the lighthouse on the flat rocks. There was a figure there, almost lost against the dark background. It was a girl with long dark hair whipping in the wind, her hand outstretched... to the rowboat. What on earth had happened? The rowboat was empty, its oars dipping into the roiling ocean.

Her stomach was churning as she wandered along the hallway in the hope one of the other paintings might offer some clue to the older woman's past. Most were landscapes with red ground and blue skies or else townscapes with heat haze. Images of the Australian outback.

But there were two which were different.

The first was a cemetery. It was large and cluttered with hundreds of headstones and in the background were buildings like those in an inner city suburb. A beam of sunlight rested on one headstone. There was writing but far too small so Sadie took a photograph. She'd look later on her computer screen.

The other painting was of a house at night, its lights all on. Well, the back of a house with a ramp leading from the back door. The aspect was from a distance and looking up as if from the bottom of a hill.

'Driftwood Cove.'

It had to be the cottage Sadie had been drawn to and even as her emotions pulled at her, a tingle of excitement ignited. She took another photograph.

Letting herself out of the cottage, she hoped to find Rebecca in her rocking chair but she wasn't there. Short of waiting here, which might upset Rebecca, there was nothing more Sadie could do. Not right now. She headed for her car and when she turned it to leave, saw Rebecca on the pier. Percy sat at her side while she stood, arms wrapped around herself, staring at the rowboat.

It was the loneliest thing Sadie had ever seen.

THIRTY-FOUR

Sadie reread the email from the studio, the one Lina had told her about, not fully believing her eyes. But there it was. The studio had been sold to another – much larger – and everything was on pause while the changeover took place. There were positive signs for the documentaries with a date set in a month to have a meeting with all the parties. For any projects which did go ahead there'd be considerably more funding and wider distribution.

She dialled Lina.

'Well, about time. Began to think there was no internet or phone coverage in your little town.'

'Funny coming from someone who has been too busy to talk for days. I just read the email.'

'Exciting times ahead,' Lina said. 'I've been offered a job as head of their research department.'

'Oh, Lina! Congratulations!'

'Thanks. Pumped, actually. Money is better than what I've made freelancing but it will be strange to be an employee.' She laughed. 'Unsure if I can do as I'm told.'

'And what about our studio's staff? Owners?'

'Some have been offered jobs but most are going their own way. Not everyone wants to work for a major studio with all the hierarchy and departments but the way I look at it, I finally get a bit of security in my life. Now all I need is a decent apartment like yours and I'll be in bliss. Bit over the flat-sharing.'

Lina deserved this. She was incredibly talented at her job and would be an asset in the new structure.

'What about you, Sades? Excited or blah about this?'

'Unsure. I'm happy for you though.'

This added a whole new element to think about. Working with a big studio would offer opportunities she'd longed for, as long as they let her have the freedom to dig deep into social issues the way she always had.

'Anyway... I did find out something about your mystery woman. Actually, doubt it is anything but I searched for the name Meyers going back to just over one hundred years ago in case I got anything which might lead to her family.'

'Good thinking.'

'You really could have used Trove for this. Plenty of good information there if you look.'

Lina was right. But Sadie had already searched Trove – the massive database which housed Australian historical information – and come up empty-handed.

'Anyway, there was a Mary Hamilton – née Meyers – who lived in Melbourne and died about eighty years ago. I'll email the info shortly. She was only youngish, early thirties. There was a funeral notice. Survived by a husband and two children. That's pretty much it and although the age might fit as Rebecca's mother, it's a stretch that they're connected.'

'In Melbourne? Do you know which area?'

'Screenshotted the notice and it's on its way. I have to go, Sadie. Zoom call in five.'

'Before you go, if I stay on here a bit longer, are you okay to keep apartment-sitting?'

'Are you kidding? Stay as long as you want.'

A minute after Lina hung up, her email arrived. There was little more in the screenshot than Lina had said. Name of the cemetery and that the service would be graveside. No flowers. Donations to the Spastic Society of Victoria.

Sadie leaned back in her chair. Why there? Obviously it was a good cause and in the nineteen fifties would have needed every penny they could get but if there was a personal connection, then was it Mary? Or one of the children? The society had changed its name some time ago but would they have records going back so far?

Too many questions.

No wonder Rebecca had clammed up.

'Are you home, love?'

'Yes, Mum. Be right down.'

But when she reached the bottom of the stairs, the front door was wide open with no sign of her mother apart from her handbag being on the sideboard near the door. She pulled on shoes and went outside.

'Can you move your car into the garage?'

Sadie followed the sound of Pam's voice, finding her unlocking the tilt door at the front of the garage.

'Did I hear you correctly?'

'You did. Got your keys?'

'Be right back.' Sadie sprinted inside again and grabbed them. In the time she'd been home that door hadn't been opened.

Pam was inside, carrying Dad's boots in one hand as she wandered back to the entrance. 'Go on. There's a storm coming tonight so it's best to get that fancy car of yours out of the way of damage.'

Once Sadie had parked the car she noticed the bottles she'd meant to give to Rebecca. She carried them out with her. Pam stood in front of the van but her eyebrows rose seeing the bottles.

'I forgot to give them to Rebecca.'

'Ah. Well, pop them down for a minute.'

'Okay.' Sadie placed them on the ground beside the boots. 'What's going on, Mum?'

Pam's hands tugged at each other. 'Since you arrived you've asked a lot of questions about the van. Why wasn't I driving it to work. Why didn't I want to own it. Offering to get the tyres fixed. And all along I kept putting off telling you the one and only reason why I haven't laid a finger on it since the day of your father's funeral.'

Little hairs on Sadie's arms stood up and there was an insistent prickle behind her eyes but somehow she kept her body still and mouth shut.

'Ron had a heart attack. You know this from the death certificate and me telling you. But there's more, Sadie. We'd had an argument. Probably the worst one ever because I yelled at him and told him... well, things I'd bottled up for a long time. He stormed off, just like he used to but hadn't for a while. He'd been so much better. And he picked up his keys and slammed the front door. I expected him to go for a drive and come back.'

A block of ice was stuck in Sadie's throat.

'After a bit I came outside because I hadn't heard the van start. It was there, here, and he was behind the wheel. I tapped on the window. Wanted to say sorry for yelling and tell him the kettle was on if he'd like a cuppa. But he didn't respond.' Pam's face turned white and her eyes were huge. 'Daddy died in the van, love. And it was all my fault.'

Sadie reached her mother just as she sank to the ground. She held her tight against her chest and rocked Pam as months of guilt and regret and sorrow poured out.

'Not your fault, Mummy. Never yours.'

. . .

'All we seem to do lately is weep and wail. I'm past that whole menopause thing so really don't have an excuse.'

'Well I'm not but you know I don't do emotions as a rule.'

It might only be five in the afternoon but Sadie and Pam sat on the front verandah with a bottle of wine open. Both had cried until there was nothing left. Then Pam had cried again when Sadie closed the garage door. And now her mother had clear eyes and a ready smile. Amazing the power of tears.

'I have to tell you something, Mum.'

'Not a question though?'

Sadie laughed. 'Nope. Just a comment. The other day when I met Bess, Annette, and Marge? Annette started to say something about you finding Dad but was cut off by Bess and marched away. I guess my face showed surprise. Anyway I did puzzle over it and figured there was a lot more to what happened than I'd been told and I actually had no idea how to broach it.'

Pam reached over and squeezed her hand. 'From now on, we have to be honest with each other. And I'll start. The other day I found a folder on the inn's computer. You know your father kept everything organised whether for the accountant or bills or customers. But this one was called Starfish and it was inside a folder he kept for church matters.'

Goosebumps rose on Sadie's arms.

'I have no idea why he did this but the folder contains copies of emails and photographs. All of the ones you told me you'd sent.'

'He kept them?'

Pam nodded and released Sadie's hand. 'Without ever showing me. I do wonder... the couple of emails from you which I had seen earlier made me cry and he hated that. I missed you dreadfully and my only explanation is that he was protecting me in some mixed-up way.'

'Oh, Mum.'

'I know. But now we can look at them together. When you want to. Having you home has been difficult, if I might say. Confronting. Worrying. And absolutely wonderful.'

'Thanks... I think.'

'The last bit is all that matters. Every day I feel a bit stronger than the last. I'm actually excited to see what Daniel will do for the inn. And the only part of my life which is sad is knowing it won't be too long before you go home.'

Sadie filled Pam in on her conversation with Lina and her mother's eyes brightened.

'You'll stay longer?'

'For another couple of weeks, yes. And I have a lot to think about. Since I came back to Rivers End I get the feeling the universe is sending me a message and it keeps getting louder.'

Pam's smile filled Sadie's heart.

'For now though, you and I need to just enjoy this evening. Wine, home delivery – no arguments, we're ordering pizza in – and maybe we can play some music.'

'And dance?'

'And dance, Mum.'

* * *

For the first time in ages, Sadie slept in and so did Pam. When they ran into each other in the kitchen it was mid-morning and her mother was in a flap about getting to the inn to clean up after the latest guests before the next ones checked in. Rather than eat, they both went to the inn and Sadie helped. She'd had a couple of people respond to her job ad and had interviews planned for later in the day so at least there was hope of reducing the workload soon.

After making sure her mother had fresh coffee and something in the fridge for lunch, Sadie turned onto the road to Driftwood Cove. Overnight she'd been unable to stop thinking of the paintings and despite the hot and humid day knew she had to visit the town. She'd not got as far as Palmerston House before pulling over.

Rebecca was standing at a bus stop.

Her head was down and her shoulders drooping and for once, she looked her age. Whatever the significance of today, it weighed heavily on her and Sadie wasn't about to leave anyone, especially this lovely woman, alone when they were distressed. She climbed out of the car and Rebecca raised her eyes, showing her surprise when recognition dawned.

'Good morning. Well, almost afternoon. I was on my way to Driftwood Cove so would you care for a lift? Much nicer than the bus or standing in this heat.'

'Why are you going there?'

'Um... oh, I was keen to take a look at a couple of the houses Dan is building. He's going to help Mum with the inn.' It was only partly a lie.

'The bus will be along soon.'

'But my car is more comfortable. Come on, I'll drop you wherever you'd like to go.'

Although uncertainty flickered in Rebecca's eyes, she followed Sadie and settled in the passenger seat, careful to secure her seat belt.

They drove for a while in a silence which Sadie was reluctant to break. If Rebecca needed to be in Driftwood Cove today, then at least it wouldn't be on a bus. She glanced across.

'I have my handbag today. And Percy was fed this morning.'

'Oh... of course. I didn't think otherwise.'

Rebecca gave her a quick look with a smile. 'I'll find my own way home, but I appreciate the lift.' Then her smile faded and she turned back to watch the road ahead.

Once Sadie parked in the now-familiar spot near the park, Rebecca was out in a few seconds, having had no trouble finding the handle, which amused Sadie. She'd tell Pam that next time there was a complaint about her 'fancy' car.

'Which way are you heading, Rebecca?'

There wasn't an answer. Rebecca was staring at the gift shop. Hadn't she done that when Dan was about to drive them home the other week?

Then without a word, Rebecca crossed the road, not even checking for traffic. Sadie hurried to catch up, thankful for the quietness of the town today. The storm Pam had predicted hadn't eventuated last night but all day the humidity had risen and in the distance, dark clouds were looming. At least Rebecca had her hat in her hand, and there was a bottle of water peeking out of her handbag. But her mind was somewhere else. Or some time else.

Rebecca stopped outside the gift shop, palm on the glass of the big picture window, eyes moving across the display. With a shake of her head she stepped back and then went to the door and pushed it open. Sadie grabbed it before it closed and followed her in. Rebecca was at a wall filled with shelves, scouring it for who-knew-what so Sadie waited quietly. When she couldn't find what she wanted, Rebecca approached the counter and after a few seconds, a middle-aged woman appeared from the back of the shop with a welcoming smile.

'Oh... you're not Mrs Murphy,' Rebecca said.

'Mrs Murphy? Goodness, that's a blast from the past. I'm sorry, dear, but she sold the shop to my parents many years ago and sadly, she's also long gone.'

'But, she's keeping something for me.'

'Let me know your name and I'll take a look on our customer order shelf out the back.'

'Becky.'

Before the woman could move, Rebecca went very still and just as quickly, she rushed from the shop.

'Wait... I can check.'

'Excuse me. I'm with Rebecca but she's on a bit of a mission. Do you happen to know how long this shop has been here?' Sadie stepped forward.

'About seventy years. Is your friend alright?'

'Just reliving her past. You don't happen to know of a Meyer family who lived here once? Becky Meyer?'

Rebecca crossed the road again and was heading for the beach.

'Doesn't ring a bell. No Meyers at all in the town to my recollection and I grew up here.'

'Thanks, and sorry about that.'

Sadie got to the beach just as Rebecca stepped onto the rocks leading around the cliff. The incoming weather was whipping up the waves and while a low tide might make it a safe route on a calm day, it was too risky at the moment. What had been a breeze earlier was now a hot wind filling the air with sea spray.

She ran across the sand. 'Wait! Rebecca, you need to stop.'

It was only when a wave broke over the edge of the rock that Rebecca paused, hands going up in front of her as if expecting to be dragged back into the depths although it was nowhere near her.

'Becky!'

Sadie finally caught up and took Rebecca's hand. Confusion filled the other woman's eyes as she let Sadie lead her back to the sand and then, under the trees. She sank onto a bench and drank from the water bottle when Sadie opened it. Once she'd had her fill, she replaced the cap and returned it to her bag, then gazed at Sadie.

'Why did you call me Becky?'

'You weren't responding to Rebecca, and you called yourself Becky in the gift shop.'

'She only lives here.'

'In this town? Becky does? In your memories?'

'I wasn't sure this was the right location, Sadie. I'd picked it on a map before I bought my home but it wasn't until I saw the gift shop I was certain.' Rebecca was herself again but her hands shook terribly and Sadie took them both in hers. 'Time plays games with the memory. I knew the name Driftwood Cove but there are others the same and perhaps I'd changed it in my head but last time I came here and sat up the hill, where the view let me see beyond the cliff, more pieces fell into place.'

A thousand questions spun in Sadie's head. Her instincts had been spot on but why was it so important to Rebecca to return?

'Do you have family here? Let me help find what you're looking for. Please, let me.'

Although Rebecca's lips moved, nothing came out. She lifted her chin and put her shoulders back and the connection between them was cut as shutters came down in her eyes. But then her face softened and she released a low sigh and squeezed Sadie's fingers.

'Would you help me get to the top of the hill, dear? I have one more place to visit.'

THIRTY-FIVE

62 YEARS AGO

Today the weather is nice again and even Aunt Ethel comes to the beach although she complains the whole time and keeps her shoes on. Charlie brings his sailboat and he and I sit in the shallow part of the lagoon and pretend to be sailors. After the boat fills with water and sinks, thanks to Charlie creating a tidal wave with his hands, I tell him that is why being in a boat is a bad idea. But Aunt Ethel overhears.

'You might think differently about an ocean liner, such as the *Marconi*. Spacious cabins with staff to make your bed. Mine has its own living area and balcony as well. Several restaurants including one which is fine dining with formal dress. A swimming pool.'

Sounding worse by the minute.

'Becky doesn't like the ocean, Auntie.' Charlie begins blowing bubbles on the surface.

'Travelling on a luxury ship is something most people will never experience. You really should come with me and discover what the world has to offer.'

Charlie's head shoots up. 'Becky lives here, Aunty. She belongs to us.'

I can't help giggling but I don't like the way the conversation is going.

Dad scoops Charlie out of the water and onto a towel. 'Becky doesn't belong to anyone but Becky. She is part of our family, of course, but the time will come that she'll leave home to start a life of her own.' He gives me a smile. It doesn't help.

'Why would you leave, Becky?'

'Not leaving, Charlie.'

'But one day. And who will bake cupcakes if you go?'

'I'm quite certain your father could bake cupcakes, Charlie,' Aunt Ethel pipes up. 'He used to be quite a capable person. Lived on his own before he met your mother and kept his house nice and tidy and cooked his own meals. But when she came along, he handed everything over, didn't you?'

Dad looks stern. 'You forgot to mention that thanks to my beautiful wife, who loved nothing more than being at home with our children and refused to let me do anything on week-days other than concentrate on my career, I got into a position to provide financial security for my family. How else would I have been able to buy this place and work mostly from home rather than being away all the time? I'm not the one using our inheritance, Ethel.'

Charlie's eyes were wide and his mouth was open. Neither of us ever heard Dad stand up for himself but we both knew the truth. He and Mum loved each other which was all that mattered.

Aunt Ethel sniffed. 'You believe you are doing the best for these children and certainly Charlie's school is helping his mobility. But poor Rebecca deserves a chance to shine rather than be your unpaid housemaid.'

'I am *not* a housemaid!' My voice rises as I almost throw myself out of the lagoon. 'I love helping out.'

'And, she would learn how to be a young lady.' The look from Aunt Ethel sends a chill up my spine. 'However, what I said is unfair and I apologise. Becca, I know you love helping and you are so good at doing the drudgery around the home. Cleaning, cooking, taking care of your father and brother. Wouldn't you like to do some things for yourself? Challenge yourself?'

My hands are tightly curled up and all I want is to scream at her stupid face with its orange lipstick and blue eyeshadow but Charlie begins to cry so I find some deep strength inside and lower my voice. 'I'm about to begin to go bike riding with a friend. And I sketch. I love art and am going to paint a lot of important pictures which will be hung in galleries all over the world. I'm happy with my life, Auntie.'

I'm not waiting around for more arguments and go to cuddle Charlie. Dad's head has dropped and out of all of this, seeing him like that worries me more than anything.

It took a while for Charlie to settle down. He hates raised voices and arguments and each one of us said sorry to him. We all went back to the house and got cleaned up and for a while, things were quiet. I was with Charlie in his bedroom but I think Dad went to his study and I really don't care where Aunt Ethel was.

'Grown-ups are loud, Becky.'

Charlie leaned against the window sill. He'd been looking out at the column for a while.

'Sure are. And I was loud. Sorry.'

'Brave, bold, Becky. I liked what you said. You want to be with us.'

'Yes I do.'

He gave me a little smile then his brow wrinkled in thought. 'If you want to do other things then Dad and I are good alone. Not as good. But we'd still be family even if you weren't here. Wouldn't we?'

My heart aches and I kneel beside him. 'Always family, Charlie. The three of us.'

'The three of us. Good.'

For a while we are quiet, looking out of his window. The sea is calm today. A really pretty deep shade of blue and there's not a cloud to be seen. Something glints in the sunlight on the column. A bit like last night with the tiny lights I saw. There has to be an explanation but I'm not about to go out there and find out. In a few more hours, Aunt Ethel will go away again and we can forget about her. I wish she would decide never to visit again. Maybe she'll die or something.

I play with the thought.

She might fall overboard. No, drowning isn't nice.

But if she went to sleep in her cabin after the bed was newly made by the staff and she never woke up, well that wasn't so bad. She'd never know.

'Becky, why are you smiling like that?'

'Like what?'

'Scary smile.'

Scary thinking. I shake my head and get up. She's Dad's sister and I guess he loves her and would miss her. And even though I don't feel guilty about those thoughts, I can never share them with anyone.

Dad makes dinner a bit earlier than usual and after we eat and wash up, he and Aunt Ethel say they have to talk in his study for a while.

'What about, Dad? Are you buying us a pony?'

'Good grief, no. A kitten is enough,' Dad says. 'We have some grown-up paperwork to look at. About family stuff.'

It happens every time she visits and Dad had once explained it was something about a trust fund their parents had set up a long time ago. It was to do with Aunt Ethel's school and

I didn't really understand. Dad came from Perth and moved to Melbourne to study and work and had never been back again.

'Will we play a game later?' I ask.

'No. Your aunt and I will be a while. You and Charlie go ahead though.'

We don't get a chance because Tim taps on the back door before we decide what we want to play. He won't come in. His hair is wet and he's very happy about something.

'Can you come down to the beach? All of you?'

I peer past him at the almost dark sky.

'Dad's busy tonight. Why?'

'Well you and Charlie then. I've got something special to show you. It's for Charlie.'

Of course, Charlie overhears and before I can protest we are walking down the hill. I have our torch and Tim has a much larger one which I carry because he has Charlie on his back.

This is the first time I've been down here this late. There's only a bit of gold in the sky from the sunset but it is light enough to see a rowboat pulled up on the sand. Tim goes right to it and sits Charlie on one of the seats. Charlie lets out a whoop and I feel my stomach turn.

'What's going on?'

'I wanted to do this last night but the storm stopped me,' Tim says. 'This is my real birthday present, Charlie.'

'Boat is good.'

'We are going to row out to the lighthouse,' Tim says.

'Oh no we're not!' I reach for Charlie who folds his arms and shakes his head.

Tim has something in his hand. A life jacket. 'Charlie can wear this because I can adjust it for his size, I think. He'll be perfectly safe and so will you. The water is calm and we'll only be a few minutes.'

I shake my head. How could I even consider this?

'Come on, Becky. Brave, bold, Becky.'

'But Charlie, what if something bad happens?'

He's smiling at me and so is Tim like they feel sorry for me and I remember what Aunt Ethel said about challenging myself. I glance up at the house. What if she and Dad are talking about me going to Perth? What if I find my bags are packed when I go back and my whole life changes?

'It's for my birthday, Becky. I'll protect you.'

I have to take control over my own future. I'm not scared of the dark and I'm not scared of trying new things. Not much, anyway. If I do this, I'll prove I can be more than a housemaid. And Dad said that a boat would be a safe way to reach the lighthouse.

Before I can change my mind I'm helping Tim pull the rowboat closer to the sea. Then he puts the lifejacket on Charlie and says I should get in.

My heart is thudding so much it hurts and I don't think I'm breathing at all. Not seeing into the water in the dark lets me pretend it isn't there and when Tim gets in and starts rowing I can't believe I'm in this little vessel. I'm facing the beach and the lights from our house are getting further away but still are like a beacon to guide me home. The rocking of the rowboat isn't awful and Charlie is chatting to Tim at a million miles an hour. As long as I don't think hard about where we are then I'm fine.

'Okay, so I'm going to jump out in a second with this rope and tie it to one of the bits of rock. Then I'll lift you both out.'

I want to say no. We shouldn't go onto the rocks and nobody is going to lift me but Tim disappears for a few seconds and then Charlie is squealing in delight as Tim swings him up. I have no idea how but I scramble onto the rock and kind of sprawl on it expecting it will move. It doesn't and the column rises up in front of me, so high it might touch the clouds on a rainy day.

Tim and Charlie are sitting nearby and we all look at each

other and laugh. We got here and it is one of the bravest things I've ever done.

'Watch,' Tim says, and points at the top.

We crane our necks.

As the last of the gold from the sunset fades, a ring of light shines from the top of the column. Lanterns, all flashing in time as a perfect beacon.

'It's real!' Charlie screams, his hands flapping so fast he almost topples over.

But Tim keeps him upright and grins at me and I'm grinning and tears are falling down my cheeks.

Charlie's lighthouse is real.

'Uh oh.'

Tim's muttered words send a shard of panic through me.

He's at the edge of the flat rock.

The rowboat is gone.

'Where is it?'

'Mustn't have tied it properly.' He flashes his torch around and we spot it, a bit more than halfway back to shore. 'I'll go and get it.'

'What? No, you shouldn't swim at night and it's so far.'

He pulls his shoes off. 'Back soon.' Tim hands me the torch and dives in.

'Nice diving, Tim.' Charlie shuffles to the edge on his behind. 'Rowboat left without us.'

'Tim should have tied it better and now we're stuck here.' I sound cranky because I'm scared. Tim was confident and calm but now I can barely see him as he powers through the ocean. 'Where are your shoes, Charlie? You shouldn't have taken them off.'

'Don't be cross.'

I give him our torch and use Tim's to find the shoes and go to pick them up.

'I'll help get the rowboat, Becky.'

What a silly thing to say. I need to calm down. This was a lovely gift from Tim to Charlie and the rowboat will be back soon and once we're home we'll laugh about it. I glance up at the beacon of flashing lights. What a kind person Tim is to have climbed up there and put lanterns on to make it real. I'll go and sit with Charlie to watch out for the rowboat returning.

Charlie isn't where I left him.

Our torch is there.

'Where are you?'

There's no answer.

I scream his name.

He wouldn't have got into the water. He just wouldn't.

There's something in the sea and it comes into the light of the torch, floating toward me.

The lifejacket.

Charlie isn't in the lifejacket.

He's going to drown. Like Mum drowned.

Brave, bold, Becky.

I kick off my shoes and drop the torch and take a deep breath and jump.

THIRTY-SIX

NOW

'We're going to get soaked in a moment. Would you prefer to sit in the car for a bit?'

Rebecca stood just inside the front gate of the same cottage Sadie had visited. They'd been there for ten minutes or more, Rebecca seemingly unable to move any closer. Thunder was grumbling away as dark clouds loomed overhead.

'No. I have to see...'

'See what?'

Holding on to Sadie's arm, as she had been since they stepped onto the property, Rebecca carefully followed an overgrown path of stepping stones to a narrow verandah. Instead of going to the front door, Rebecca released Sadie and placed the palms of both her hands onto one of the windows.

'I was distraught that my father uprooted us from our apartment in Melbourne. Heartbroken. He tore me away from my mother's grave where I used to go and talk to her. I was twelve when we moved here that wet spring day. When the removalists were leaving I stood on the other side of this window and wished with all my heart to go with them.'

Mary Meyer-Hamilton's daughter. She had to be.

'How long did you live here?'

'Only a few months.'

'You went back to Melbourne?'

Rebecca dropped her hands. 'I've never been back there in all these years.'

The rain began in earnest, tapping on the metal roof.

'We should go in.' Rebecca tried the door, which was locked.

'But we don't know who owns this anymore.'

'If the lock hasn't been changed then I imagine that I do.'

With that remarkable announcement, Rebecca stepped out into the rain and leaned down to turn one of the stones in the path. Sadie went after her but Rebecca had found what she wanted and was returning. Back on the verandah she held up a very old key and then wiped it on her shirt. Inserting it into the lock she seemed to hold her breath but it turned and the door opened.

This was surreal. Rebecca knew where the key was to a house which was close to being demolished. She'd guessed that the town she'd chosen to live near was one where she'd spent only a few months as a child six decades past. And she thought she might own the house. Sadie could not have written a book any stranger than this.

They went inside, leaving the door ajar as they stepped into an open living area with a large kitchen on the other side of a long bench. There was some furniture, old and dusty, and the smell of neglect and abandonment permeated the room.

'I made so many meals in there. Sometimes three a day for us all. Cupcakes and cookies and cakes for Charlie.' She laughed shortly. 'He'd have liked that alliteration. And burned my arm once. It made him cry more than me. Look, I covered the scar.' It was a small lighthouse tattoo.

Rebecca moved through the house room by room, sometimes reaching for Sadie's hand. 'We used to play board games all the time. That coffee table was the perfect height for Charlie's cut-down chair and he'd watch television from the sofa.'

As desperate as she was to ask questions, Sadie kept her mouth shut. Rebecca was reliving the past in a way Sadie could barely comprehend and it was both a privilege and a heartache to witness.

'My father had his study in there. He was a clever man. A scientist who wrote important papers. And a kind man. At least until... well, until he wasn't.'

Rebecca bypassed one room and went into another. Sparsely furnished and covered in dust it showed signs of belonging to a youngster who loved art, if the sketches hanging on the wall and open drawing book was anything to go by. 'My bedroom. And everything I owned before I was taken away. Who does that, Sadie? Who takes a child from their family because they think they know what is best for them?'

Without waiting for an answer she exited the bedroom and then paused outside another. Its door was open just a crack. Rebecca didn't touch the door or look in but she spoke to herself. Words so quiet Sadie could only make out one or two. *Failed you. Forgive me.*

Turning her back on the room, she returned to the door they'd gone past before and opened it. 'I made a place where I could sit and talk to my mother. Even at twelve I knew she was only a memory, but she was the one thing of mine I could hold on to. Charlie didn't really remember her and Dad was too broken to speak about Mum very often but she'd visit me in my dreams.'

There wasn't much in here. An old wardrobe and a dressing table.

But Rebecca's lips turned down and her tight hold on her emotions wavered as she picked up a small jewellery box. Sadie had seen the kind. Turn the key in the back, open the top, and a ballerina would dance to music. 'I can't believe this is still here. Would you open the wardrobe, Sadie?'

Inside were a few shoes and some clothes. It reeked of mothballs.

'Everything left behind.'

'Who left it behind, Rebecca?'

She tenderly placed the box down. 'My father. I'm guessing, of course, but I expect he lived here long after... what happened. Or he might have abandoned the house but never sold it or rented it to anyone. My bedroom is just how I left it.'

Lightning flashed across the sky and Rebecca jumped. When thunder boomed overhead, she fled this shrine-of-sorts and entered the kitchen where she stood in the middle. Her face was drawn and she looked ready to collapse from exhaustion. Sadie turned on the cold tap and let the water run for a minute until it cleared.

'Glasses in the top cupboard.'

It was full of glasses and plastic tumblers and cups and saucers including a set in an exquisite pattern. Sadie collected two of the glasses, rinsed them out and filled them. 'Do you want to sit for a while?' She pressed one of the glasses into Rebeca's hands. 'Or shall we go?'

'I'd be in here and Charlie would call for more cupcakes from the loungeroom. Or he'd scoot around behind me in his wheelchair and I'd shoo him out in case I dropped something on him. He told me I'd become a famous chef one day and he was half right. I could never be famous, of course. It would have meant someone finding out my real identity.'

She finally drank the water.

'I don't understand. Why shouldn't your real identity be known?'

Forehead creased, Rebecca gazed at Sadie. 'I wonder if it really mattered. Would you mind taking me home, dear?'

'Hello?'

There was a tap on the open front door and Dan's head appeared.

Once again Rebecca jumped and her glass smashed onto the floor. Sadie guided her past the worst of the shards as Dan rushed in.

'What on earth are you both doing here? This place isn't stable.'

'I can assure you, Daniel, there is nothing wrong with this house. Not structurally. Are you here to demolish it?'

Dan took Rebecca's arm and she leaned against him.

'Not mine to demolish, Rebecca. I was heading home and saw Sadie's car. Then the open door.'

'We were just going back to Rebecca's cottage,' Sadie said. 'Would you mind taking her? I might just quickly clean up the glass and lock up and then I'll be along. Is that alright with you, Rebecca?'

There was a nod, but from the slumped shoulders and grip Rebecca had on Dan, she was spent. Dan didn't ask any more questions, but bundled Rebecca outside and then tucked her under his jacket to get her into his four-wheel drive. He ran back to where Sadie waited on the verandah.

'I'll explain later, I promise. She's so fragile, Dan. This was her home as a child and there's a tragedy she hasn't spoken of but I think she lost her brother here.'

'Shall I help you clean up?'

'No, I can. She needs to be home, I think.'

Dan wrapped Sadie in his arms and kissed her, just one quick kiss, then was sprinting through the rain. His timing had been perfect. She touched her lips. He was as perfect a person as she'd ever met. Perfect for her.

Just as Rebecca had said she'd done many decades earlier, Sadie pressed her hands against the window and watched Dan drive away in the pouring rain. Some poor cyclist in a hooded rain-coat slowly rode by... but then circled around, their face turning to look at the house as they passed. It was too far to see their features but something was familiar about whoever it was. Prob-ably a local she'd seen in the town, curious about the front door being open.

She closed and locked it. Dan coming in was one thing but she didn't wish to attract the attention of strangers.

Sadie found a dustpan beneath the sink and swept up the broken pieces of glass. The pantry was almost empty, other than a few old tins of food and a packet of plastic bin liners. She took one and emptied the glass into it, careful not to cut herself when she knotted the end.

The house was dark and sad and lonely. Where a young family once had laughed and eaten and played and slept there was nothing but the ghosts of memories and dust. Whatever happened here so long ago was tearing Rebecca apart. The jewellery box was important to her and Sadie returned to the room a young girl had created to feel close to her dead mother. She turned the key on the back of the box a few times then opened the lid and a sweet little ballerina began to twirl as music played. It juddered and the dancer stopped and started. Sadie closed the lid. This might be something George could fix.

She closed the door behind herself and hesitated. Although she'd told Dan she'd be along soon, this might be her only chance to gather more information about Rebecca's past, or at least her childhood. The floor creaked underfoot as she pushed open the door where Rebecca had spoken of failing and forgive-ness. It was another bedroom with little in the way of personal items. There were posters on the wall of nineteen seventies' pop groups. A bed stripped bare. A bedside table with a lamp in the shape of a lighthouse. In the wardrobe was a box of Lincoln Logs. Nothing else.

The window overlooked the back yard where Sadie had met

the elderly man. It was a lovely view from here of the little bay
with its column of limestone rising from the sea.

Sadie glanced at the lamp. A lighthouse so similar to the one
in Rebecca's painting. She looked at her phone for the image
she'd taken all that time ago. The one in the painting was almost
identical to the lamp. Tears misted her eyes and she was hollow
from grief of a loss which wasn't her own. It was time to go back
to Rivers End.

'She took a long shower and has had some soup and she asked
me to make sure you come and see her.'

Dan had met Sadie on Rebecca's front verandah and they
sat, holding hands, while he filled her in. The warmth from his
fingers melted some of the ice she was sure had filled her veins
on the way back. Her mind was weary from so many scenarios
about a twelve-year-old girl who had changed her identity and
none of them made sense.

'Rebecca said she'd been waiting for a bus when you
stopped. Thank goodness you saw her.'

'Has she ever told you about her brother? Charlie?'

He shook his head.

'I'll tell you.'

They both looked up, startled. Rebecca was in the doorway,
Percy in her arms. The colour was back in her face and her hair
was drying into silver waves over her shoulders.

'I'm sorry, I don't mean to pry,' Sadie said.

With a wry smile, Rebecca stepped inside. 'Of course you
do. Isn't that what journalists do? Sadie, come and have tea.
Daniel, go home. And thank you.'

Dan stood and pulled Sadie to her feet to hold her against
his chest. 'I'm being evicted. Call me, okay? When you're
finished here, or later, or anytime.'

She tilted her face upwards and they kissed and more of his

warmth saturated her body. If this kept up she'd be a blazing sun in no time. That thought was the best she'd had in hours and reluctantly she stepped away and waved as he ran through the rain. Again.

When she went inside, closing the front door, she found Rebecca staring at the painting of the lighthouse. Percy was at her feet now and meowed at Sadie without moving.

'Are you certain you want the burden of my life story in your head?'

'I'm here as a friend, Rebecca. Not a journalist. But growing up I drove everyone around me crazy with questions and in some ways, I'm still that person. That first day, when I saw the lake from the top of one of the hills and wandered through that magical forest, something happened. At the risk of sounding like I'm ditzy, I was drawn to the cottage beside the lake. And when a certain green-eyed black cat stopped me in my tracks, I was lost.'

'You have become dear to me.' Without taking her eyes from the painting, Rebecca reached out a hand and Sadie grasped it. 'I have never told anyone my story but I'm no longer willing to take it to my grave unsaid. I think it is time.'

THIRTY-SEVEN

Over a fresh pot of tea, sitting outside on the verandah, Rebecca told her story. The air was warm enough to be comfortable. Percy was curled in Rebecca's lap. The lake was misty and the rowboat rocked gently under rain which had lost its intensity. They might have been two old friends enjoying a companionable afternoon together.

But there was nothing comfortable about the older woman's story. The heartbreak of losing her mother when she was only eight. Confusion as Charlie, who was three or four years old at the time, was evaluated over and over by doctors until being declared to have spastic palsy.

'Cerebral palsy is the accepted term now although Charlie had the muscle tightness which is specific to what was known as being spastic. Back then any number of names were used by the average person, and some cruel versions. I protected him from the nastiness as much as I was able, but he still heard them. Yet Charlie had the most beautiful soul and knew he was far more than his difficult body.'

Their father's decision to move to Driftwood Cove had shocked young Becky, who feared losing the connection with her mother. Living by the sea and having to spend so much time at the beach was frightening for the girl whose mother had drowned and she'd resented her father's insistence on taking her little brother into the waves time and again. Despite this, Becky had settled in the town and was making friends.

'Tim was two years my senior and lived a few streets inland. He never judged me for protecting Charlie so fiercely and he never saw my brother as anything other than a seven-year-old kid. Then, briefly, an eight-year-old.'

She'd dropped her head and Percy woke, making a soft sound of love.

'We can talk later if you need to rest,' Sadie said.

'This is the only time I'm telling this so it is now or never.'

Even though the story pulled at Sadie's heart, there was hope in it. Hope that Charlie would continue to gain strength and new skills to help him as he grew up. Hope that Becky would do well at school and follow her dream to be an artist. Hope that the small family would find their way past the pain. But then Aunt Ethel had arrived. Rebecca's eyes had hardened. This was when everything in Becky's world had changed.

'It never occurred to me not to jump into the sea that night. Dad had made me take swimming lessons after Mum died but I'd hated them and he gave up after a while. I'd never swum in the sea and, quite frankly, was convinced I would drown. I remember going right under the surface. I'd taken a breath but the shock of how deep I dropped made me panic and I must have kicked so hard I breached the top of the water. I tried to swim but my arms wouldn't co-ordinate and I went under again.'

Sadie leaned forward, her heart racing. 'What happened next?'

'My fingers touched something above me and I held on and kicked again. It was the lifejacket and I hung on to it and kept using my legs and I managed to stop going under and even move back toward the beach, although very slowly.'

The lifejacket had been on Charlie. One vest for three kids out in the ocean at night.

'I heard yelling. People screaming my name and Charlie's. Dad and Aunt Ethel. Nobody had any light because both torches were back on the rock and by then it was quite dark. Only Tim's lanterns at the top of the column were on but they were too high and too weak to be helpful. I called out but I doubt they heard me thanks to the seawater I'd swallowed, yet out of the night Tim appeared in the rowboat and he hauled me into it. I lay on the bottom gasping and crying and he kept repeating 'sorry' as he rowed us back to shore.'

Shivers went up Sadie's spine and all the hairs on her arms were standing. The rowboat in the painting, the lighthouse, the terror of the night – all were gripping her heart.

Pain etched Rebecca's face and her fingers stroked Percy, over and over.

'When we were getting closer to the shore I saw Dad and Aunt Ethel. He was halfway up the beach and carrying something in his arms. Tim yelled that I was safe and then Dad began to run up the hill and I realised he had Charlie in his arms and I started screaming. I jumped out into the shallows and Aunt Ethel grabbed me and slapped me and then hugged me. I just wanted to run after Dad but she held on to me until I stopped struggling and told me I needed to go with her.'

'To the house?'

'She meant for me to leave home. With her.'

'What?'

'She said Dad was taking Charlie to the hospital. There wasn't time for an ambulance. Tim tried to tell me something and she yelled at him to shut up and go home and if he didn't she'd have him charged by the police for putting our lives in danger. He didn't even pull the rowboat all the way in and disappeared around the bottom of the cliff. We were alone. Standing in the waves. And I asked her if Charlie would be alright.'

Rebecca reached for her tea, which must have been cold but she drank it. Sadie had no questions. She wasn't certain she could speak at the moment.

Tea cup back on the table, Rebecca leaned back and closed her eyes. When she opened them they were shining with tears.

'My aunt was very calm then. She said Charlie was in a bad way and Dad had told her she should take me with her to Perth because I had failed Charlie. It was my fault and he knew the police would take me away from him and put me into a youth training centre so I was better off going to another state.'

Sadie's voice returned. 'How dare she!'

A smile touched Rebecca's lips. 'You sound like the young me. Always fighting against injustice.'

'You were a minor. Nobody would have blamed you and taken you away... oh. Except, your father might have been seen as unfit for allowing it to happen. I'm sorry. I shouldn't have said that.'

'Not the first time I've heard it. The way she worded it, I felt I had no choice. Dad wasn't there to say otherwise. He hadn't even stayed long enough to see for himself I was alive. Charlie was on his way to hospital which was my doing. And if I was removed from home by the authorities then so too might Charlie be.' Her voice dropped to a whisper. 'Aunt Ethel told me he would end up in an orphanage.'

Before she could stop herself, Sadie burst into tears.

'Oh goodness, child. Here, take a tissue or ten. And a cat.'

Percy appeared on her lap, and then a tissue box. How could she cry at a moment like this? Poor Rebecca deserved her attention, not her hysterics.

'And this is why we are friends, Sadie. We are connected by our empathy no matter how hard we each try to bury it. Just please, promise me something?' There was a hand on hers. 'Stop running.'

She had no idea how to answer so dried her tears and smooched Percy and that helped. Planting a smile on, she met Rebecca's eyes.

'Crying is healthy. Not that I understood its benefits for a long time. Everything was a blur for a while. I do recall Aunt Ethel packing a suitcase for me while I stood at the window. The moon came out and I saw the rowboat near the lighthouse rocks. How very strange to remember this little detail, but I wondered if it would forever go back and forward from beach to lighthouse.' She laughed shortly. 'When Aunt Ethel began packing her rented car I wrote a note for Dad and left it on his desk. I told him I was so sorry and I would come back to him and Charlie. I promised I would. And said there was a frozen lasagne once Charlie was home.'

'Even back then you were a chef. And always looking out for your family.'

'It was second nature. I found myself in the car and we were driving for a long time in the night. I had begged to stop at the hospital but she drove past the turn-off and when I kept on about it she said in a very scary voice that she would take me to the police herself if I didn't co-operate. So I cried as quietly as I could until I must have fallen asleep. I don't remember how we got on the ocean liner but looking back I must have been deeply in shock. She told me she'd phoned Dad and there was no news about Charlie except he was still unconscious. And in just twenty-four hours I'd gone from saying I would never set foot on a boat to having almost drowned and now being a passenger on the *Marconi*.'

Percy was warm against Sadie's stomach. The rain was barely a heavy mist now but from the far distance came a low rumble of thunder. Another storm.

'We'd been at sea for a day or two and I must have been

thinking things through and working out that Aunt Ethel might have exaggerated to get me to go with her. I asked about Charlie. About Dad. So she went to talk to the captain and arranged a special kind of phone call. I remember the minute she returned to the cabin. She closed the door and her face was all red and upset and I knew she had terrible news.'

Rebecca reached across and collected Percy.

'Charlie had died.'

The rocking chair began to move. Back and forward. Back and forward. And Rebecca's eyes turned to the lake.

'Dad told my aunt that he never wanted to see me again and I was never to contact him. Ever. I couldn't believe he wouldn't forgive me and kept writing letters to Dad, but I wonder now if she prevented them from being posted, and the one time I tried to phone she locked me in my room for days. A few months later, Aunt Ethel showed me a certificate which said she adopted me. It proved Dad had turned his back on me and something in my soul just broke. I went to her stupid school for girls and hated every second of the first two years. I was angry and destructive and she stopped me attending and made me work in the kitchen there instead and tried to teach me at home. To this day I do not understand her motives. And then when I was just fifteen, on the third anniversary of my brother's death, I ran away. I longed to go home but what was the point? Dad didn't want me anymore and Charlie was dead.'

'Is this why you use your mother's maiden name?'

'You have been checking into my life, young woman. But yes. My name is Rebecca Mary Hamilton. Until three years ago I lived in fear of being found out. I moved a lot. My cooking skills got me jobs. But I never had any dealings with authority, no driver's licence or credit card. And that is my story.'

With a long sigh, Rebecca's body relaxed.

'What happened three years ago? What made you stop being fearful?'

'I began dreaming about Charlie and all I wanted was to say a proper goodbye. We never had the chance. Not with him nor my father. I know my dad is long gone. How could he not be when I'm close enough to seventy-five and he married Mum when he was thirty-five? So I researched and planned and when this little place came onto the market I felt the universe calling. Sometimes one has to listen. Sometimes it takes a lot of calling. And thanks to you, today I got to say my goodbyes.'

There was little more to speak of. Sadie had her answers. Rebecca had her closure. It didn't feel like closure to Sadie though and something nagged at the back of her mind.

'Sadie? I'm so tired. I might sleep for a while.'

'Would you like me to stay?'

'Thank you but no. Go and find Dan. Spend time with your mother. Listen to your heart before it is too late.'

After helping Rebecca clean up after their tea, Sadie hugged her tightly.

Today had helped Rebecca to heal. And given Sadie so much to consider about her own life but if she knew anything, it was that she wasn't going to ignore the universe any longer.

THIRTY-EIGHT

Back in her car, Sadie sent two messages. The first to Pam to say she was okay and sorry she would have to miss sitting in on the job interviews. She'd explain tonight. The second was to Dan.

> May I visit now?

> Yes.

She pulled up in his driveway beside the four-wheel drive. The garage doors were open and Dan was inside, building something. He met her at the front of the garage with a smile and a kiss and then brushed damp hair from her eyes.

'Rebecca cares greatly for you, Sadie.'

'I feel the same about her. But what she's been through in her life... ripped away from her family by an aunt with dubious motives... living her entire life in fear of being found and blamed for the death of her brother.' She was unable to go on, not unless she was prepared to sob her eyes out and today she'd cried more than she ever wanted to.

'Will you stay a while? I'm almost finishing making some flower boxes for my front verandah. Have you eaten?'

Sadie smiled. 'I haven't since breakfast but my stomach is still churning a bit.'

'Why?'

'Her baby brother's room was the worst. She didn't go in, but after you left I wanted to check everything was left as we found it. All that's in the bedroom was a box of building blocks, some posters of pop groups from the seventies, and a lamp in the shape of a lighthouse. Charlie loved lighthouses and thought the limestone column was one when they first moved in. Rebecca bought him that lamp from her pocket money.'

That nagging feeling was back.

Dan touched her cheek. 'What are you thinking?'

'Do you know much about seventies' pop groups?'

'Almost nothing.'

Feigning shock, Sadie shook her head. 'I seriously doubt we have any kind of future then. It was the best era ever.'

'Wait. Did you just say something about our future?'

'You imagined that bit. I should have taken a photo of the posters but everything was so distressing at the time. Are you better at mathematics than music?'

Although his eyes made it clear he preferred to pursue the subject of their future, Dan sighed. 'Care to elaborate?'

'I'm sorry to do this. I have to go.'

Dan reached into his pocket and removed car keys. 'Back to Driftwood Cove? How about I drive and you calculate on the way.'

Sadie did exactly that, once the four-wheel drive was on a smoother surface than the track from Dan's house. She was thankful to be in his vehicle which was better suited for the conditions now that the rain was getting heavier.

'Rebecca said she's almost seventy-five. Charlie is five years younger. So when he died, the day after his eighth birthday, it was the early nineteen sixties. Now, I only glanced at those posters but I'm certain one of them was for Edison Lighthouse, because the name stuck in my mind when I was making connections between the limestone column and the lamp on his bedside table.'

'Where is Edison Lighthouse?'

'Oh Dan. They're a pop group.'

'Sing me one of their songs.'

'You'd stop the car and leave me on the side of the road.'

He glanced across with a smile which sent her heart racing. 'I've heard you sing, remember?'

In a canoe for two on a river beneath the stars. As if she'd ever forget.

They turned onto the road to Driftwood Cove.

Ahead, the sky was even darker than during her visit earlier in the day and a blustery wind blew rubbish and small branches across the road. As they passed a building site, Dan made an annoyed sound at a huge tarpaulin which flapped madly in the breeze, attached only by one corner and exposing a stack of timber.

'Do you mind if I drop you at the house and come back? That's one of my sites and I don't want that internal timber ruined. Shouldn't even be out in the weather.'

'Stop now if you want. I can help.'

'We're almost there. But thanks and I won't be long.'

Sadie climbed out quickly once he pulled up outside Rebecca's old home and she hurried inside after collecting the key from its hiding spot. She closed the front door but didn't lock it in case she didn't hear Dan knock. Before going to the bedroom she collected the jewellery box and left it on the kitchen counter to remind herself to take it to George. Whether Rebecca ever wanted it was another thing but if she did, at least it would work again, assuming it was fixable.

She knew she was on a mission that would fail. The silly idea in her head that somehow Charlie had survived that night was a waste of time and energy and hope but Sadie knew she wouldn't sleep tonight if she didn't discount it. She must have remembered wrong.

Until she returned to the bedroom.

Not possible.

The poster was from the release of the first big hit from the group.

Sadie sank onto the bed and searched her phone for dates. She had a passion for seventies music and had a fair idea the UK group had become popular around nineteen seventy. But seeing it on one site after another was bittersweet. The band didn't exist in the early sixties.

Did another child live here?

There was no other child in the family. Sadie's mind darted to possibilities. Rebecca's father remarrying and having more children was the obvious one but why would Charlie's lamp be here?

Drawn to the window, Sadie gazed at the limestone column. With the storm almost overhead, waves were whipped up and crashed against the flat rock until it was almost submerged. But the night of the disaster had been fine and the sea calm, according to Rebecca, and the distance was swimmable.

The back of her neck chilled. Someone was watching her. She spun around but nobody was in the bedroom.

'Dan? Are you here?'

There was no reply and she returned to the window.

The man from the other day stood at the edge of the garden, staring at her. A hooded raincoat billowed around him from the wind rushing across the bay. And then he turned and vanished down the slope.

Sadie ran through the house and fumbled with the back door, finally unlocking it and flying out onto the small deck.

'Please wait!'

She was careful not to slip on the wet ramp but once on the grass, sped up, sprinting past the basketball hoop and shed and almost falling headlong onto a narrow, sandy track when the ground abruptly fell away. Somehow she kept herself more or less upright. The man was at the bottom, oblivious to her pursuit.

The rain stung as heavy drops turned into a downpour, soaking her through in seconds and blurring her vision. When the ground evened out and she was on sand, she paused, wiping her eyes. He was nowhere to be seen. Surely he wouldn't be so reckless as to go around the rocks at the bottom of the cliff?

Sadie was almost at a shallow lagoon when lightning cracked through the sky and hit the limestone column, turning the air green for a second. Thunder followed with a crash overhead which rocked the ground.

'Come here!'

She followed the shout to the entrance of the cave. The man stood just outside it, gesturing for her to hurry. As soon as she was close he shouted again, 'Go in.'

Fear of being hit by lightning overrode her normal sense of caution and she dived through the narrow entry. It was surprisingly large inside. Firm sand was beneath her feet and a few scattered rocks were large enough to sit upon and she chose one, sinking onto it and pulling her hair back so she could see.

He followed her in and dropped his raincoat on the ground and they sized each other up. He looked a little older than Rebecca. And he was, without doubt, the person on the bicycle earlier in the day. As little as Sadie knew, even after the revelations of the afternoon, there was one person he might be.

'Are you Tim?'

Half-expecting a terse reply, Sadie barely heard his answer over the storm, but she could read his lips. He'd said yes. The earlier chill at the back of her neck shot all the way down her spine.

In order to better hear him, Sadie rose and covered the distance, keeping at arm's length not because she felt threatened, but so she didn't intrude on his comfort zone. He didn't move but watched her through eyes which were partly curious and very wary. This was the person who'd befriended Charlie and later Becky. Who'd never judged her for trying to protect her brother but had been instrumental in his death. Or had he?

'I saw you ride past the house earlier. Did you happen to see who got into the four-wheel drive out the front?'

'Daniel.'

'You know Dan?'

'Renovating mine and my ex-wife's house. He's a decent bloke.'

You were married to Marge? Oh my goodness.

'He is. What about the woman?'

'Only saw her for a second. My eyesight is pretty good for an old fellow but I reckon I'm going to get someone to check it. People don't come back from the dead.'

Forcing her legs to hold her up as they began to shake, Sadie chose her words with great care. 'Why would you think Rebecca is dead?'

'You're a journalist. Seen you on telly and you've done good but now I have to wonder if you know your stuff. Becky ran away from that old crow of an aunt and then when Mr Hamilton was about to leave to go to Western Australia to look for her, a death certificate turned up.'

'But... no, that's not possible.'

Aunt Ethel showed me a certificate which said she adopted me.

How many fake certificates had the woman made?

'Tim, do you know anything about Aunt Ethel formally adopting Becky?'

Tim scowled. 'Adopting? Mr Hamilton would never have agreed. All he wanted was his daughter home but that woman said Becky was happy at the school and not having to cook and clean all the time. We didn't believe a word of it but going over there was nigh impossible at the time. Every time Mr Hamilton phoned that woman had a reason why Becky was unavailable. But Becky had left a note on his desk saying she was coming home soon.'

'Well, she was forced to leave by her aunt and she was never happy there. She cooked and cleaned at the school rather than studied.' Sadie had dropped her head and thought her words were low enough to be drowned out by the rain but then her wrist was grasped and she raised her eyes. Tim was furious.

'You're lying. How would you even know such a thing?'

'Because she told me. This afternoon, Tim. It was Rebecca you saw earlier.'

He released her and staggered back, the colour draining from his face. 'But... but why didn't she come home?'

'Because her father said he never wanted to see her again after Charlie died.'

'Is that what her aunt told her?' Understanding replaced the shock then Tim dropped onto one of the rocks, tears streaming down his face. 'Our Becky is alive?'

'She changed her surname and hid who she is for decades, afraid her father would be prosecuted for neglect over Charlie's death.'

Anguish filled the old man's face and he barely got the words out. 'She lived her whole life thinking her brother died that night?'

Thinking her brother died?

Dan was there, just inside the entry. For how long, Sadie didn't know but his eyes were on her, steady and comforting and giving her the strength to ask the final question.

'How could she think otherwise when her aunt told her he was dead?'

'I can assure you, Miss Forest. Charlie Hamilton is alive and well.'

THIRTY-NINE

Strands of seaweed moved with the current, the visibility better at last after several days of rolling storms. It was barely dawn and just light enough for Sadie to be amused by the juvenile whiting as they chased each other around the pylons of the jetty. Lungs burning, she surfaced and drew in long, slow breaths of salty air until her heart rate settled to a normal beat.

Lately, her heart had raced or thudded or completely stopped. Perhaps not the latter but it felt it at times. It was more than the discoveries about Rebecca's life. More than uncovering age-old deceptions. And a lot about coming to terms with her own past.

She rolled onto her back and floated, eyes wide to take in the big beautiful sky above with its changing palette of gold and pink and orange. Oh, how she loved this time of day and the velvet caress of the water.

She'd spent most of last night awake, going over every aspect of her life from her career and apartment to her mother and the revelations about her father. Rebecca had counselled her to follow her heart. To listen to the universe. And to stop running.

And that was the part she had the most trouble with because, until recently, her career was her only anchor.

A flash of movement from the top of the jetty was followed by someone diving into the sea nearby. A moment later, Dan surfaced.

With a grin, Sadie paddled closer. 'I thought you didn't approve of swimming unless it was broad daylight.'

He didn't bother answering, gently pulling her hands around his neck and gathering her in his arms. When they kissed, they sank into the calm water, slowly rotating until their air ran out. They resurfaced, spluttering and laughing, and then kissed again.

Once they were back on the jetty, watching the sunrise, legs dangling over the end, Sadie told Dan about her most recent findings of the Hamilton family history. Rebecca had mentioned bits and pieces over the past couple of days which led Sadie to her own investigation.

'Ethel Hamilton died a few years after she sent Rebecca's home-made death certificate to her brother. What a cruel and evil thing to do. Tim told me Mr Hamilton never really got over the death of his daughter, especially after he'd not even got to say goodbye on that dreadful night. That not a day passed he didn't blame himself for not going to Perth and bringing her home instead of listening to the lies of his sister. I've yet to discover the details of what happened to the school but it appears to have closed shortly afterwards. Her own niece was not the first girl she'd put to work in the school. There are a number of reports of irate parents making complaints to the education department. My friend Lina is doing some digging around for me and I will ask Rebecca for permission to write a piece about it. But only if she is comfortable.'

'Sounds as if this Ethel lived the high life at the expense of others. Where did Rebecca go after she ran away?' Dan's face was so sad that Sadie touched it, and then his lips flicked up for a moment.

'Hitchhiked to Kalgoorlie and found work cooking in a pub. Nobody cared about her age or asked for identification and after a bit she began working on some of the big stations. Never stayed anywhere for long. Somewhere along the line she did something she'd seen her aunt do at the school and forged some documents to get herself a bank account. She only used to deposit money into it, always keeping enough cash out to live on. Gave her enough to build a small business catering and running cooking classes in Mildura and then buy the cottage.'

The sun was up now, warming Sadie's skin and illuminating a perfect blue sky.

'Back then records weren't on a computer database. There was no internet to search for people or to verify facts. Births, deaths, and marriages were kept quite secret as far as outsiders gaining information. I imagine Rebecca did whatever she had to in order to stay away from legal documents and trouble.'

'*And* friends and having her own family. She once told me her life was solitary and she'd made peace with that many years ago,' Dan said. 'She had nothing to go home for. How heartbreaking to believe your brother had died and you had some hand in it, no matter how innocently. And to be told her own father never wanted to see her again. So many lies. Family is important. Love is important.'

As if to prove his point, Dan leaned over and gently kissed Sadie's lips.

They'd never spoken of their feelings. It seemed ridiculous to even think about a future with someone she'd only known a matter of weeks. And even more not to think about it.

'I didn't sleep last night, Dan. My head is mixed up working out what to do next. Do I go back to my life in Sydney and career? Do I look for alternative ways to do my job that allows me to live here? Or is it time to refocus my life completely? What would you do?'

All the time she spoke, Dan's eyes never left hers. And she couldn't read them.

From further down the beach, the bark of a happy dog crossed the water. Sadie smiled and got to her feet. 'Big day today.'

He reached up a hand and took hers. 'You don't need my help deciding your future, Sadie. There is no right or wrong decision.' His lips touched the back of her hand. 'But life can disappear before we know it so why not choose happiness?'

Sadie left him on the jetty and wandered along the tideline to the stone steps. At the top she looked back. Dan was in the sea, swimming strongly a long way out. A great love of the ocean was another thing they shared.

Choose happiness.

It had its merits.

She'd not returned to the cemetery since the first day home but she had no choice today. If she was to move forward then she had to make the steps on her own.

Mum must have been here recently going by the fresh geraniums. She sat for a while beside her father's resting place, braiding her hair before it dried. From her bag she took the little jewellery box from her father and opened it to withdraw the starfish necklace. George had done a perfect job. She put it on.

'Last time I was here I was pretty angry with you,' she said, 'and I'm still not entirely okay with how you lived your life but holding on to all the pain isn't helping me. And it doesn't matter to you now. What does matter is that you and Mum had better years at the end. She only thinks of those, not the horrible stuff, and you might not have deserved it but she loved you all along.'

The starfish was cool against her skin and she touched it. 'This reminded me of the love we shared. I lost you when I was about twelve even though you were physically around. My friend Rebecca lost her dad at the same age but she never saw him again. I'm going to try to only see you in my head as my real dad. The one who taught me to swim and stay safe in the sea. The man who believed in me. Wherever you disappeared to, we both missed the real Ron Carson and I hope wherever you are there is comfort. I'm going to keep an eye on Mum, although she's doing a great job now she is finding her own true self. So, I guess I'm saying I forgive you. And I... I love you, Daddy.'

With nothing more to say, she got to her feet and stretched. Some of the hollowness was gone. And for the first time in years, there was peace in Sadie's heart.

Once the storm had eased the other day, Tim, Sadie, and Dan had returned to the house. Tim was reluctant to come inside and only did so because he needed to sit for a while. Dan collected a blanket from the four-wheel drive and wrapped it around the elderly man. They'd talked at length and when they'd finally parted ways as night fell, Tim had asked Sadie to hold off telling Rebecca about Charlie until he'd spoken to him. It was a delicate situation needing gentle steps to reconcile two lost lifetimes.

Every day since the visit to Driftwood Cove, Sadie had visited Rebecca.

And every one of those visits was to a woman pretending nothing had happened.

She'd make a pot of tea and sit chatting about the garden, or accompany Sadie on a walk around the lake, trailed by Percy. But apart from the odd snippet she volunteered, anything Sadie raised made Rebecca clam up and cut the visit short.

This afternoon has to be different.

Sadie parked to one side of the cottage. Rebecca was at the end of the pier with Percy. She'd taken a foldable chair and sat in the pleasant warmth. Before too long, autumn would nudge summer away. Percy trotted to greet her with a welcoming meow as Sadie strolled along the pier. The lake was at capacity after so much rain, almost level with the bottom of the timber boards.

'Four days in a row. Are you checking up on me?'

Sadie didn't answer, but dropped onto the pier to sit cross-legged. She had rehearsed a dozen speeches and still had no idea how to explain what was going on.

'What a pretty necklace. Is that a sapphire?' Rebecca leaned down a little to see.

'Much to my surprise, it is.' Sadie lifted it so the other woman had a better view. 'My father had this made when I was ten. I thought the world of him but only two years later he turned his back on me and we never got a chance to put things right.'

Rebecca sat back abruptly.

'This morning I sat at Dad's grave and forgave him. It felt good. Did you know that your father is buried in Driftwood Cove graveyard, the one near the little chapel?'

The older woman drew in a quick breath.

'There's some other things you need to know.'

'No. No, I do not. The past is the past and I've said my goodbyes so please just leave things alone.'

Percy stalked right up to Sadie and glared at her.

'You told me you named all your cats Percy to remember someone special. That was Charlie, wasn't it?'

'Sadie, stop. Please, stop.'

Reaching up to take one of Rebecca's hands, Sadie smiled. 'I know this is hard. But there's new information which affects you. The other day, after I left when you wanted to sleep, I went to see Dan. But I remembered seeing something in your childhood home and he and I returned there.'

'That afternoon? In that horrendous storm?'

'Yes. And I know you didn't go into Charlie's bedroom, but I did.'

Snatching her hand back, Rebecca glowered at Sadie as Percy had done.

In the distance, the familiar rumble of Dan's four-wheel drive approached.

'Be as cross with me as you want but in a couple of minutes it will be forgotten.'

'I believe you have lost your mind, child.'

'Quite possibly. The lighthouse lamp was in Charlie's bedroom, and a box of Lincoln Logs. Oh... no tears, Rebecca. Not yet.'

'I'm angry. Not sad.' Rebecca wiped her eyes. 'What do you mean, not yet?'

'Do you remember Charlie having posters in his room?'

'Of course he didn't.'

'Well, there are some. From a pop group which was only started in the very late sixties.'

Rebecca pushed herself to her feet. 'So some other person had his room. Why would you torture me this way?'

Dan pulled up on the grass halfway between the cottage and the lake and he jumped out.

'What on earth is he doing? Come on, Percy, these two children need to have a piece of our minds.' She only made it a few feet before a passenger alighted from the back seat.

Rebecca stopped dead as Tim gazed at her, then raised a hand in greeting. Sadie caught up and rested her hand on Rebecca's shoulder. 'You know him?'

'Except it can't be. Tim?'

'It is Tim.'

Dan opened the front passenger door and helped another man out. He was almost as tall as Dan but his legs, while muscular, were bowed. Dan collected a pair of elbow crutches and the man slipped his arms into them and immediately began to power over the grass.

'Becky! Brave, bold, Becky!' Charlie's voice bellowed across the distance.

Rebecca was running, almost stumbling on the uneven boards in her haste to bridge the gap between them but when she reached the grass, she stopped dead, both hands over her mouth and tears streaming down her cheeks.

Charlie let the crutches drop to the ground, and gripping Dan on one side and Tim on the other, he half ran and half flew. 'Becky. Do you recognise me?'

'Oh my god, Charlie. Charlie, Charlie.'

Rebecca opened her arms and then Charlie was right there and they held on to each other, rocking back and forth as they wept.

It was too much for Sadie and she squatted and buried her head in her arms. Percy climbed under her elbows and tapped her face with a questioning meow and then Dan's arms were holding her with a gentle, 'You did good.'

FORTY

Dan was the only one who seemed able to function properly, organising everyone to go into the cottage and sit at the kitchen table while he made tea and coffee. Sadie had tried to help but her hands kept shaking and tears periodically fell and in the end she'd followed Dan's suggestion that she sit and leave it to him.

Rebecca hadn't let go of her brother's hand once and kept gazing at him with sheer disbelief. Up close, Charlie looked younger than his years with a distinguished streak of silver through his otherwise dark hair. His smile was contagious and warm. Tim was quiet, his eyes moving from Charlie to Rebecca and occasionally to Sadie, with a small flick of his lips.

'Tim gave me an idea of what happened to you after I jumped into the water that night to help get the rowboat. That you were taken away by our awful aunt and lied to about me. And about Dad. Oh, Becky, I'm so sorry.'

'We were all lied to. But *I'm* sorry, Charlie. We should never have been out there in the first place.' Rebecca turned her eyes to Tim in a long, serious gaze. 'You tried to tell me Charlie was alive, didn't you?'

'Yep. Your auntie terrified me and I figured you'd follow

your dad and Charlie to the hospital. He never came close to drowning, Becky.'

'I swam all the way to the rowboat even after the life jacket fell off. But I'm glad it did because you'd have drowned otherwise.' Charlie leaned closer to Rebecca. 'I heard Tim yell that you were okay and wanted to wait for you but Dad was in a flap. Flapping, floundering, father, he was that night.'

That made Rebecca laugh. 'Have you never stopped using alliteration?'

'Not really. My wife still laughs at me when I use it even after forty-five years.'

'Wife?'

'Wife, three kids, and seven grandkids. Becky, you've got a whole family just hanging out to meet you.' His smile widened even more. 'Jean and I have a home just outside Melbourne overlooking Port Philip Bay and there's plenty of room for you to visit whenever you want.'

Percy, who'd been unusually quiet and stayed on the floor near Sadie's feet, suddenly jumped onto Charlie's lap and regarded him with serious eyes.

'Well hello. And you are welcome as well. Although, I'm not certain how Percy will feel about a carbon copy intruder coming into his house,' Charlie said.

'Charlie, did you say you have a cat called Percy?' Sadie found her voice again.

'Of course. Every cat I've ever owned is Percy. Black fur, green eyes. Why?'

'Meet Rebecca's Percy.'

His mouth dropped open and he stroked the cat's fur with great concentration. 'Having cats helped my fine motor skills, Becky. I've often thought about us ganging up on Dad about getting a kitten until we wore him down. We got our first Percy when I was ten.'

Dan made sure everyone had their drink of choice and

leaned against the kitchen counter. He'd been a rock through all of this. Never once had he doubted Sadie's theories or tried to stop her search for the truth. He'd simply trusted her and been there when she needed him most. His easy-going view of the world was rubbing off on her. Not today so much, with her emotions out of control, but more and more often she was conscious of being calm under pressure. Less reactive and worried. He caught her watching him and winked.

'We have so much to talk about. All three of us,' Rebecca said. 'Are you going to stay here for a while?'

Charlie and Tim exchanged a glance. 'Neither of us was sure how big a shock this would be for you. I had a bit of warning at least. I'm staying at Palmerston House for the next night or two and Jean is there as well.'

'Your wife is with you... I cannot wait to meet her. And Sadie and Daniel, you have to come as well.'

'Me? Oh, you don't need outsiders, Rebecca.'

'I really will tell you off if you say things like that. Charlie, this wonderful young woman is the reason we're here together. She chipped away at little clues only she could see, always careful not to cause me upset. Well, most of the time. Sadie has made me a bit cross once or twice.' Rebecca's smile said otherwise.

'You never get cross, Becky,' Charlie said.

'Actually, there was a time after you cut your foot that you became quite demanding. I'd spoiled you with too many treats and extra attention because I felt guilty.' Rebecca released Charlie's hand and pushed her chair back. 'I can't believe I have these.' She opened the fridge and extracted an airtight container.

When she removed the lid, chocolaty richness filled the air. 'I never thought I'd hear your voice again, Charlie, or see your face. And time has changed us so very much, but so very little.'

Joy radiated from her face as she pushed the container closer to her brother.

He grinned and began to laugh when he saw the perfectly iced cupcakes and then his eyes welled with tears and he whispered, 'Cupcakes, Becky. More cupcakes.'

* * *

'You look exhausted, love. Please go and sit in the living room and I'll bring us both a drink once I've washed up.' Pam flicked the end of a tea towel at Sadie. 'Shoo.'

Sadie needed no further encouragement and gratefully sank onto the armchair she'd taken as her own. It wasn't physical tiredness, but emotionally and mentally she was drained. In a happy way. She'd ended up excusing herself from going to Palmerston House today. There was a family who needed to get to know each other and begin a long journey of healing and discovery. Tomorrow she'd meet Jean and again spend time with Charlie, Tim, and Rebecca but for now she yearned for a chance to recharge her own batteries.

'I went to that new wine bar today, Sadie.'

'Excuse me? You went to the wine bar?'

Pam looked pleased with herself as she placed a bottle of wine and two glasses on the side table. 'You do know they have a little shop filled to the brim with local wines and spirits?'

'I do, yes. But how do *you* know this?'

'Well, one of the new owners dropped by this morning with a very nice little brochure. It includes a bit about the shop, a bit about them, and more about their wine bar. Even the menu, which I think we should try.'

Somehow, Sadie kept herself from bursting into inappropriate laughter. Whoever had stolen her mother had done a brilliant job of replacing her. This Pam Carson was adventurous and curious.

'So, it already opened? I thought that wasn't for another week?'

'Early opening for local traders only. Secret code for the front door.'

Pam's lips twitched.

'I see. And you dropped in.'

'I did. They're offering a discount until the official opening and I took advantage of it.'

'Mother. You weren't drinking during the day?'

'Sadie. No. But I did buy a few bottles of wine and make a booking for dinner for Friday night. For three.'

Pam poured two glasses of deep golden wine. 'There you go, darling. You have earned it.'

'Cheers, Mum. And thank you.'

They both tasted the wine and both sighed in contentment.

'Three?'

'Well of course. You, me, and Daniel.'

'Why Dan?'

Her mother's expression was comical. She clearly had something to say and no idea how to broach the subject. It wasn't the Pam of old who kept her mouth shut so as not to upset anyone. No, this was about her picking the right moment to have a bit of fun.

Well, it wasn't now. Not when Sadie was so bone-weary.

'He works too hard and could use a night out,' Pam said.

Sadie scoffed. 'That man is never on a construction site unless it is to show me what he's building or tie down a tarpaulin. He flits about from place to place but really, Mum, have you ever seen him with a hammer?'

Actually, Sadie had. He'd been building flower boxes at his house.

'Regardless of your opinion of him, having known him for all of a few weeks, he is going to turn my inn into a destination stay and I would like to talk to him over a lovely meal supporting a brand-new local business. Anyway, he already agreed.'

'In that case I'd better agree as well. And thanks, Mum. Sounds nice.'

'Bit different from the first time you suggested we eat out.' Pam's face was serious. 'I was a mess when you arrived and now... well, I have you to thank for my new outlook on life.'

'Me?'

'Yes, love. You came home not knowing what to expect and stepped up when it was obvious I wasn't coping. Apart from feeding me and restocking the fridge every time I turn around, you've got me back in my garden and making plans for the future. I know you have your own life to think about but always know you have a place here. If you ever want it.' Pam squeezed Sadie's arm then settled back in her chair.

'That means the world to hear, Mum. I'm proud of you.'

'All this mutual appreciation is going to make me tear up, Sadie. And you look as if you don't have a tear left in you.'

Sadie managed to grin. 'I have never cried so much as today. Seeing Rebecca and Charlie throw themselves into each other's arms... there's a whole lot of love there.'

'Have you considered becoming a private detective? Not the type who snoops around people's dirty laundry, but one who finds lost family and friends and reunites them. Who else would have started with a stranger who'd left their handbag at home and ended up with a tale of terrible lies, unbearable loss, and the most wonderful discovery of family?'

Not a bad idea.

Sadie yawned. 'I'm done for the evening. Do you mind if I go and fall into bed?'

They embraced and Pam picked up one of the paperbacks on the table. At the door, Sadie watched her mother for a moment, heart filled with love for her own small family.

* * *

Sadie was at her laptop before sunrise, the aroma of her freshly made coffee reminding her of early morning breakfast meetings at Circular Quay in Sydney... but without the bustle and noise.

By now she should have been back at her apartment and starting preliminary work on the next documentary. Her few weeks' break was the longest she'd ever not worked and wasn't nearly long enough. With the sale of the studio she'd bought herself a little more time. And she had an idea.

She sent two emails. The first was to the new studio. Thanks to Lina she had the contact details of the programming director. Sadie kept it brief, mentioning the concept she'd had about showcasing the new Rivers End facility as part of the series which she hoped would still go ahead under the new management.

Then she reached out to a woman in Melbourne, an indie producer. She wasn't part of a big studio or backed by a streaming service but knew her way around documentaries as well as anyone Sadie had ever met – and all those years ago had given Sadie her first chance in front of a camera. This was a long shot but Sadie was paying attention to her gut these days, more than ever. Dan and Rebecca had both spoken of listening – to her heart, her instincts, the universe. Whatever the description, it all came down to finding her path.

After closing the laptop, she took her unfinished coffee out into the garden. The air was fresh and cool and before long it would be too cold to be outside so early, sitting on the bench near the roses. But for now it was perfect. The sky was still filled with stars and only a hint of the coming day lightened the horizon. Magpies serenaded her as the birds greeted the dawn and in the distance, a pony whinnied.

Beats cars and buses and sirens.

A light went on upstairs. Mum was up and ready for her

own busy day at the inn. She'd even hired someone from the interviews who was starting today. And tonight was dinner at the new wine bar. With Mum. And Dan.

Sadie stood and stretched, enjoying the feel of her muscles moving. Rivers End was good for her. And it was time to cook breakfast.

FORTY-ONE

Dinner for three began with drinks for seven. Rebecca, Charlie, Jean, and Tim were keen to catch up and celebrate and the beautiful new wine bar was soon alive with laughter and swapped stories.

'We arranged for a local Uber driver to look after us tonight,' Jean said with a smile, as Charlie and Rebecca broke into peals of laughter over a shared memory. 'Such a nice woman who has promised she'll be in the area all evening. She's already been running dear Tim back and forward to his home as well as Rebecca to her cottage.'

Pam and Jean had immediately hit it off and there were plans in place for Pam to visit when she went to Melbourne. Not bad for a person who'd rarely left her hometown. And whenever Rebecca could tear herself away from Charlie, she'd talked to Pam, trying to fill in years of history and continually stopping when her eyes would shine with unshed tears yet again. It was a happy time tinged with inevitable grief for the lost years.

'You're being very quiet.' Dan's arm leaned on the back of Sadie's chair and every so often he'd play with her hair. She longed to lean against him but there was so much to be said first. So much to sort through.

'At heart I'm a people-watcher.'

'At heart you are a woman of deep compassion and empathy.'

Sadie shot him a surprised look. 'Empathy?'

'You take on the pain of those who matter to you. And their joy. I see it in your eyes as you observe the sheer emotion between a brother and sister parted for most of their lives. You are happy and sad for them.'

'Rebecca said the same.'

'She's wise. And I had no idea she could laugh so much, Sadie, and that is your doing. Life will never be the same.'

There was a wistful tone to his voice and he dropped his arm and got into a conversation with Tim. Whose life would never be the same? Rebecca's for sure. And Charlie's. Even Tim's. Small towns intrigued Sadie and it wasn't just from growing up in one. There were stories to be told if you dug a little beneath the surface. Did Dan mean his own life? Melancholy Dan was new.

Her phone beeped and she opened the email she'd been waiting for, heart racing a little. It was short and to the point and it made everything a lot clearer.

After a while, the others stood to leave for their dinner at some fancy place in Green Bay. There were hugs all around and Rebecca held onto Sadie.

'Charlie and I went to our father's grave. I told him I'd never forgotten him and had sent letters and I now know he probably never received them. But at last I've been able to tell him goodbye and it is you I have to thank for that.' Rebecca stepped back and reached for Charlie's hand as he went past. 'And for this.'

. . .

Pam, Dan, and Sadie ordered meals to share from the tapas menu and as the wine bar rapidly filled with other local traders, their table fell silent while they ate.

'I'm planning on walking this lovely meal off tonight,' Pam announced. 'That is, once I devour their sampling plate of desserts.'

They'd walked down, all three of them, Dan canoeing to the same spot he'd collected Sadie from on their dinner date at the jetty. Now was the time to talk to them both about her decision but her mother was too busy talking about Jean and Rebecca to interrupt. Dan's hand slipped under the table to take hers and although he didn't look at her, he was smiling.

The wine bar was going to be a huge success and welcome addition to the township. Pam actually hugged one of the owners, the woman who'd dropped the brochure in, and Sadie couldn't be happier. Before long, her mother would have more friends than she knew what to do with.

Outside, Pam grabbed Sadie's shoulders and kissed her cheek, then did the same to Dan. 'Go on with you both. I'm planning on checking the inn before I go home.'

With that, she turned and walked away. Strode really.

'What if I run after her?' Sadie whispered.

'Don't ruin her fun.'

'So...'

Dan took her hand. 'Walk on the beach?'

They took their time. Lots of window shopping followed by a leisurely stroll to the bridge and then following the path beside the river.

On the other side of the tunnel they both removed their shoes and it was all Sadie could do not to giggle like a child about to open a gift. Underfoot the sand was still warm from the day and when she gazed at the sky, the myriad of stars told her everything she needed to know.

Fingers entwined they wandered along the tideline,

allowing the water to swoosh over their ankles and stopping to kiss every so often. At the lagoon they sat on its bank, feet dangling in.

'I know this isn't Becky and Charlie's lagoon but it still feels special. Did you know Charlie called it their lake? So their house was the cottage by the lake,' Sadie said. 'No wonder Rebecca bought her own version.'

She glanced at Dan.

'At dinner I heard back from a producer in Melbourne. She's a tough lady. Doesn't take on a lot of projects. But she likes the one I pitched.'

'About?'

'The place you're building. And why we should raise our expectations when it comes to protecting our elderly.'

Dan drew in his breath.

'Yeah. Kind of a big deal. And my dad is helping with this because with his trust fund I can use it to help this happen by investing in the production by offering scholarships for young film crew to learn on the job. And I want to. Not so much for him though.'

'Then who is it for, Sadie?'

'For me. Dan, I'm moving home... to Rivers End. I can commute to Melbourne to work a few times a year but I have a lot of ideas and want to make a difference across a range of projects. I wasn't thinking big enough.'

'You make a difference just by breathing.' Dan lay on his back. 'Look up there, mermaid.'

She joined him. The stars were insanely gorgeous. Brilliant and pulsating with hope and expectations.

'A shrine of stars.'

'A lifetime waiting to happen, Sadie Forest.'

Sadie snuggled against his chest. 'And I don't want to waste another minute.'

A LETTER FROM THE AUTHOR

Huge thanks for reading *The Cottage at Whisper Lake*. I hope you were hooked on Sadie and Becky's journeys. If you want to join other readers in hearing all about my new releases and bonus content, you can sign up for my newsletter!

www.stormpublishing.co/phillipa-nefri-clark

If you enjoyed this book and could spare a few moments to leave a review that would be hugely appreciated. Even a short review can make all the difference in encouraging a reader to discover my books for the first time. Thank you so much!

Some stories demand to be written and Becky's was one of those. She'd been with me as a character for a long time – a stoic and protective young person who would do anything for her brother and father. But until I began to write *The Cottage at Whisper Lake*, Becky's story went no further than the fateful night at Charlie's lighthouse. Once I met Rebecca – adult Becky – I knew I had to find out what happened next. How might such a tragedy affect a person? Would they completely lose their authentic self? How would they overcome such grief? Sadie wanted those answers as well and even though her need to find them came from a desire to help Rebecca, she had every bit as much to gain. I love exploring the resilience and power of the human spirit and am grateful my characters found answers and hopefulness at the end.

Thanks again for being part of this amazing journey with me and I hope you'll stay in touch – I have so many more stories to share with you!

From my heart to yours.

Phillipa

ACKNOWLEDGMENTS

Many years ago I created the seaside town of Rivers End, along The Great Ocean Road in Victoria. After writing a few books set there, I moved onto other projects but my heart never left it. When I was given the opportunity to write a new series in and around the same town it was a dream come true. For that I have to thank Kathryn Taussig from Storm for encouraging me to return to dual timeline women's fiction in a setting I so love. To my incredible editor at Storm, Emily Gowers, I can't express how much I adore and value you! From the beginning you've believed in me and you 'get' my stories. I know my books are in good hands with the entire Storm team. Special thanks to Oliver Rhodes. I also have to thank my fantastic fellow authors for such a welcome.

At home I get so much support from my family who believe in me even on the days I lose sight of my dreams. Thank you always to my husband Ian and sons Alex and Nick. You rock.

And to my friends and readers I send love and thanks for being a vital part of this wonderful journey. Special acknowledgement to Joanne Barton from my reader's group for helping name Driftwood Cove, and every person who has helped in ways big or small.

Printed in Great Britain
by Amazon